BOAT TROOP

BOAT TROOP

AN SAS THRILLER

By Johnny "Two Combs" Howard

McBooks
Press

Guilford, Connecticut

McBooks Press

An imprint of Globe Pequot, the trade division of
The Rowman & Littlefield Publishing Group, Inc.
4501 Forbes Blvd., Ste. 200
Lanham, MD 20706
www.rowman.com

Distributed by NATIONAL BOOK NETWORK

British Library Cataloguing in Publication Information available

Library of Congress Cataloging-in-Publication Data

Names: Howard, Johnny, author.
Title: Boat troop : a Sas thriller / by Johnny "Two Combs" Howard.
Description: First McBooks edition. | Guilford, Connecticut : McBooks Press,
    an imprint of Globe Pequo, 2022. | Summary: "Within two weeks of the
    Argentine invasion of the Falkland Islands, it is the mission of four men
    to gather vital intelligence with Argentine patrols everywhere. The rest are
    tasked with a suicide mission-an attack on the Argentine airbase in the
    mainland. In charge is a man unafraid to risk the lives
of his men in search of greater glory"— Provided by publisher.
Identifiers: LCCN 2022002897 (print) | LCCN 2022002898 (ebook) | ISBN
    9781493066223 (paperback) | ISBN 9781493068999 (ebook)
Subjects: LCGFT: Novels.
Classification: LCC PS3608.O9244 B63 2022 (print) | LCC PS3608.O9244
    (ebook) | DDC 813/.6—dc23
LC record available at https://lccn.loc.gov/2022002897
LC ebook record available at https://lccn.loc.gov/2022002898

♾️™ The paper used in this publication meets the minimum requirements of
American National Standard for Information Sciences—Permanence of Paper
for Printed Library Materials, ANSI/NISO Z39.48-1992.

To Shaggybagarags
Long may your windsocks blow

PROLOGUE

Sitrep A: 29/3/82: 08.00 hrs: B: Troop to cancel training. Move to Gibraltar: C: Heli lift 17.00: D: RV SAS liaison GHQ: Gib.

Sergeant John 'Blue' Harding was like every SAS trooper – a sucker for a fastball, the adrenalin buzz of approaching action even more of a turn-on when he was left to speculate about the nature of the operation. He listened as Luke Tuikabe, Graunch Powell and Digger Patterson boxed the options endlessly, shouting above the noise of the heli. The big Fijian, Luke, was the most excitable of them all, throwing his huge frame around, laughing, threatening to pick up the other pair, a feat of which he was easily capable.

Blue, when they included him, just sat back, said nothing and smiled. He'd been in the Regiment longer than these guys. He knew that whatever they thought they were up for it would be something completely different. The law of King Sod said this: that if the four of them had spent the last two weeks on an 'O' class sub, working their bollocks off, practising float-on, float-off drills in an eight-man Gemini inflatable, then wherever they were bound for now was likely to be halfway up a mountain and as dry as a witch's tit. When he heard the BBC World Service, Blue found out he was well wrong!

CHAPTER ONE

C in C Fleet to Flag officer 20 Flotilla 3/4/82: A: Break off Exercise Spring Train: B: Proceed with all dispatch to RV Fleet Auxiliary & Carrier Group: C: Effect immediate.

Three weeks later the four-man team came ashore on the Murrell Peninsula. They crept into the rock-strewn inlet of a river, so small that nobody had bothered to even give it a name. After weeks banged up in a nuclear sub sailing at flank speed, with only one trip to the surface to pick up an air drop, even this hole was a welcome sight. The airdrop had delivered the kind of kit the huge military store at Gibraltar had been unable to provide. That was one of the joys of being a badged trooper. The Headshed never stinted you when it came to equipment. It was help yourself and sign here!

Their task had been outlined to them by the SAS liaison officer. They knew what they had to do and had chosen accordingly. As well as standard requirements they'd added pre-prepared cam netting that they had woven on to chicken wire; secateurs for cutting; two pocket scopes, plus high-power binos were added for long-range observation. Weaponry included a GPMG and 1000 rounds of ammo, plus their own personal weapons. Individual choice was allowed. But each man, when selecting what to take along, had to consider the needs of both himself and the patrol. And it all had to be carried. What they were engaged on was non-aggressive, but within that set of parameters they had to be able to hold their own in a fight. The four men had thought it through, and given themselves every option that they could think of to make the recce a success.

The pallet dropped from the Hercules had provided some very pleasant surprises. The latest cold weather clothing; duvet jackets and new on the market Gore-tex trousers, admired in shops and catalogues but not easily affordable. There was a whole pile of the latest American kit: a brand new Satcom telephone link, improved night sights and spare batteries to fuel them; two M203 Armalites with 40mm underslung grenade launchers, giving a lot of firepower at a low weight. The attached condoms were only a joke because of the note that came with them. It read, 'For four of the biggest pricks I know!' and was signed 'Clarkie'.

HMS *Scylla* was a Swiftsure Class SSN, 4500 tons, capable of thirty knots submerged. It carried a crew of 116 accommodated in a space that would have been cramped for two-thirds of that number. The addition of four Pongos using up bed space, doing press-ups in the gangway, was not greeted with glee. A big boat, *Scylla* needed a lot of water under her keel. She wasn't designed for work close inshore. And in an area where the enemy had complete air superiority, running on the surface was risky, even in the dark. Safety for a nuclear sub lay in deep water.

The skipper, after long discussions with Fleet HQ in Northwood, agreed to run in only far enough to make a landing possible. That meant inside an arc of ten miles. It was his call as to time and place. He would surface and open his deck hatches only if the conditions justified it and there was no risk of water from a heavy sea getting into his boat. That left the four-man patrol with one bugger of a trip in the Gemini, especially using 40hp Johnston outboards, engines that were well prone to breakdown.

The air had a hint of ice in it, made colder still by the stiff breeze. They'd come to the surface under a bank of heavy black clouds, tinged with silver where a strong moon illuminated the edges. The sea-state was what the Navy called good, which in the latitudes of the Falkland Islands meant ten-foot waves with crests a hundred metres apart, which had a big effect on the pitching, rolling deck, hard enough to work on when it was slippery, wet and stable. But even with that amount of unwelcome motion the huge mass of the sub's hull created an area of less troubled water in its lee. It was this area into which the Boat Troop patrol would launch.

The inflatable and equipment came up through the torpedo room hatch, pushed up to the deck level by the matelots. The SAS troopers used the central hatch to get out and receive them. The sections of the Gemini base were swiftly laid, with Luke Tuikabe working furiously on the foot pump to inflate the surround, while his fellow troopers loaded the pre-packed Bergens and the outboards. Even after three weeks of inactivity the manoeuvre was carried out smoothly and with speed. It took less than ten minutes from the point at which the captain called action stations to the moment when *Scylla* blew her tanks. The huge cigar shape of the hull sank beneath the waves, the conning tower pulling away as the boat reversed.

That left them floating on an empty sea. But they didn't hang about. Almost as soon as the hull of the inflatable hit the water the engine was fired up and they were moving. The big green compass, which Blue used, glowed strongly. Taken from an old Spitfire fighter, it was strapped on the inflatable just in front of where he sat on the port side. The luminescence rose and fell through twenty feet as they crested each smooth-topped wave.

No one spoke, first because it wasn't good practice. Even if this was a manoeuvre they'd carried out a hundred times, it only worked when everyone concentrated. There was another factor. Each man knew this was no training exercise: it was for real. They were hyper-alert, and that went especially for Blue Harding and Luke Tuikabe, who'd fought a real enemy in Operation Storm.

Digger and Graunch had seen no battle action since joining the Regiment. But they'd faced danger many times. And all four had trained hard, aware that in doing so they made fighting easy. Yet no amount of talk or encouragement can encompass the feeling of going into action, for the first time or the tenth. These troopers were so alert and fired up that, underneath their dry suits, their skin was tingling.

They'd only covered half the distance when the outboard packed up, spluttering and coughing before finally giving up the ghost. Raiding the stores at Gibraltar, and able to pull out a spare Johnston, they'd elected to take it. This foresight was celebrated with quiet expressions of 'Thank fuck!' In the dark, bobbing about in the water, it was no time to undertake running repairs. But neither could they just dump the bastard over the side. The fault could be simple, easy to repair given time, and there was no guarantee that the second one was any more reliable. With the minimum of movement they carried out a procedure that they'd all had to manage too often, and changed over to the spare engine.

Even an eight-man boat wasn't spacious when it was loaded with four troopers, a spare engine and fuel, plus heavier than ideal Bergens. Necessity demanded they bring in a hell of a lot of kit, this for a multi-tasked job that was of an unknown duration, landing on a part of the shore so far from anything that only shit luck would put them close to any patrols. They'd discussed the idea of a permanent coastal guard, but one look at the map showed that was not an option. The shoreline of East and West Falkland must have run to over a thousand miles. They'd been gifted scant info about the Argie forces. But it was enough to establish that they didn't have the men to cover all that terrain.

With so much time to talk it through, the plan the team decided on covered all the foreseeable risks. Without elaborating, Hereford had let them know that for days, if not weeks, they would be the only reconnaissance patrol on the island. Any information was valuable, but particular attention was to be paid to the standard of Argentine troops. Numbers and locations were the priority. Equipment levels, both unit and individual, were required, as well as relative strengths and capabilities. What additional radar, and what range might it provide? Were they a complete garrison, settling down to just hold their gains, or still in the process of being reinforced, an army preparing for battle? What about morale and readiness, and the skills of their officers?

Heavy armaments came next, artillery and ack-ack strength, coupled with accurate data on the defences round the airport. Were they digging in around the main population centres, adopting a defensive posture, or looking mobile? Minefields were a certainty, their location a strong indication of preferred tactics. Were they laying booby traps, and what was the state of their training when it came to an air threat? But if the observation was passive, the intention clearly remained aggressive. They were tasked to make an appreciation as well, based on that same information, and that included the answer to a key question: what were the prospects for a sudden, medium-force landing close to Stanley?

No four-man patrol, forced to move only in darkness, adopting observation posts that might have a very limited view, could find all this out. The Headshed were well aware of that! They were working on the principle that if you don't ask you don't get. Blue Harding, as patrol commander, knew the score. It was broad-brush stuff. Get in, get around, find out what you can; give us who come in behind you something to work on.

The trip, even without the need to replace the outboard, was too slow. They were under scudding clouds, some moonlight, heading into a blustery west wind and tricky currents. That added an hour to the time they allotted to get within earshot of the coast. Not that they could hear much with a half gale whistling around their lobes. But that was no bad thing since it applied equally to anyone on the flat and silent shore.

Luke Tuikabe and Digger slipped over the side. The other two troopers used their Armalites to cover the beach in front of them. Protected by their dry suits, they swam in to the shore. On land, a few minutes were allotted to orientation. Then they headed along the shore to check out the area to a total width of some two hundred metres, first to the left, then to the right, staying together to provide mutual support. Satisfied that the area was secure, they sent a torch signal to Blue.

The outboard made little noise as they eased in, the beach party over the side again, getting ashore to set up a defence. The priority was to find a cache, and that had to take account of the ground and the threat. This was not densely populated land, regularly patrolled. It was the middle of nowhere. They had no information to say that the Argies had patrol boats. But that was a possibility that had to be taken into consideration. The danger came from the air. The Headshed had told them that the main supply to the islands was by flights from the mainland, with distribution by helicopter. So finding a spot that was free from air observation, one that they could return to with speed if necessary, was task one. A slight overhang, not visible from land, was perfect, even if it took a while to find.

Removing their dry suits, they emptied the dry equipment bags and donned cold weather kit. It took little time to unload the inflatable. Everything was pre-packed and in their Bergens. These weighed nearly 120 pounds. The heaviest individual item was ammo. But there was food too, water bottles, medical kits and dry clothes. They had their normal patrol radio, a PRC320, carried by the patrol signaller, Graunch Powell. But Hereford having gifted them the new Satcom, that too had to be transported.

Neither featherweight nor small, taking up almost the entire space of one whole Bergen, it was gifted to Luke Tuikabe. Distribution was as fair as possible, taking into account individual capabilities. The Fijian also had half the belt ammo from the machine gun. Graunch had fussed like a mother hen when the Satcom was loaded. He'd spent so much time

7

playing with it on the way down that Blue Harding gave him some of the condoms, so 'they weren't left carrying the kids!'

Even with a total of sixteen hours of darkness they had to move fast. They hid the deflated Gemini, folding it flat and stuffing it under the overhang, following that with the cans of spare fuel they would need to get away. Both outboards were sealed into the custom-made Allison bags and placed on top. That completed, Blue called them together. After a quick map appreciation, he ran over the main points of their orders. He established the direction of march and detailed the stops they would make, designating this beach as their primary emergency rendezvous. Then it was Bergens on, weapons at alert and an eight-kilometre tab to their primary LUP. They needed to make up some time, which just added more to what, given the weight they were carrying, was going to be a 'bad trip'.

Standard operating procedure usually put the patrol commander at number two, ahead of the signaller and medic. But John Harding never worked that way. He liked to be out ahead, using his own five senses instead of someone else's. Why wait to be told you were compromised, when you could see or hear it for yourself, and save valuable seconds by taking the appropriate action?

The wind was cold and strengthening. The wet peat bog that ran along behind the shoreline sucked in their boots, a situation made worse by the rough tussock grass when they reached a drier surface. They halted every thirty minutes, and stood rigid, listening hard, each weapon covering a different arc, eyes searching the darkness for any sign of movement. Compasses were checked and distances aggregated. Each two-hour stop was designated a rest halt, a chance to ease the straps on the Bergens, as well as the pain they were inflicting on the skin of their shoulders. They didn't remove the heavy packs, just fell back to sit against them so that the pressure was relieved. At no time were they any less alert. Blue, without lowering his weapon a centimetre, sipped some water, gave the patrol another ERV to replace the distant beach, carried out all the standard checks, then stood up and set off again.

In one way it got tougher as they hit the foot of Mount Round, the wind seeming to gain in velocity with every step that took them higher. But at least the ground was better: loose scree mixed with big boulders – noisy if you slipped, but a faster route to where they needed to go. It was the patrol commander's decision to basha up or go for distance, his job to decide where the maximum safety lay. That was helped when the wind dropped completely on the inner side of the hill, making tabbing a lot easier. Blue chose to go on, and the four men pushed up a blind valley full of rocks, the site chosen for what they hoped would become a defendable, well concealed patrol base.

Picking a spot to lay up, in the dark, had all the usual risks. First they made a Bergen cache, guarded by Luke and Digger, while Blue and Graunch searched out an LUP. Perfection was possible but unlikely, and really it came down to experience as to which point was chosen. They required cover from ground or aerial view, cover from enemy fire, and a clear exit to dead ground, all that in limited time.

They had to stick with the notion that the Argies were spread thin, hopefully more concerned with preparing defences around the main strategic positions on the islands. It was unlikely they'd be out patrolling all night to look for infiltration teams they had no idea had arrived, especially in an area in which little of value could be observed. What they chose in the dark could be improved upon once seen in daylight, or they could move altogether. The stag was reduced to one man while the others worked to provide a hide.

Having got warm from tabbing to get here, it would have been nice to light a fire and to stay that way. They might be out of the wind but the air temperature was close to freezing. But heat, hot food or drink was out of the question. This was a hard routine operation. Blue and Graunch Powell, using the one-time pad, encoded the Sitrep. Then Graunch set up the comms and sent off the morning Sked on the radio to confirm they were ashore and in their primary position. By the time that was completed, it was near 07.00 hours. Under a sky tinged with grey, the four troopers stood to and watched as daylight came to reveal one of the most miserable landscapes any of them had ever seen. They stayed in position till half an hour after full daylight.

From the side of the hill they occupied the land stretched towards Mount Low, at near 900 feet the dominant feature of the Murrell Peninsula, grey rock capped with a light dusting of snow. The valley was green by contrast, but it was the colour of ground too wet, not gentle pasture. Hemmed in by hills, they couldn't see much to the north or south. What was in view was either that flat bog-like grassland, or bare

9

hills dotted with rocks. Knots of sheep grazed intermittently, filthy grey fleeces doing nothing to brighten up an outlook that even in full daylight was made oppressive by lowering grey skies.

There were times when you stayed silent, when even if there was no apparent danger, it might just be around the corner. Not here! They could see for miles.

'Who in the name of fuck would want to live here?' demanded Digger when they stood down. 'It's a pisshole.'

His already thick London accent was heightened by his disgust. Digger was a small bloke, compact, with a round face and bright blue eyes. His disrespect for anything called authority was legendary, and the natural Cockney wit seared into those he chose to take the piss out of. He also owned the dirtiest mouth in B Squadron, the greatest number of expletives reserved for any football team that dared to play his beloved Tottenham Hotspur. Digger was cagey about how he'd come to end up in the Regiment. He claimed to have once been a jockey. If his ability to stay on a horse was anything like the way he fell off bar stools after a few beers, he must have been a godsend to anyone wanting to fix a race.

'Just thank Christ it's empty,' said Luke Tuikabe.

'It ain't empty, mate,' Digger replied, grinning at the huge, stocky Fijian. 'There's a cochell of Argies out there who all like a bit of black. They're just dying to fuck your arse.'

'Cochell? Is that a betting term, Digger?' asked Graunch.

Graunch considered himself the resident egghead, much inclined to use French words instead of English. He never had a chat but a *'petit bavard'*, and when he went to the bog it was for *'un piss ou un merde'*. Given he had a Brummie accent as flat as a saltmarsh, it never quite came off. Normally he avoided it on an operation, but he knew it annoyed Digger.

'You must be thick if you don't know it's Cockney.'

'Sounds vaguely French to me.'

'Pie and mash sounds French to you.'

Graunch farted. 'How does that sound?'

It was Blue who replied. 'Let's get out of sight.'

'Too fucking right,' said Digger. 'But if you don't mind I'd like somewhere away from that dirty-arsed bastard.'

That lacked his usual humour, carrying an element of real dislike.

Digger and Graunch had a feud going, to do with a woman they'd both tried to get hold of in Hereford. It didn't help that Graunch was one of the ugliest blokes any of them had ever seen. He had a flat face, with huge, hairy, lobotomous lumps above his eyes, a broad nose and thick red lips that were forever cracked and dry. The idea that he'd pulled a bird anyone else fancied was bad for the ego. And Digger had one the size of Wembley. They'd nagged at each other all through training, then for three weeks in the sub. They'd keep it up here probably. But Blue wasn't concerned. They were pros, so it wouldn't interfere with the job.

They were static, so each man looked to his own needs. If you operate on foot, then common sense tells you to look after them. A lot of things can make you uncomfortable, but sore feet must rank amongst the worst. It was socks off and wrung out, sprinkle with dry powder and make sure it gets between the toes. Re-dress and put your boots back on – all that before they even thought about water or food.

Normal procedure – in fact the SAS rule – was to stay out of sight during daylight hours. But life wasn't like that. None of them was happy about the state of the LUP. They wanted it to be a secure patrol base, one where they could leave half their kit, going out and returning with a very good chance of finding it uncompromised. So, mainly toiling on their bellies, with a pair stood to all the time, they worked hard to cam it up. It was Blue who called a halt, deciding it wouldn't work. He ordered a rest, knowing that they could find a better spot when darkness fell. They stood to an hour before, ready to leg it if threatened, and only relaxed two hours later.

Given the number of rocks and boulders, it seemed as though they were spoiled for choice. But if the Argies, patrolling, started getting aggressive, this would be just the kind of place they might examine. Better to dig out an observation post. It was paramount that what he decided on could not be seen from the floor, overlooked from the hills behind, or spotted from the air. It needed to be dry, and likely to stay that way when it rained.

Sure that no human life threatened their position, they moved up the hill to dig, choosing a point where the ground bobbled slightly. That meant the roof – supported by wire, and fronted by fine netting – would not show up as being strange. On the slope, most rainwater should run past, rather than flood the place, though sniffing the air it seemed as if

11

snow might be more of a problem than rain. The ground was rock hard from the continuous cold, and it was a calculated risk, given the noise it created, that had them hacking at it with entrenching tools to break it up.

Underneath the crust it got easier, and a careful distribution of the spoil left no trace of the digging. Luke rigged an extra poncho inside that he'd borrowed from the submariners – no mean feat in a ship so crowded that the crew had to hot bunk to get any sleep. It lay half along the deck, the rest lifted over to cover the chicken wire roof. That in turn was layered with cam netting then covered in the same rocks they'd shifted to start their dig. Graunch mixed some water and soil to colour the front net so that it too blended in.

Once completed, Blue checked it out, above, below and from the sides, aware of the imperfections. This wasn't like the jungle where you could build a hide so well cammed that a man two feet away couldn't see you. There was no way on such a bare slope it would hold up under too close a scrutiny. But they had a clear view of the approaches, and if the enemy got that near, the team would be long gone. If not, they'd be engaged in a firefight they'd expect to win.

Another bout of sleep was called, difficult for four restless individuals. They were all still hyped up, alert in every fibre, burning energy at a terrific rate. One trooper stayed on stag while the others slept, but no one got much rest. The following morning was a repeat of the previous night: all stood to again half an hour before sunrise, everything packed for a quick bug-out as they examined the empty landscape. The sky was a grey, overcast slate colour, the air cold and damp, with the wind now gusting from the south, which made the landscape look even less inviting. An hour later they withdrew into their hide, where the morning Sked was composed and, using the standard patrol radio, fired off into the ether. Graunch finally got to set up his Satcom in the middle of the afternoon, calibrating the angle of the dish with great care from the grids on top of the container.

It was intended really as just a repeat of the Morse transmission they'd already sent, a chance to test out the kit and see if it was as good as the Yanks claimed. But it turned out better than that, the voices from Hereford clear and precise. The Headshed dropped heavy hints about the airport, behaving as if the guys didn't already know it was the main target for observation. There was no chat, just hard information, quickly dispatched. Whatever else, the kit worked brilliantly, which made it a pity that it was too heavy and bulky to transport easily.

The Satcom would be left here, and used sparingly, since all the overlinks in outer space were not yet *in situ*. Apart from that it was too bloody big. The main news sent, on both transmissions, was that they would stand to half an hour before darkness, and prepare to go out one hour later. No Skeds would be sent until they were in a new position, unless they were on the emergency frequency. And that would only be used if they were in deep shit.

Blue Harding was cold, even in his thick Gonk bag, designed for the Arctic. Having the cover on didn't help much. The sleeping bag seemed to suck the chill in from the surrounding earth. And two hours' sleep didn't feel like much – about as satisfying as the cold rations and water he consumed. The four ate as they drank, each man mentally checking his own list. They would carry water and food for three days, plus emergency rations, medical kits and the equipment to construct another hide. Added to that they would load enough ammo and grenades to make them a very hot prospect in a contact. No one could ever be sure they got the balance right between eating, trauma kits, fast moving and heavy firepower. That too was about experience.

'Right!' Blue said. 'O Group.'

As patrol leader he was employing Standard Operational Procedure. Go through the main aims of the mission, time after time, detailing tasks. Make sure everyone knows his own job, as well as that of the other team members. These were the orders he'd issued on board *Scylla*. But everyone present had contributed to them, in a Chinese parliament that, trapped on the sub, had lasted a long time. That was the Regiment's way. Orders were agreed, not imposed. He had the map in front of him, using a half concealed torch emitting just enough light to give vision.

'We don't even try for the airport on this jaunt. We've got to find out what kind of stunts the Argies are running on their patrols. Are they numerous and are they serious or relaxed?'

His finger traced the line of march, watched by three pairs of eyes.

'We will route through between Beagle Ridge and the Murrell Heights. Task, to look at Argie positions on the northern approaches to Port

Stanley. I want to establish a forward LUP as close as possible to a point agreed between the two beacons covering Blanco Bay. Artillery and anti-aircraft positions a priority, minefields and ground troop locations a secondary. Remember, all that high ground we'll put behind us overlooks Port Stanley on a clear day. Contact to be avoided, no shooting unless whole operation is compromised. Stay away from the locals as well as enemy.'

Blue looked up to check in the dim torchlight the eyes of the others – little blobs of white in their heavily cammed faces. They knew the problems – not surprising the way Hereford had pratted on about it. If compromised, they'd kill the enemy. But they all knew that the locals might well pay the price for their aggression. The Argentine Army had a poor record when it came to civil disobedience. There had been a so-called 'dirty war' going on in their own backyard for years, the Army on one side and the *Peronistas* on the other, with thousands of men, women and even children just disappearing. One of their favourite tricks, it was rumoured, was to drop people who disagreed with them out of helicopters into the sea, so far from land that their smashed, drowned bodies would never be washed ashore.

And they also knew they were working without any knowledge of how the info would be used. But that was standard too, and not worth worrying about. Only the guys in the Headshed, collating the news and views, could decide what to do with anything sent back. There might be a para drop planned; a rigid boat attack by marines; even a high-altitude low-opening drop by the Regiment. As Blue had been saying for weeks, 'We send it in quick and send it in right.' Digger always added a dirty rhyme.

It made no difference what Hereford said: Blue reckoned he had to kill the sentry. Never mind his orders, he was left with no choice. Silencing the Argentinian soldier would have done no good. The guy would just wake up later and yell the place down. There was no way to take him with them as they withdrew. What could he do with a prisoner? Right up to the last second, Blue had hoped that the gloom would keep him hidden, which it would have done if the stupid sod had stopped a few feet off.

It is possible to scream silently, which Blue did inside his head. 'You dumb, fuck, bastard!'

Why had the Argie moved when he should have stayed on station? Had he seen or heard something and come to investigate? The other sentry close enough to cause them trouble was moving away, and this arsehole should have done the same. Instead he walked towards the beach. Was he stupid or just being butch? It didn't matter now, because the guy ended up standing right above Blue, his cock out, sighing as he opened his glans to piss.

Blue Harding knew he would look down, if for no other reason than the strange sound of the stream hitting his clothing. Having made his decision, he acted quickly. When the muddy shape, barely visible, moved, the guy's body and head jerked forward. Shock stopped him from producing an immediate shout. Blue's speed, as he jammed a hard fist into his windpipe, brought out a terrified gasp, but that was all. The knife was already halfway to his ribcage as Blue hit him again, this time a sweeping forearm blow that half-turned the victim. He was trying to yell, emitting a rasping sound through his smashed voice-box, as the arm took him round the throat. Blue's knee was in his back, arcing him like a bow. The knife was aimed down, hitting the point just below the rib cage, then it was pulled up to slice into and through the heart, as well as the blood vessels and arteries that supplied it.

Digger was coming from the side in a fast crouch to slam the butt of his Armalite into the man's ear, no doubt hoping the combination of weight and blows would drop him like a stone. He was too late, but he caught the body. Both men dropped the sentry slowly, to control the noise, then turned towards the huts that lined the back of the beach, weapons up and ready to rake the doorway, with Blue to the front, over the sentry's head.

'Fuck!' whispered Blue, after a few seconds.

'Not right now, thanks,' Digger hissed.

Weapon still pushed forward, the Cockney's free hand reached out to the sentry's neck, feeling for the pulse by the carotid artery, the smell of stale tobacco and wine, tinged with the odour of skin and fresh urine, filling his nostrils.

'We've got about a minute to get out of here,' he whispered.

'A bit more,' muttered Blue.

They'd timed the guard routes along with the routine of the NCO for a long time before crawling forward. Unless he or the second sentry did something surprising they had more than that. The NCO was inside the hut, the other guard along the path that ran behind the beach. But that still begged the question.

'Leave him or take him?'

'Either way he'd cause a search,' hissed Digger.

Blue looked towards the door of the huts that lay behind the unlit beacon above Blanco Bay – a possible landing site if the force wasn't too numerous. There were several dozen men there, part of the teams laying mines along the exits from the beach below, one of them the NCO they reckoned to be in charge, since there was no sign of an officer. They could try to take him if he did his rounds, which would increase their evade time. But that might just compound the sin. Likewise the second sentry, who must have reached the end of his designated route by now and be beginning to turn. Two bodies instead of one. And even with what he'd just done, Blue knew that silent killing was not as easy as it looked in the movies. There was always the risk of noise.

That would be bad news, since they'd slipped through an artillery position to get this far, one that was right on their route to safety. All Blue's training told him not to panic. He knew he had to make a decision, as well as approximately how long he had to do it. He'd been trained to take his time, better that than make a mistake. And since Digger had benefited from the same instructors he stayed silent, leaving his patrol leader to think it through.

'Dead,' was all he whispered in Blue's ear, as he took his hand off the sentry's neck.

Blue reckoned just leaving him was the worst thing he could do. That NCO would see he was off his beat. It was odds on the body would be found before they had a chance to put any distance between this spot and the secondary LUP. The first thing the Argies would do was send up flares. In this flat, featureless landscape that was a major bummer, even if they got clear of the gunners on the way. It virtually guaranteed he and Digger would have to stay away from Luke and Graunch, hiding up waiting for their return, for fear of compromising them.

Not that they would be safe, stay or run! There had to be some kind of field communications here. The Argies would put out an alert that might

16

make it impossible for any of the four-man team to sidestep a firefight. It was bad enough at night. By morning, the whole place would be crawling with troops, and the helicopters they'd seen earlier that day ferrying supplies would be out hunting them. Taking him along, even for a short while, lengthened the time, the mystery of a disappearance acting to slow down the reactions. But carrying the body would slow him and Digger even more. It was a fair guess that a torch would show not only the mess of his bowels, but also the trail of blood they'd leave as they dragged him off.

They had been in the act of measuring the layout of the minefield, crawling on their bellies trying to build up a picture they could transfer to paper at a later stage, showing the location of the mines themselves, plus the dimensions of the safe corridor the Argies had left so that they could make their way to and from the beach. They were crouching in that corridor now, one that should have been taped off at this stage for reasons of safety. It was the fact that the Argies had failed to do that which gave Blue the idea of making the approach.

'Has he got any grenades?' Blue whispered.

Digger didn't ask why, he just went on to his belly and crawled to the side, his fingers feeling under the still body, the swear words soft, filthy and constant under his breath.

'Got one. Christ, it's an L2!'

'Give.'

'What's the plan?'

'Roll him over.'

'An explosion?'

'No fuckin' choice.' Blue gasped. 'Get ready to leg it.'

Digger got to his feet and stepped well away. He was moving as Blue began to haul on the pin. Blue looked once, to check that Digger was at the spot where the safety corridor turned at an angle of ninety degrees. Then he dropped the L2 beside the body, hauling on the cadaver's greatcoat to pull him on top. He knew he had four to seven seconds to get clear, but allowed himself two long paces back on to what he knew was mine-free ground.

It's amazing how much ground you can cover in seven seconds, even in heavy, muddy boots. He made the angle in five, was abreast the hut when he finished his count, and on his belly when the grenade went off.

The explosion was muffled by the corpse, but still loud enough to crack in their ears. Digger had got behind the hut, and Blue joined as the blast subsided.

Both men crouched as the door on the opposite side flew open, throwing a shaft of light across the minefield. They didn't look at it directly, but obliquely, the need to keep night vision intact paramount. But it was easy to imagine the scene – the shattered body, the great plume of settling dust that should cover any trace of the killing, the fear and precautions of the others who would take great care in their approach, thinking one of their number had mislaid an anti-personnel mine. Would it occur to any of them to look around? Even if they did, coming from a well lit interior, they would not see Digger and Blue, on elbows and knees, crawling away.

And in daylight they'd realize it was probably a grenade. These things did happen, and that was what Blue was counting on. No matter how often you told soldiers not to play with their dangerous toys, they did so. Accidents happened! With no evidence of outside involvement it should just suffice. If it didn't, they'd just have to deal with it.

Graunch and Luke were waiting at the secondary LUP, a mile from the explosion, on a slight rise that gave them some view across the bay towards Stanley airport, eyes searching the darkness for any sign of their mates. Already hyped up, the dull thud of the exploding grenade had the adrenalin operating at maximum, providing heat to cold limbs and an extra dimension to the sharpness of their senses. They had a routine for this, to stay in place until a threat was perceived. And in a situation where any one of a dozen explanations was possible, there was little point in speculating as to the cause of the explosion.

There was little ambient light looking south, just enough to show the figure standing with his rifle held up and horizontal in both arms as a shade darker than the background. No one spoke, or issued any call signs. It wasn't necessary. The shape was the agreed signal that allowed Blue and Digger to enter the LUP, a quick pat all that was necessary to let them know how happy Graunch and Luke were. Once in and secure it was question time again. To stay, or bug out of what could now become a very hot area. They lay waiting for a full hour to check on any pursuit. If there were one, they would try to evade it without compromising the mission. If they couldn't do that, they'd fight.

Faint in the distance they could see lights moving, including those of a truck that had been brought up to illuminate the area. But the enemy didn't come any closer, and the hairs on the back of Graunch's neck, which had been standing up for the last hour, began to subside.

CHAPTER TWO

Sitrep A: 21/4/82 04.00 hrs: B: Mt. & Bt. troop D Sq.: C: Visual S. Georgia: D: No substantial enemy force opposing: E: Landing Sea & Air imminent.

Brigadier Cornelius Hosier tapped a finger on one of the red staff officer's tabs that adorned his shirt collar, unaware that the officers sharing the room with him saw this as a gesture designed to emphasize his recently acquired rank. Had they voiced that notion he would have laughed, and pointed out that as Director of Special Forces he had no need of such flummery. The pause did, however, help to cover his own dilemma, which was simple. Given that his country was engaged in an operation that might lead to a full-scale invasion of the Falkland Islands, what precisely was his role? For the first time in years he had no clear executive function, this compounded by an imprecise supervisory one.

As an ex-squadron commander, he knew enough about the Regiment to take an active part in discussions regarding operations. The trouble was there was no one to discuss them with. Jamie Robertson-Macleod, the CO of 22nd SAS, had taken himself, plus the entire command of G and D Squadrons, off to Ascension Island, even including the Regimental Sergeant Major. Elements of D Squadron, at this moment, were approaching South Georgia, within hours of making a landing. Those left behind in Hereford, A and B Squadrons, whose officers filled the room, were not yet committed. And it was a telling indictment of his dubious status that he had no idea whether they would be. Which left him high and dry when it came to what to say to them.

'Typical bloody Jamie!' he thought savagely, recalling the barnstorming nature of the man, a trait which had led him to organize the attack on the Iranian Embassy without consulting his then superior. Hosier's predecessor had taken the news of such an action with seeming equanimity, behaviour that puzzled the new Director. But there was a great deal he didn't quite understand about Sir Anthony Luffenden, the man he'd replaced. Not least was his reluctance to point out to the powers that be his own function in the operation. There seemed to Hosier little point in being head of a unit, taking any brickbats flying around on their behalf, if you couldn't also take credit for their successes.

The handover had been uncomfortable, but then these things always were. Luffenden, an ex-regimental CO, was too indulgent of what he cheerfully referred to as the SAS ethic – that method of behaviour which meant that, if a trooper disagreed with his superior, there was no requirement for him to be even marginally polite when pointing it out. The Regiment was getting too full of itself, and Hosier considered that things needed tightening up. He'd hinted at some of his aims, only to have the stiff-nosed, short-arsed bugger warn him off from too much interference.

'The Director's role, old chap,' Luffenden had said, in his clipped Old Harrovian tone, 'is to advise and facilitate.'

'Interference,' he thought savagely, his mind still on the Embassy siege. 'An officer commits the unit to a major action in aid of the civil power, and doesn't even try to inform his superior. There would have been no advise and facilitate there, Sir Anthony bloody Luffenden. I would have carpeted the sod for that, and no mistake!'

The soft cough from the acting regimental CO, Gerry Tooks, brought him back to the present. Cornelius Hosier, aware that his face threatened to reveal his thoughts, deliberately relaxed his jaw muscles. Then he turned his large brown eyes on to Tooks, recalling that when he'd first served with the Regiment the man had been a staff sergeant. To have reached his present army rank of major was not unusual. But to be serving as a troop commander in the SAS, having been an NCO in the unit, was unprecedented. Now he'd gone and landed the job of acting CO.

It was luck, of course. A case of being in the right place at the right time when the balloon went up, with no other officer of sufficient rank on the base to quickly take over. For all that, to Hosier, it was an unwelcome development. He had very strict ideas regarding how far ex-rankers should be indulged. A couple of captains in the room had risen from the ranks as well, and it was interesting to note that, in the main, elevation to officer status did nothing to round off the rough edges. The rest were a mixed bag, some from the best regiments in the Army, others middle-class chaps made good.

'I came up from London for a purpose.'

He had a strong voice, which still carried a faint trace of his mannered Scottish accent, the product of Fettes College, plus early service with the Argyll and Sutherland Highlanders.

'I can tell you there are quite a few people at Northwood who've got the squitters about the whole Task Force idea. Not the Navy, mind. Galtieri and his cohorts have vindicated their whole existence. They're so damn cock-a-hoop that even I'm searching for a loo when they're about.'

He waited for the laughter that sally should have produced, and was forced to hurry on when it didn't come. 'We have to be ready to support Jamie if and when the call comes, with equipment or men, whatever he requires.'

'Of course, sir,' replied Archie Grosvenor, the recently appointed OC of A Squadron. 'Will you be staying for lunch?'

From anyone else that 'of course' might have been taken as an insult, the underlying proposition being that the whole function of 22nd SAS was instant readiness. But not from Major, the Honourable A. S. Grosvenor. Nicknamed 'the Duke', even though he wasn't related to one, he had that self-assurance that comes from old money, Eton and membership of a black button regiment. It produced an air of ineffable social superiority that managed to make the remark sound perfectly natural.

'Can't Archie, I'm afraid: have to be getting back to Northwood. The PM is due to visit this afternoon, so it's all ranks dolled up for kit inspection.'

'A quick drink, sir, surely?'

'If my chopper's ready.'

It was Gerry Tooks who replied, his voice a low growl that was habitual. 'Refuelled and waiting.'

Hosier absentmindedly fingered his staff tab again, picked up his sand-coloured beret, then stood, drawing himself up to his full height of 6' 1". Cornelius Hosier worked hard at looking imposing, aided by a square jaw and hard, high cheekbones. Rigid self-control measured all his actions and the thin pale lips were never allowed to relax to more than a half-smile. Only the brown eyes were different. Not soft – more feline, watchful and wary.

'Then just the one, Gerry, to toast the boys off South G. Can't indulge in any more. Wouldn't do to slur when the PM asks me what the Regiment has up its sleeve. And you can tell me what's been happening to the chaps you've already got in place on East Island. Harding isn't it? It will do no harm to give Mrs Thatcher some good news. She's tending to look a bit grey around the gills at present.'

'What the fuck did he want?' asked Don Grant, as the Gazelle lifted off from the helipad, carrying back to London the man known to the entire regiment as 'Jock the Sock'.

Gerry Tooks grinned as he dropped his saluting arm. He knew his Squadron Sergeant Major hated the Brigadier. He wasn't alone in that: it was an emotion felt by most people in Stirling Lines. But 'Lippy' Grant had served closely with 'Jock the Sock', and was in fact credited with giving the new Director his nickname. The earning of that monicker was a tale he would recount time and again after a few drinks in the mess. And if he got really pissed then the depth of his loathing would surface, interspersed with bitter anecdotes about Hosier in particular and, if there where none about, 'Ruperts' in general.

'He was just paying a courtesy call, and asking about Blue and the boys on the East Island.'

'He could have done that on the phone, boss. Why heli all the way up here?'

Gerry Tooks smiled. 'Maybe he's lonely. Missing the camaraderie.'

'Rupert words like that never sound quite right when you say them,' Lippy said.

That nipped rather than stung. Even having risen to his present rank of major, Gerry Tooks was still a bit uncomfortable, especially with troopers like Lippy Grant, who'd known him as a sergeant. Sometimes he wondered if putting himself on offer for another tour with the SAS had been a wise decision. Perhaps he should have just stayed in his own regiment, and accepted the ceiling that was likely to impose. But he couldn't help his ambition. And he'd realized before most that, if you wanted to progress in the British Army, service in the SAS Regiment was becoming a must. That had been true before the Embassy siege. But after that stunning, very public success, it was doubly so.

'Hosier's out the loop, I think.'

The venom of the response made the harelip scar on Don Grant's square face stand out stark and white. 'Then I reckon thank fuck for that, boss.'

'Jamie's stuffed him good and proper by going south himself. Jock the Sock's livid with him for attaching himself to the Commando Brigade. With Julian Thompson around, Jamie doesn't even need the Brig's rank to clear his orders.'

Gerry Tooks guessed that the absence of Lieutenant Colonel Jamie Robertson-Macleod, known as JRM, was no accident. He was a very determined character, who'd earned a degree of respect from the troops he led. He was also a rare beast to the Major's way of thinking: a good officer, outspoken and direct, who looked as though he was going to get somewhere in that dog's breakfast they called the British Army – which was still, to Gerry's way of thinking, Lions led by Donkeys. JRM knew what Jock the Sock was like, knew that the new Director would have encamped himself at Hereford and tried to take executive control if he'd stayed still. So he'd done the only sensible thing and moved his HQ to a place where Jock the Sock could only reach him by radio.

Up until Luffenden's departure, six months before, the role of Director Special Forces had been more than anything a convenience. The Army was still a hierarchy, even to the indulged troopers of the SAS. The chain of command required that an officer of staff rank pass the Regiment's requests up to GHQ. That same chain demanded that any orders flowing in the opposite direction also carried the imprimatur of a Brigadier. Numerically, the inclusion of the Territorial Army units 21st and 23rd SAS, plus the Special Boat Service, excused the truncated nature of the command. Hosier hadn't waited a day to let them know he wasn't satisfied with the *status quo*. He was a man who liked to command. So he'd lost no time, when he received his appointment, in seeking to expand the Director's brief.

Naturally the unit CO, who saw his own prerogatives being breached, had resisted this. Autonomy was an important and very attractive part of the SAS commander's role, and one that JRM was particularly keen to preserve. No harsh words were exchanged, either in private or in public.

Quite the opposite! Polite tones were adhered to at all times. But there was no disguising the conflict. And both men manoeuvred with great cunning, calling in favours from everyone they knew with influence, each assiduous in the pursuit of what he considered the only true path.

Lippy Grant made a scoffing sound that, for Gerry Tooks, killed off the train of thought. 'Don't kid yourself that'll stop him, boss. If there's a bit of glory going, Jock the Smelly Sock'll find a way to nick it. He was like that as a brand new Rupert, and he ain't changed. He could write a medal citation from doing service in the shithouse.'

You couldn't say that Lippy Grant looked abashed at that point. Such a thing wasn't in his nature. But the eyes flicked away, evidence to Gerry Tooks that, momentarily, the SSM had forgotten he was talking to a Rupert. It was an ongoing bone of contention amongst the troopers that only officers could write medal citations. And some of them did so shamelessly. This meant that SAS commanders were often heavily laden in the chest decoration department while the men they led were ignored. It wasn't that the troopers hankered after gongs. But they hated to see them going to officers who'd done nothing on a dangerous operation but issue the orders, while the men who had carried out the actual task received something like a Mention in Dispatches. Gerry himself had railed against it before being commissioned. He now tried to avoid temptation in his present position as OC of B Squadron.

'Be grateful Blue Harding's new toy wasn't on stream,' Gerry said. He was keen to change the subject. Slagging off brigadiers, even in the loose associations that were the currency of the SAS Regiment, was not a good idea. 'Otherwise he would have been on the phone giving out orders.'

Lippy did a fair imitation of Hosier's voice, catching just right that strain of Scots in the almost pure Oxbridge tones. 'It would be a pipping notion, chaps, to carry out a wee raid. Why not nip into Stanley and collar General Menendez.'

'He did say how lucky we were, over his whisky, that the Argies seemed subdued.'

'That won't last,' Lippy growled. He'd been less than keen on the operation that sent them in, seeing his 'boys' hung out to dry, all alone and with no support. 'As soon as the lads hit South G the bastards'll get the message. Then they'll be shooting off at anything that moves.'

'They'll manage, Lippy. They're a good team. And as soon as South G is over, they'll have so many patrols in it will be like Piccadilly Circus.'

'Is that the word?'

'It's not public, but yes.'

'Mind if I tell Sam Clark? He and Blue are best mates.'

Gerry looked at Lippy long and hard. They'd served together in Borneo, the Persian Gulf and spots around the globe that were called deniable. The way officers and OR's related to each other was very much an individual thing in the Regiment. But it was relaxed and informal, first-name stuff, and all were as one in trying to resist Hosier, keen on a bit more of the old Green Army bull. 'Yes sir, no sir, three bags full!' was not the way the SAS worked. Gerry Tooks, having come from the ranks, couldn't have played it stiff even if he'd wanted to, especially with a man he considered an old friend.

'Would it make any difference if I did?'

Lippy grinned. 'Not a lot, boss.'

The message about increased nervousness was one that Blue Harding and his guys got as they set out to recce the airport. The Argentine night patrols, as well as their sentries, had been lax to the point of sleepiness on the way in to Blanco Bay. That had changed on the way out, either because their ploy with the grenade hadn't worked, or the mere sound of an explosion had livened the sods up. But by the time they set out, twenty-four hours later, for the next job, the whole landscape was crawling with troops.

Their return signals from the Headshed had been quite snappy about the dead Argentinian. Clearly they were not pleased. Another dead body was a definite no-no! And again they'd stressed the need for information regarding the airport. But the man on the ground had the power, and it was his decision to go for it, not theirs. In fact, the Headshed carping was more inclined to make him extra cautious than super keen. But within that too was the knowledge that he and his patrol only knew what was necessary. What was happening in the big outside world, especially as it related to the re-taking of these islands, was a mystery to them.

Part of the problem was that they were based to the northwest of the Murrell Heights and Mount Low. These locations, if an invasion was imminent, were of some tactical importance, covering as they did the northern approach to Port Stanley. The Argentines should have a post on the summit, to overlook the coastline. They certainly now had aggressive patrols on the lower inland slopes, which more than halved the team's rate of movement.

To compound their difficulties, the weather had changed, ushering in a spell in which wind and temperature dropped and the sky cleared. In daylight, the terrain was thrown into sharp relief, at night creating a moon state that hampered easy progress. It also lit up the lower slopes of the hills that they had to traverse, the loose scree at the bottom creating a zone of maximum exposure. On the polder and peat marsh any slight activity picked up in the distance could be mistaken for a cow or a sheep. Not so the barren slopes. If they were spotted on those the Argies would know they were human.

But all four were, at least, fully acclimatized now, if being dirty and more than a bit smelly could be described that way. It took only a few days for the patrol to reach optimum operational pitch. Digger still tried to be funny and his feud with Graunch rumbled below the surface. But when it came to the job they were well in tune with each other. So much so that, once out and tabbing, communications became almost telepathic. Blue and Luke Tuikabe were the same, able to confer with no more than a tap and a pointed finger, the odd soft grunt added for emphasis.

The airport was a bastard to get close to, and had been the subject of a lot of discussion on the way down. As their primary target, it was natural to want to land as close to the strip as possible. But the damn thing was, excepting Port Stanley itself, the most heavily defended spot on the Falklands. It lay on what was almost an island, with only a narrow, dog-legged causeway to provide access. Around it was the ground which, logic demanded, on such a barren island, would contain the bulk of the Argentine troops.

The integrity of the mission was paramount, the ability to remain undetected and operational for weeks. There is guesswork in any mission, not just the one they were planning. The decision to base themselves in an area that was close to Stanley, without being on top of it, gave them some protection from the enemy. The hope was that it would put them within a single night march of their numerous tasks. But they soon discovered how far out that assumption was. The next probing run that they tried, given the care that had to be exercised, took so long it cut down drastically on their time on target. Another forward LUP had to be built.

Choosing a site was murder, even worse than the main LUP. The spot, about five miles from Stanley, was close to a stream between Drunken Rock and Mount Longdon, in an area with serious enemy traffic. They had to scoop out a shell scrape, a minimum of nine inches deep, close to the edge of a stream, using the slight fall of the bank to ensure that it didn't show as an elevation in daylight. The displaced sod and cam netting would be used to cover the top, the excess soil going into the stream to be washed away, so leaving no trace of their presence.

The digging was easy, the earth at what was nearly sea level much softer than that on the hillsides. Carefully they cut out a section of the grass-covered topsoil, which was laid to one side. Digging out the black earth had to be done slowly, pushing the entrenching tool rather than hacking with it, most of the work done by feel. They rotated places to prevent themselves from getting too cold from standing stag or too hot from digging. It wasn't long before they had to stop digging, having hit the real bummer, water. But the shell scrape was just enough to conceal the patrol, if they lay absolutely flat.

Blue decided, as a test, to use the forward hide to probe the barracks at Moody Brook and the defences around Wireless Ridge, falling back to it before first light. That they achieved with limited success, since the area around the old Royal Marine base was a bustling hive of activity, while Wireless Ridge, commanding one of the only two flat approaches to the island capital, was crawling with Argies. The ridge line was being prepared as a major defensive system, with clear signs, even in the dark, of preparations well under way to provide for heavy weapons and dug-in infantry positions.

But when it came to composing the morning Sked, they had even more interesting information. The Argentine soldiers, especially those exposed on the tops of the hills, had lit numerous fires. They tended to huddle round in an attempt to keep warm, which had acted as an aid when it came to avoiding contact or compromise. Nothing was more telling as evidence of low ability. Good soldiers, led by proper officers, didn't start fires at night. They got into their trenches and foxholes then sat out the hours of darkness, with enough men awake and alert to spot any incoming threat.

The SAS did that during the day. Once concealed, they had to remain through the eight hours of daylight, in prone position, unable to observe much in the way of approaching danger. The drill was simple: you didn't talk, eat, smoke or fart. You stood stag one hour on, three hours off. It was even more miserable than any of the team had anticipated, cramped together, four men in what would have been tight for two, as the water from the ground seeped up around them, chilling them to the marrow. The man on stag, lying behind the GPMG, was no better off than the others. Sleep was only possible to the exhausted. Silence was essential, the first hint of a snore and they pinched on the sleeper's nose. Hard as it was, this, to Blue Harding, was the very essence of the job.

To enter and stay in the Regiment fitness was essential, initiative and intelligence vital. But the real sort out for a badged trooper was the mind-set to stay in maximum discomfort, without letting concentration slip. Then, at the end of a body-numbing spell of total inactivity, to still be able to operate at peak.

'The sooner we get back to the Hilton the better,' growled Digger. Darkness had fallen, everyone was awake, and they'd just completed the stand-to. Those few words said it all. The primary LUP was no palace, but compared to what they'd just endured it was paradise.

'Luke.'

The Fijian, in response to Blue's whisper, lifted the cam netting, and with it the sod on top, the whole lot rising no more than two inches. He was right above the stream, which glinted in the moonlight yet still managed to be black. A good look round followed. Not that he could see jack shit from such a low elevation. After a ten-minute still period he eased himself out and lay flat on his belly, weapon out, right by the side of the water. The others followed, taking up their positions to cover the ground until they were sure they were safe. At Blue's signal, they all began to stretch, working to get both blood and warmth back into their stiff limbs.

Normally, the next steps would have been discussed in the LUP. But the icy, underground cold made that undesirable. It didn't matter what the rules said. This was common sense. Blue wanted his guys alert and at peak when he read out the orders, route of march, target details and tasks. Normally, when patrolling, features like roads and bridges were avoided like the plague. But on this job there was no choice. They had to tab three miles, picking their way through the incomplete defences of Wireless Ridge, then cross the first road within a mile of Moody Brook Barracks. The second road was even more difficult, since there was little space to work in as they passed between Stanley itself and Sapper Hill, in one place less than fifty yards from the nearest occupied dwelling.

Yet the area was quiet, the locals shut up in their houses, the invaders round their petrol fires, or in tents and barracks, no doubt wondering why they'd bothered to liberate such a dead-end island. Oddly enough, there were fewer Argentine patrols close to Stanley than they'd met on the outer rim. Blue reckoned that they had to be inside a defined defensive ring, one in which the enemy felt really secure. The thought of how wrong they were made him grin.

There was another road to cross to bring them onto Stanley Green, a flat expanse of land that was nothing like what it sounded. It was soft and bog-like, a real pain to traverse as the troopers' boots dropped through the topsoil into mud underneath. They stopped for the fourth time to check their distances and establish their location, before turning north towards the narrow causeway.

The heavily manned guard post, and the barrier that blocked the road, came as no surprise, since the flames from a fire inside an oil drum had given the troopers plenty of warning. That showed that the Argies had added concrete posts to form a chicane to slow any vehicles going in either direction, and posted sentries on both stretches of the approaches. Some of the troops on the islands were supposed to be regulars, according to the sigint they got from Hereford. But it didn't seem that way once contact was made. The guards on the causeway were just the same. Their lack of skill made them easy to spot. When they moved, which they did too often, it was noisily. A couple even called to each other to share a soldiers' joke. One was actually smoking a cigarette, his cupped hand failing to hide the glowing end, the smell of which drifted in the night air to torture the cancer candidates in the patrol.

There was still no way to get round that guard post, given the limited land that lay on either side of the causeway, regardless of how badly it was manned. The east shore, Rookery Bay, facing the South Atlantic, was bound to be defended, and laced like Blanco Bay with new-laid

31

minefields. There was seawater on the west side too, the inner arm of Stanley Bay. This was as close as they could get, the point nearest to the strip where they could observe, not only some of the flying activity, but the traffic between the town of Stanley and its airfield. Blue and the others, having agreed an ERV, were going to have to split up, and lie up throughout the day in the open, with only the shallowest trench and cam netting to hide them. Even then they'd hit water on this low bog land. Being soaked through would be bad news, but it looked as though they would have no choice.

And the really low elevation would strictly limit what they could observe. Noise would help. They were close enough to the airfield to hear planes and helis landing and taking off. And within striking distance of the road so that trucks or marching boots were audible. They would have no notion of airport defences unless the Argies ran a drill, and started firing off their ordnance. Even then, they'd have to be very flush with kit to go blasting off with anti-aircraft missiles. The job was to get as much as possible, air activity and the buildup of troops. To get any more would require the presence of several teams in the area, with the Headshed able to cross-reference their reports to build up a better picture.

Well spread out before daylight, each man had dug out his own shell scrape, using his personal cam net to cover it over. Luke Tuikabe, huge of frame, had the biggest problem. Blue, thinking about the four of them, wondered what it would look like from the air. For all he knew they would stick out like four fresh turds on a Swiss pavement. But that had to be dismissed, as he heard the first Hercules come in, and he peered through his high-power binos, trying hard, at over three-quarters of a mile, to see what was being unloaded once the plane taxied to a halt.

The helicopters were the worst, flying as they did in no fixed direction, and with a frequency that underlined the way they were being used to transport men and equipment. Graunch, closest to the harbour, observed two vessels come in. Though he could only really see their upperworks, silhouetted against the huge silver fuel storage tanks, he pegged them right away as cargo ships. He watched as they crept towards Stanley Harbour. No doubt they would tie up there and be hurriedly unloaded. But in this low landscape they'd be sitting ducks. The only thing missing now was the flyboys to sink them at their moorings.

Throughout the day Blue, Digger and Luke observed several planes

32

arrive. Some clearly carried troops, who marched in loose order over the causeway to reinforce the men around Port Stanley. Carefully each observer noted their bearing, seeing in their slumped shoulders and general lack of interest an even greater indication of low morale. Yet these jundies were supposed to hold the Falklands against a pretty potent threat.

If order of battle info was loose about the Argentines, the same couldn't be said of the British Army. The enemy must know there was a whole Parachute Brigade available, and they would know the lift capacity of the Royal Air Force down to the last Hercules transport. Then there were the Royal Marines to complete the war-winning scenario, which would have the airborne troops dropping to take the airport; that combined with an RM amphibious assault; both followed by an airlift of battle-ready troops and equipment on to the now-captured airfield. Crete all over again!

It sounded terrific until you took in the distances: a flight of four thousand miles from Ascension. What idiot would sail eight thousand miles to take back this craphole? But if the Argies were any good, they should do the necessary and prepare for the near-impossible. The evidence that they might wasn't there. But that could be because of his inability to see. Troops should already be dug in round the exterior of the promontory, trenches covered over so that they were hard to observe. The temptation to go in and take a look was strong, and Blue spent some of the quiet time considering the angles.

He knew there was a wire mesh fence, which would provide an easy way through. He also had a rough layout of the airport. A low-traffic field like Port Stanley was probably something of a dumping ground, littered with rusting, unrepairable equipment. Could that provide points of observation and a grid area covering the field? They would have that, as well as the long tussock grass, as cover. It didn't take long to scrub the idea. They were too few, and the job was too dangerous, running as it did right across their primary duty to stay undetected.

As soon as darkness fell the four troopers RV'd. After mounting a stand-to, Blue issued the orders to get them out of this location and back to their secondary LUP. At first light he would encrypt a message detailing everything they'd seen, as well as what they'd picked up on the way in. The Headshed could then build up an intelligence picture to pass on to the RAF and the Navy.

They spent the next day in the secondary LUP, with the Sked sent off before they could even try to look to their needs in food and comfort. They needed to remain in the soaking backup post, recalling base that night to check that the job was complete. It was a relief to find there was no 'message for you' signal posted as they tuned in the set. That meant that a return to the airfield was probably deemed unnecessary. Then they tabbed back to the Hilton in a light, penetrating drizzle, four exhausted men who never forgot their drill for a second. The place might look secure, but they couldn't just walk in. It was Digger and Graunch forward, while Luke and Blue provided cover. Only when they received the news that it was safe to do so did the patrol commander and the Fijian come in.

Then, in a hide that was at least partially dry, they could do something about their feet, which had been in water for four days. A change of socks and drying powder only helped so much. Their feet were in a bad way. But once you've done everything possible, that's it. Then it's time to lay down to eat rations, drink some water and take turns at sleeping, waiting for nightfall again, and a signal to tell you the nature of your next task.

'He should pull them out, I think,' said Gerry Tooks, scanning the now-decoded intelligence that the patrol had sent back. 'Get someone to work on this and make it neat before we courier it to Northwood.'

'If we get them out quick enough,' added Lippy Grant.

He had to shout over the noise of a pneumatic drill as he followed his troop commander from the comms room into the main planning room. This was brand new and still smelling of fresh paint. The whole Hereford base was in the process of being rebuilt, which was just dandy considering what was happening elsewhere in the world.

'They can brief the prunes from D and G before they go in.'

The soft hum of the air conditioning had a reassuring quality, as did the lights that illuminated the large maps of the South Atlantic. So far the Regiment was performing well, if not perfectly. D had got ashore at South Georgia, though they had lost several boats and a couple of choppers doing it. The submarine threat, which could have jeopardized the whole shooting match, had been dealt with that day when a Lynx

34

sent a Sea Dart missile into the tin can's hull, forcing it to beach. It looked as though the resistance on the island was about to collapse, giving the forces their first bit of Falkland success.

'Get a signal off to Northwood, Lippy. Ask the Navy what they have close enough to get our boys out. Then get a message on the evening sitrep to JRM's HQ and suggest we extract them to brief his teams. Add that we will be talking by Satcom later, so we can pass a go message to Blue then.'

Lippy grinned. The signals should have been the other way round. 'You think he'd leave them there?'

'I'd rather not chance it,' Gerry snapped. 'He won't like having no one ashore at all. But even Jamie will see the sense in pumping them before he sends in his major recces.'

'Fuck me, boss,' Lippy replied. 'I wish I was down there with them.'

'So do I, Lippy, so do I.'

Gerry reflected, in the ensuing silence, that since they meant it, they must both be fucking crazy.

The tab back to that beach was a worse trip than the one in. The team were past their peak, still fit and capable, but tired after days spent in fitful sleep, and nights occupied marching, infiltrating, and exfiltrating Argentine positions. No matter how well you tried to take care of yourself, the risks of things like dehydration or hypothermia were always there. The razor-sharp edge had gone off their performance, and all four were working on sheer will power to retain their effectiveness. With a RV already scheduled, they had a deadline to meet. But that couldn't be allowed to compromise anything. The Argentines mustn't know they'd been there at all, even after they were gone.

The LUP was left pristine, with no trace of their ever having occupied it. The march was carried out with the same adherence to procedure as they'd used ten days before. The listening or rest stops were fixed and had to be just as alert. Blue still issued and re-capped his orders, checked compasses, distances and map references. The actual approach to the cache on the beach was made with as much caution as any approach they'd made since landing.

The Gemini was retrieved and reinflated with the foot pump, the outboard topped up with fuel while Graunch had a look at the original, the one which had packed up, only to pronounce it useless. They took it with them only to avoid discovery. They were back in their dry suits and on water within an hour, Blue setting the course with his old Spitfire compass, to make the meet with the frigate that was tasked to pick them up. As soon as they were in the arc of the rendezvous, Blue fired up the flashing beacon that guided the rigid raider to them, a boat that took them in tow and back to its mother ship.

CHAPTER THREE

Cabinet Office to Fleet HQ Northwood: 1/5/82. The War Cabinet consider the presence of a capital enemy ship close to the Falklands total exclusion zone a most serious and unacceptable threat to proposed operations. You are hereby instructed to engage the Belgrano with all available force at your disposal.

Damp, still cold and carrying eight days' growth, the four troopers didn't get to a shower until they were aboard *Hermes*. That meant as a group that they didn't attract close company, either on the frigate that lifted them out, or on the chopper that ferried them to the command vessel, *Fearless*. Even Jamie Robertson-Macleod stayed well downwind as they were debriefed. That took over an hour, and by the time they'd finished telling him and his staff about the ground, the Argies, the airport and the weather, the whole cabin was full of the stench of the seriously underwashed.

The Green Slime posed most of the questions, his job of intelligence officer giving him the lead role in milking the returned troopers of information. But every time he paused to make a note, either the CO, the Operations Officer or the G Squadron OC, Major Sam Cullis, put their oar in. Plied with questions, tea and cigarettes in equal measure, they found themselves repeating the same answers over and over again.

Ground description; anticipated tabbing times as opposed to proposed; making and camming of hides; Argentine troop movement; establishment of vehicles; level of personal armament; unit complement of heavy firepower; location of anti-aircraft, radar, any missile batteries; mapping of troop concentrations, bunkers, equipment observed; morale; level of training; weather; effects of elevation; water tables; availability of food from natural resources; all put a dozen times. It wasn't anything Blue and his boys objected to. These Headshed guys were just being careful, making sure they had the full monty, and not just a fleeting impression of what recce life was like on the Falkland Islands. When they put the next patrols in, their initial actions – and some of their targets – would be based on what was said in this cabin.

What would happen with the information wasn't their concern. But Blue could draw some conclusions from the drift of the questioning. You could never quite trust a Rupert, men well schooled in keeping things to themselves. But it seemed to him that they were very seriously adrift on info about the Argentine Order of Battle. The things they concentrated on showed a need to correct this, and given the difficulties of moving on the Falklands it looked like some of their mates were in for a cold, hard time. The best way to gather intelligence was to pile in the numbers, get them into a good position, and keep them there to report back on a daily basis.

'That satellite phone, Powell,' said JRM. 'Worked a treat. Gerry Tooks says it was as if you were standing right next to him.'

'Christ,' said Digger, under his breath, 'what a bloody nightmare.'

'*Merveilleuse*, boss,' Graunch replied, throwing a glare at the Cockney. 'But it's *une grande mère* to hoik about.'

'Then you'll be glad to get shot of it?'

Graunch tried to look disinterested, but he didn't manage it very well.

'Or would you like to keep it?' The question was posed in a way that indicated such a thing wouldn't happen.

'*Certainement*,' Graunch answered, in a tone of voice that appeared to be already saying goodbye.

'Sorry,' the Colonel said. 'But we've only got two of the buggers. And there are a few ops coming up that will just suit that kind of kit.'

Graunch was all innocence. 'Will they have time to learn how to use it, boss, that is before they're put ashore?'

The Green Slime looked at Graunch suspiciously. Perhaps he was wondering how this Brummie boy with the terrible French had sussed the Headshed's intentions. That was typical of Intelligence. They were so seriously short on brains, they assumed everyone else must be the same.

'They can learn from the manual, Powell. You did!'

Robertson-Macleod must have known what was coming before Graunch replied. He was a good-looking man, who knew it, tall with that sort of blond hair that had natural streaks in it, bright blue eyes and the kind of smiling charm that had earned him the nickname 'Sundance'. He didn't look charming now. He looked like the hard-nosed bastard he really was.

'*Une prob*, boss. I don't have a clue where it is. Might be aboard the sub, or *peut-être* it just got left in our hide.'

If ever an expression screamed lying bastard, it was the one on the CO's face. That brought a little hope to Graunch's own look. But that changed as Robertson-Macleod suddenly grinned, showing teeth that did nothing to dent the movie star image he was so very conscious of.

'The wonders of science, Graunch. We got another one with a manual and access to a photocopier.'

'*Quelle chance*,' Graunch responded, trying to sound sincere. Never the chirpiest of guys, he now sounded like a man who'd forgotten to post his winning Pools coupon. Blue guessed that inside that ugly head of his, he was screaming 'fucking Rupert' to himself.

A quick discussion followed, while everybody made sure that they understood what favour or faults the new kit had. Graunch, for all his disappointment, described it carefully, adding that once the Yanks had additional satellites up, the link would become an absolute must. There had never even been a hint of malfunction, vital because nothing destroyed the integrity of an operation more quickly than badly performing kit. That didn't mean slagging off the PRC320. One operation, in which the movement had been minimal, was not a true test of the Satcom's ability. Any radio that had a proven track record of working was better than a Star Trek gizmo that might play up.

When that finished, Robertson-Macleod broke the meeting up, turning to address Blue Harding, who was leaning back, so low in his chair that he looked smaller than Digger. He didn't miss the slight flicker of annoyance. JRM wasn't used to other ranks lounging in his presence, regardless of the time he'd spent in the Regiment. It was always a problem for Ruperts, who did specified tours then returned to their original units. The contrast between the standard Green Army bullshit and badged trooper attitudes was never quite resolved. Officers generally preferred men who stood to attention and saluted.

What Robertson-Macleod saw was the very opposite. Having been Blue's troop commander when he passed selection he knew the subject quite well. There wasn't a lot of traffic in the gossip department between officers and men. But there was some, and the soldier JRM was looking at now tended to generate quite a bit. Under the dirt there was a man who was as hard and good as he was himself. If Blue Harding didn't have movie star looks he had the style.

Off base or operations he was Mr Cool. He spent the kind of money on clothes some guys spent on home improvements, bought the latest electronic kit when it hit the shelf and was the oracle on fashion and rock 'n' roll music. He was smooth on a dance floor too, and a lot of his fellow troopers didn't like him for that. Blue was not the kind of guy to leave alone with any women you held in high regard. He'd been married three times, which showed he was better at the theory of pulling birds than the practice of keeping women.

But on an operation he was respected. Not only was he good at his own job, he had natural ability when it came to getting the best out of others. The trouble, for Robertson-Macleod, was that annoying air that Blue had, which told even someone as high ranking as him, in no uncertain terms, that he knew his strengths. But whatever he thought, this was no time and no place to pull rank.

'Right Blue. I don't know if you've been told. We retook South Georgia last Sunday, so all our ops are going to be on the main islands from now on. You lot are the only people from B Squadron here ...'

'How's that?' demanded Digger. 'B should have been on standby as soon as D became engaged.'

'It was decided to deploy G Squadron instead,' said JRM.

Digger was glaring now. There was a Guards Mafia in the Regiment, especially amongst the Ruperts, that definitely looked after the squadron the rest called Woodentops. G was sponsored by the Brigade of Guards, being the butt of many jokes, as well as much resentment, from the men who saw themselves as the three originals. The worst thing was the way they imported some of their bullshit. It didn't take too much thinking to figure out that, with a real war to fight and glory on the table, the Mafia had bumped G up to the head of the tree. If there was any success going, the Woodentops would be desperate to hog it. No imagination was required, either, to guess how their fellow B Squadron members had taken this. They must be fucking livid!

Why they alone, of B Squadron, were here, was obvious. They'd been doing float on, float off when the shit hit the fan. And they'd been within a cough and a spit of a sub heading south. But Digger asked anyway, forcing JRM to confirm. He always did with authority, because, as he liked to put it, 'You got to keep the fucking Ruperts on their toes.'

'D and G are on *Hermes*,' Robertson-Macleod added, 'so you can attach yourself to one of them for sustenance.'

Digger was still miffed, which gave what was meant as a joke a very hard edge. 'That's like asking me who I like to room with, Frankenstein or Dracula.'

'Shut up, Dig,' said Graunch.

Jamie Robertson-Macleod grinned again, not in the least put out by Digger's interruptions. 'I shouldn't worry, cobber. You'll hardly have time to wipe your arse before you're off again.'

It was a measure of the respect that JRM generated that Digger didn't respond with a put down. Normally, and as a dyed in the wool Londoner, if anyone called him cobber, hinting that he was an Aussie, he gave them a mouthful of abuse. He'd got his down-under nickname from a drunken nocturnal adventure in Hereford, during which he'd pinched and driven around in a JCB. It was not a good idea to steal a JCB digger in a quiet rural town. Fortunately he'd abandoned it before the local filth caught up with him, and the subsequent questions they'd put to the Boss had been fielded for lack of evidence. Mad as he was, JRM stuck to the rule: the Regiment looks after its own.

The main deck of *Hermes* was packed with stores: great cases of spares, trucks, Land Rovers and artillery. There were Sea Kings and Harriers too, some undergoing maintenance, others stripped near the workshops for serious repair, the sparks from welding guns creating an area of bright light in the otherwise poorly illuminated area. The ship was pitching and rolling, shuddering throughout its whole frame as the bows dug into the huge South Atlantic rollers. At least here, in this vast hangar underneath the flight deck, they were out of the wind, which had made their crossing hairy and the landing so tricky. And the blowback of spume from the bows had soaked them with spray before they made it to shelter.

Not that they were then entirely dry, given the amount of water dripping from the overhead metal. *Hermes* was an old ship and it showed, especially since the kind of painting and maintenance that was carried out on peacetime service had been abandoned for the duration.

Bulkhead doors didn't quite fit and had to be shouldered shut; rust was showing through where the thick layers of grey paint couldn't contain it. It sounded ancient as well, creaking and groaning as though it was about to fall apart and drop them all into the South Atlantic. The crew looked just as grey, with sallow complexions and depressed spirits that seemed to match the ship they served in.

They didn't have to ask directions. Anyone they met on the way down would wrinkle their nose and point to a companionway or a bulkhead door. That led them to the main deck, the heart of the ship, and finally to a screened-off area towards the bows where they'd rigged a heavy cable to hold tarpaulins, this set aside to accommodate the SAS 'pongos'. Here, towards the front of the main deck, which stank with a mixture of oil, aviation fuel and seawater, the motion of the ship seemed exaggerated, each dip into a trough sending the men staggering towards the nearest thing they could hold on to. Behind the heavy tarpaulin screens there were two distinct areas with an avenue down the middle, both deserted, one for D Squadron and another G. There would be little traffic in between even when the guys were around. For Blue and his men the preference was simple. There was no way the smooth operators from B Squadron would volunteer to basha up with the Woodentops from G.

Just then, a voice, which seemed to come from the bottom of a sleeping bag, solved the problem. 'What the fuck are you doing here?'

'Is that you, Grizzly?' asked Blue.

The face that emerged was clean-shaven, but even in the dim overhead bulkhead lights Blue could see the parchment coloured skin and thick growth that had earned Billy Cook his nickname. He was wearing a woolly hat, and underneath that lay a mat of pepper and salt hair. His body, chest, torso, back and legs was coated in more hair, all jet-black. Billy also had a voice so deep he made Lee Marvin sound like a soprano. He and Blue had been in the Green Jackets, and had done selection around the same time, in the middle of winter. Not only could Billy sink ten pints a night and rise in the morning to do his tabbing, with all that hair he could have gone out naked in the snow and still got through. Blue liked him, and had hoped they would end up in the same troop. Why they hadn't was a mystery, known only to the fucking Ruperts who ran the Regiment.

'We're on holiday, mate,' said Digger, as *Hermes* slammed into another roller, the lifting of the bows causing those standing up to perform a sudden sideways dance to keep their balance. 'Got a real cheap offer from a bucket shop.'

'Well you certainly found the biggest fucking bucket in the world,' moaned Grizzly, pulling himself free of his Gonk bag just as *Hermes* thudded back to drop into the subsequent trough. 'I didn't know the mavericks from B were on this job.'

'I told you we wanted the South Pacific,' whooped Luke Tuikabe. He followed that with a hard punch to Digger's shoulder that produced a big frown. 'That's the last time I let you book my vacation, man.'

'Somebody give this fuckin' ape a tree to climb, please. That's all he needs to feel at home.'

Hermes rolled suddenly as Blue replied, but the troopers had their feet spread wide now, and rode it out, though the sounds of metal bending and cargo straining at its bindings forced him to raise his voice. He was trying to sound normal, but it was clear from his complexion that he wasn't happy with the motion of the ship.

'We got a fast ball from Gib, mate. They knew you'd need some real soldiers around to make sure you lot didn't fuck up.'

'From the smell it was a shit ball, not a fast ball.'

'We're looking for *une place à mettre la tête*,' Graunch added, tapping his forehead and beginning to slip off his Bergen.

Grizzly Cook flicked his hand. 'The heads are that way.'

'Jesus Christ!' Digger exclaimed, 'D Squadron makes a fuckin' pun.'

'Seriously, Grizz,' added Blue, dropping to his knees to ride out the new roll of the ship. 'The Headshed told us to basha up with you lot.'

'That'll cheer a few people up,' Grizzly replied, giving Blue a knowing look. 'Still, there's no birds around except seagulls, and nobody will mind if you fuck one of them.'

Digger couldn't stay silent. 'You ain't seen this man chat up a lady albatross.'

'Nope,' Billy Cook replied. 'But I've seen him carry the odd one around. I can never understand why you elbow the nice ones and marry the dogs.'

'Breeding, mate!' snapped Digger. 'He can't cope with it.'

Blue flicked his head to the other area, belonging to G Squadron, now more defined by the neatness of the layout. 'So you're goin' to bang us in with them are you? And I thought we were mates.'

Grizzly Cook was on his feet now, swaying easily on well-attuned sea legs to contain the motion of the ship. 'Naw. I wouldn't do that to you. They might start talking to you about a career in the Army.'

'They did that at Shorncliffe, old mate.'

Grizzly, with a complexion that was near to sallow and deep lines in his face, wasn't long in the smiling stakes. But that name, and the association with the Woodentops, nearly made him look as though he was suffering as badly as Blue. No one remembered their first days in the Army with any affection. Eight weeks of being shouted and sworn at by moronic bastards, the instructors from the Brigade of Guards. It coloured the way you thought from then on.

'Not that there's many of them about,' Grizzly added. 'Most have heli'd to the frigates to go on ops. The four that are left are to be lifted out at sundown.'

Hermes did a corkscrew then, not only lifting but also sliding sideways so violently that not even Grizzly could quite handle it. He managed to stay upright, but only just, while the others, even on their knees, had to throw out a hand to remain stable. From some distant place they could hear the sound of something breaking, either crockery or glass.

'Sundown!' exclaimed Digger. 'Have you put your barnet on deck, Grizzly? The sun's never fucking come up.'

'Where I come from the sun never stops shining,' said Luke.

'I know,' Digger growled. 'It's such a fucking paradise you flew ten thousand miles to get to the UK.'

'The women is easier, man, especially for a guy that's got somethin' to offer.'

'Like a pineapple for a brain.'

'Where we've been is no fuckin' paradise, that's for sure,' moaned Blue. 'It's so fuckin' miserable we should pay the Argies for taking it off us. And water? Can you get your hands on any plastic sheeting, Grizz?'

'What?'

'Find some before you go ashore, man,' Luke insisted. 'We've just been over the Headshed telling them how fuckin' wet it is.'

'And cold, mate,' added Digger. 'Brass monkeys ain't in it.'

Graunch chimed in, so passionately he used no flat-vowelled French this time. 'If you're in a hide on the flat ground, you need fuckin' water wings.'

'I know we ain't got any.'

'What about the matelots?'

Blue looked at the great tarpaulins that cut off this section of the deck. Grizzly got up and fingered them too, but he pulled them back to reveal the packed main deck. The metal floor was running with water that only got halfway to one side before the ship rolled to bring it coursing back again.

'I bet half that shit there is packed in plastic.'

'I make you right.'

'Two ticks,' he said.

The speed with which Billy Cook moved, and the ease with which he found what he was looking for, testified to one heavy fact: this was not the first time he had indulged in a little light-fingered acquisition. The plastic sheet he found was out of the packing case, folded and in his Gonk bag in minutes, a look of pure innocence as he turned back to face Blue Harding.

'Can't upset the matelots, mate. They are not a happy bunch.'

'We noticed!' said Blue.

'Must be 'cause there's a war on,' Digger replied.

'Will you give us a full brief, Blue?'

The ethic of the Regiment said you didn't enquire, you never asked a man where he was going or where he'd been. That was pure bollocks, typical Rupert-speak. They could be so tight-lipped they wouldn't pass on the location of the bogs in a strange pub. Blue was a trooper, and would happily pass on what he'd learned even to the Woodentops of G Squadron.

'I'd rather do it after a shower, mate.'

Grizzly rode the wave as he held his nose, making his deep voice sound Dalek-like. 'I wasn't goin' to insist on it bein' delivered before.'

Northwood was a place to make anyone schizoid, a pleasant house in rolling grounds, that once entered became like a set for *Dr Strangelove*. Below, in the underground Operations area, the air conditioning hummed quietly, giving a peaceful air to what was a war room. There were actually two rooms: the one used for normal operations, the other a special high-security suite that was designated as solely for the control of Polaris-carrying subs. But the Navy, forced to share their premises with the other services because of the combined nature of the operation, had commandeered that for their private deliberations. The lights in the main area were bright and fluorescent, and the numerous Wrens the pick of the Navy's lovelies. Cornelius Hosier hated the place. Not because he didn't like a good HQ but because he wasn't running things.

In fact, with all the brass around he was a mite junior. Admirals abounded, tall beetle-browed Radcliffe and tubby little Onslow top dogs, a Shautzer and a pug, lording it over the mere mortals that surrounded them. Hosier had already nicknamed them the Kennel Club. But there were generals and air marshals too, all in best bib and tucker, wearing medal ribbons and thick lanyards. This caused him to wonder if his attachment to camouflage jackets and jungle boots made him look like a bit of a tit. Whatever, it was better than regulation uniform, which even with his red staff tabs, in these surroundings, would have condemned him to total obscurity.

There were other officers in his predicament, too high to be denied access, but too low to be consulted regarding operations outside their own specific sphere. From them, he'd accepted the congratulations for the capture of South Georgia with becoming modesty, even though he'd had no hand in either the planning or execution of the action. Indeed, the word 'Rejoice', so tellingly used by the PM outside 10 Downing Street, had begun to dominate his vocabulary in the last twenty-four hours.

Right now there was something going on that had the matelots on tenterhooks. Hushed conversations were taking place between officers as they exited the Polaris Ops room. Convention denied Hosier the direct enquiry. His hints had been ignored so comprehensively that he'd been tempted, just to wind up all these salts, to pick up a phone and loudly demand to be put through to General Galtieri.

'It seeped out of course,' he informed his wife over dinner. 'These things always do. Had it from a young Wren, who just drooled over the old SAS monicker and insisted trying on my beret.'

Aware of the look he was getting from his wife, who knew perfectly well why he traipsed around in combat gear, he continued hurriedly.

'Seems the Argies have a cruiser called the *General Belgrano*. Odd that, callin' a ship after a soldier.'

'Did we not once have an HMS *Wellington*?' his wife asked.

'I believe we did. Anyway, this tub is stooging about outside the exclusion zone. The Kennel Club had their knickers in a twist about the bugger. Got some kind of green light from the PM to take action, but they wanted it to be more specific. A clear order, no less.'

Miranda Hosier listened intently. She was a loyal wife, ambitious for her husband, quite prepared to be angry on his behalf even when there were doubts about the rightness of his cause. Had anyone accused her of a modicum of bias, they would have faced the full force of her not inconsiderable wrath. This would have been delivered in a voice that made field marshals take notice; one that had been honed by the fight to become head girl of her very good private school with no academic ability whatsoever. To her way of thinking, and a fact she imparted to all of her friends, Corny'd been treated abominably, appointed to a supervisory post just as all hell broke loose. The daughter of a general, she knew that opportunity was a fickle thing in the Army, and that reputations were rarely enhanced behind desks. Since most of her companions were also espoused to soldiers, they nodded politely, while plotting their own husbands' advancement. But one thing they would all have agreed on. The Navy were stuck up, out-of-date fools, while the Royal Air Force were an absolute, spendthrift shower.

'One wonders what the Navy is for, darling, if it's not to sink ships. Surely with all the billions they've wasted on Polaris missiles, they have the means.'

'Politics, my dear. The PM and the War Cabinet have to give the go-ahead. From what this Wren told me, it seems the bloody thing is not only outside the zone, it's sailing in the wrong direction.'

'Surely Maggie Thatcher won't let nonsense like that deflect her. Good god, Corny, they're the enemy after all!'

'There are people around the PM without her cast iron pudenda.'

'Really Corny, that is a bit barrack room.' Miranda didn't object to her husband swearing. After all, he was a soldier, of necessity masculine in habit. But she did like to remind him occasionally that vulgarity was a privilege that she bestowed.

'Sorry, my dear,' the Brig replied, with the automatic tone of the frequently guilty. 'Anyway, I thought I'd nip back to Northwood and see what's up.'

'Stiffen the old sinews, what?' his wife barked, swinging her wine glass. 'That's it darling. That's it precisely.'

Miranda Hosier put the knife in with an ease born of long practice, her voice so low it was near to a masculine growl. 'Or is it that pretty little Wren?'

All Brigadier Cornelius Hosier could manage, in response, was a slightly goofy smile.

He was still at Northwood, sharing a pink gin with the Wren lieutenant, when the news came in. He was then given cause to wonder at the cheering that erupted in the officers' mess. As he pointed out to Miranda, 'A brand new state-of-the-art nuke sub had clobbered a ship as old as the Ark.'

Mind you, he had to join in the celebrations, being in the company of a naval officer. But he did notice, as he sipped and flattered, that there were a few wiser folk around. Sailors who shook their heads at the loss of life when the news came in that the *Belgrano* was sinking. These were men who had lain in their own bunks sweating in terror at the prospect of drowning. They couldn't 'rejoice' even when their enemies met that hideous end.

'I have my car outside,' he said to his Wren, who was showing interesting signs of a desire to celebrate this naval triumph. 'Can I drop you off?'

'Super,' she replied, throwing up her arm, and sinking the contents of her glass in one throw.

They didn't cheer wildly on *Hermes* either, the crackling announcement from the skipper greeted with excited, but subdued murmuring. Men were expiring in the same water that was under their heaving keel, a thousand freezing fathoms. The crew, nearly 1400 strong, were sailing into battle, a conflict made more real by the destruction of the Argentines' most prestigious ship. *Hermes* was the command vessel for the Task Force! She had prestige too, enough to increase the likelihood of a retaliatory strike by an enemy sub.

Blue and his team paid little attention. Now washed, shaved and smelling of carbolic they sat in the galley, eating and talking, surrounded by the men of the two active squadrons, answering questions, fielding the endemic inter-unit insults, and baiting Digger about the chances of Spurs winning the FA Cup. Grizzly, in the more serious moments, told them that most of his guys were on the way back from South Georgia, and since that had been partly a Boat Troop operation for D, they discussed it at length.

'Hi, shitface!' said Grizzly, looking over Blue's shoulder.

Turning round, Blue was faced by Lew Stradler. A scaley, Lew worked on the Regimental Signals. He'd set up the SAS comms link on *Hermes*, causing much resentment by the way in which he'd bagged himself a cabin in the process. Grizzly'd already mentioned it, and told them about the *Whitehouse* and *Fiesta* pictures that covered the walls.

'How are things in the wank parlour?'

'Don't you start, Grizzly,' Lew replied, his dark-skinned face breaking into a grin. 'I've had the skipper at me to stop you lot on the flight deck. Says he can't hear the rhythm of the engines for you lot pumping away.'

'Use it or lose it,' said Blue, who'd recovered from his original bout of discomfort on coming aboard.

'You should know, slippery,' Lew replied.

'What do you reckon on Spurs, Lew?' asked Digger, knowing the scaley was a fellow supporter.

'Can't lose, Digger.'

'If I promise to be nice to you,' said Digger in a fey voice, 'can I share your cabin? Then we can talk about tactics.'

'You'd have to wear a skirt to get in my cabin.'

'You hear that, MacLoughlin?' Digger called to a huge man who sat at the end of the table. 'If you've got your kilt with you, shit-stabber Lew here will let you into his bunk.'

When it came to a sense of humour, the Army barmy guys of G were not well supplied. And of all the people in G, MacLoughlin was one of the worst. Huge, ginger-haired and an ex-Scots Guardsman, he was a bad man to tangle with. And since he had a voice that was too high for his massive frame, he was very sensitive to remarks regarding his manhood. That was, of course, to Digger, like a red rag to a bull.

'Ya wee Cockney shite,' he barked, his already red face deepening in colour. 'Shut yer gob or ah'll claim ye!'

'Lew,' said Digger, looking puzzled. 'You do comms. Can you do a bit of decoding and tell me what that ginger-haired Jock bastard said?'

'I think he says he wants a kiss,' said Graunch. 'He must have heard about you fuckin' ex-jockeys all being poofs.'

'After you,' snapped Digger, ''cause if he plants one on your ugly mug we'll know the bastard's blind as well as dense.'

'Children,' hooted Blue.

'Tosspots the lot of you,' said Lew, as he waved a piece of paper in his hand. 'I came to tell you what this said, arsehole. Grizz, you're stood down for at least twenty-four, since the South G lot won't be back till then.'

'I'm heartbroken,' growled Billy Cook.

'Blue, you and your team are on the same standby as G. They're sending through orders for you later. The good news is you'll be going by chopper this time.'

'At night?'

Grizzly saw Blue's eyebrows shoot up. 'You'd better eat some fuckin' carrots.'

'Don't let him wind you up, Blue,' said Lew. 'Some of the heli pilots got hold of PNG kit before they sailed.'

'Brilliant,' Blue responded, recalling the trip he'd had in the Gemini. Just thinking about the way they'd been tossed about made him feel slightly sick again. 'That means we'll arrive dry.'

CHAPTER FOUR

07.00: From: Flag Officer: Fleet: To: HMS Sheffield. Relieve HMS Coventry. Effect immediate.

Certain they were going out that night, the four would have slept all day if it hadn't been for the alarm. But when you're on a ship, and you hear a rumour that another has been taken out by a missile, snoring your way through the excitement isn't on. And when an aircraft carrier goes from a defence watch to full action stations, the racket would wake the dead. It was klaxons blaring, alarm bells ringing and sailors rushing in all directions, presumably to positions that they knew, even if it didn't look that way. That was all over in five minutes. And if it hadn't been for the noise the ship itself was making, as the plating expanded, twisted and contracted in the heavy seas, it would have been possible to say that silence had descended. SAS troopers had no function, and with action stations called it seemed daft to just sit on the main deck surrounded by their guns and ammo. But they had no choice. Had they gone up and tried to help out they would have just got in the way.

So they repaired once more to the galley, empty and silent, and set about making a brew. When *Hermes* stood down, that earned them a few glares as the matelots returned to their stations. The sailors had been less than friendly when Blue and his team came aboard, which had earned a few of them the edge of Digger's tongue. Grizzly had provided the soothing oil, explaining that it was not hostility, more indifference. Sure they'd seen the guys on TV doing Princes Gate. But the Special Forces had come aboard in gear very close to standard Green Army kit. They looked nothing like black-clad Embassy siege teams, and were thus just standard Pongos. Communication couldn't come from the troopers because it wasn't allowed, and probably some officer had told them to stay clear of these weirdos. And the poor sods were really on edge, already tired from doing watch on watch off, with constant alerts to make sure they never got a decent kip.

Matters were made worse, especially for the ratings, by a lack of information. They'd announced the *Belgrano* on the PA. Whatever had happened they should do the same now. These guys were only human. The best way to allay their very real fears was to tell them all. But the naval Ruperts were keeping things to themselves, so speculation was rife. Blue, bleary eyed as he watched the matelots running to their posts, wasn't even sure if one ship had gone down in ten seconds, let alone the six or eight one of the ratings had screamed out to another.

Everyone knew that the Argies had sea-skimming missiles, French-built Exocets, and the planes to deliver them. It was on the bloody news! Now, as the ship reduced to a lower level of readiness, it was filtering down from the bridge that a vessel had been hit before the crew knew the Exocet was coming in. Even if it turned out to be true, no one bothered to reassure the poor bastards from the flight deck to the engine room of *Hermes* that with Harriers from *Invincible* flying Combat Air Patrols, there was no way the Argies could shoot off at the flagship before they were engaged.

The seeming calm of him and his mates must have rankled too. The matelots were jumpy, the pongos laughing and joking. There was always a gap between the attitude of any badged trooper and another serviceman. Most of the sailors had joined to see the world and to drink in exotic ports. They craved a life of cheap booze, with easy-going tarts on their laps. The double payoff was that moment when they could swagger as they returned home, to lord it over the berks who'd never been further than the pub at the end of the street, lighting up their lives with tales of twenty-pence blow jobs. These pongo spooks were different. They liked a fight, and expected one, even if peace reigned throughout the world. In other words, they were nutters, and best avoided.

'What's that?' asked Digger.

He'd come across MacLoughlin on the main deck, now open to the elements as the lifts carried helicopters up to the flight deck. The ginger-haired Scotsman glared at him, his habitual frown deeper than normal. You could see in his eye that he was still thinking that there must be a quiet place, away from prying eyes, where he could give Digger the kind of good news which would shut him up. But then Luke Tuikabe was with the Londoner. He was as big as the Jock, probably even stronger, and for all the smiling nature of his behaviour, a real evil bastard in a fight.

MacLoughlin had been bent over a huge wooden crate when Digger first saw him. Only his size and temper saved the Scots Guardsman from a boot in the arse. Now he was stood upright, and was holding a tube five foot long, with a mass of electronics at the front.

'They caw it a Stinger.'

'I heard about it. Yank job?'

'Aye. None o' that wire shite you have wi' our bits. It wurks oan infrared heat.' MacLoughlin lifted it onto his shoulder, and squinted through a sight at the empty, grey sky above the lowered lift. 'Accordin' tae whit a'hve been telt ye just hold it up and hoik the trigger.'

The Londoner, who looked like a dwarf beside the gigantic Jock, peered along the barrel, unable to see what was inside the casing because of the Scotsman's massive hands.

'OK MacGenius, where's the trigger?'

'A dinna ken, dae ah,' MacLoughlin snorted. 'A huv'na read the book yet.'

'Luke. Would you do me a favour?'

'What's that, man?'

'Nip up to the bridge and say to Sandy Woodward not to light his pipe. Tell him if he does, ginger Jock here, who never reads the instructions, will stick a heat-seeking missile up his arse.'

They knew only too well what was happening at Northwood. They had their own comms link with *Hermes* as well as the ships that had gone to the aid of *Sheffield*. Soon they had an addition to that. Satellite television had been patched through from the main networks so they could see on the screens before them the terrible damage the Exocet had inflicted on the frigate, a burning smoking hulk, already listing badly. Grim as it was, Cornelius Hosier took some quiet satisfaction from the way it had wiped the cockiness out of the top naval brass.

Most of the men in the Ops room had risen to high rank on a diet of expectation rather than action, training for a conflict that never happened, shots fired in practice rather than anger. Talking about taking casualties was vastly different from actual loss. Real blood, and death barring an accident, was alien to them. That applied to half the officers from the other services. But he'd seen blood spilt for real; in the jungle, in desert sands, and in half a dozen places he was not allowed to mention. Like all men who'd actually experienced action, he loathed people he perceived as armchair warriors.

'Well we're not that now.'

'Sorry, old boy?' asked Toppy Monckton, an RAF group captain who had once flown him and his men in and out of various trouble spots.

'Thinking aloud, Toppy. That this is the real thing for most of these chaps.' The voice dropped an octave, to emphasize the gravity of his words. 'No longer a game, if you take my point.'

The Group Captain looked at the screen, with the ship burning fiercely as the fire hoses from her consorts played over her hull. 'Poor sods.'

'Should have seen the damn thing coming, surely?'

Monckton shrugged. 'Easier said than done, old chap. I don't know how good their counter-measures are, these days. Long time since I played at sea-skimmers. But they've come on in leaps the last few years and that Exocet's a real bugger, even if it ain't the very best. Fast, poor radar profile, and with a stability that has allowed the Frogs to experiment at firing it off very low. Evidently they have succeeded.'

Monckton went into a long explanation about sea-skimming missiles in general, and Exocets in particular. The claim that he knew little was soon laid to rest. He knew the damn things intimately: weight, speed and construction. As the comms crackled and whirred in the background, he reeled off a stream of depressing information. He used his hands to highlight the manoeuvres with which RAF had tried to outwit the Navy, adding with an arch smile that they'd always won. He then added his opinion of the way the Argies must have deployed them.

'Firing at short range, planes coming in below the horizon with their own radar off, so that, as targets, they'd show only when they hopped up to fire. Have to do that so the Exocet radar can lock on. Result, the first you know about the attack is when your radar picks up the plane just as the bloody missile is fired. That is now coming towards you, locked on to your own system, at over six hundred miles an hour.'

'So how d'you stop it?'

'Chaff and that sort of stuff helps. But another missile is better, and most Navy ships haven't got the new kit to take it down.'

'What kit is that?'

'Sea Wolf. Specially designed to operate at low level. All the old stuff, like Sea Dart is designed for sky work, which is where they expected the Ruskies to come from. We've told them more'n once that there's bound to be another way, and quite possibly another enemy.'

'I dare say they'll deny you ever said that.'

Monckton frowned. 'Without doubt, old chap. Never do to let on that they were warned. Thank Christ the Argies have got limited range. Only the Super Etendards can deliver the bugger, and they seem to lack extra fuel tanks. Just as well. If they had those the whole bloody task force would have to steam home.'

This led to another long explanation, full of Mirages, Skyhawks, Super Etendards, spare fuel tanks and fighter ranges and poor warship design. This was spiced with the odd question from Cornelius Hosier. A naturally curious man, he was fascinated by all aspects of warfare, believing that you could never tell when some small piece of information, apparently useless, could be the difference between success and failure on an operation. And Toppy had all the time in the world to answer the enquiries, for as he put it, he had, 'Bugger all to do!'

But as he chivvied the RAF man along, Hosier's mind was beavering subconsciously on another level. It was some time before he realized which way he was taking the conversation. It was really only when Monckton let on that the intelligence estimates of the number of missiles the Argies had were just that – good guesswork rather than hard intelligence.

'Can't be sure if they've not got dozens of the bloody things.' The Group Captain nodded towards the still flickering television. 'The Frogs are bein' very cagey about letting on, though it's to be hoped pictures of the poor bloody *Sheffield* might jog their memories.'

Hosier opened his mouth to speak, but stopped himself, then added a meaningless insult to the French armed forces, which covered for his true thoughts. In a matter of seconds he had worked out two things. The level of the threat those missiles posed to a fleet at sea, as well as a way to handle it, the plan complete in seemingly every detail. But he wasn't about to tell Toppy Monckton. In fact, he quickly decided not to tell anyone until he could present an actual plan. A voice broke his train of thought, though the words started another.

'Admiral Radcliffe, the PM is on the secure line.'

Barney Molesworth being in the South Atlantic wouldn't turn out to be such a bad idea after all.

Gerry Tooks looked at the signal the following morning. It was a request from Brigadier Hosier to be sent the latest data on Hercules C130s, details of the mid-air refuelling capabilities, correlations of airspeed, information on the prevailing wind patterns south of Buenos Aires, plus an update on the strength of B Squadron.

'I told you,' said Lippy Grant, when Gerry Tooks passed it to him.

'He's just playing silly buggers,' Gerry scoffed.

'He's fuckin' well equipped to.'

Tooks grinned. 'I was in the mess with him one night, after a formal scoff for HRH. The Sock was a bit pissed, and he was waxing on about that film *Patton.*'

'I saw it. The Yanks win the war without any help, yet again.'

'Don't knock the Yanks, old son. The kit and signal intelligence that they've given us to fight this little skirmish is priceless.'

Gerry Tooks was aware that Lippy Grant was looking at him strangely, wondering where all this was leading. 'You know the scene where the Jerries have just broken through in the Ardennes, and the brass are sitting around wondering what to do.'

'And old Patton produces a plan.'

'Jock the Sock loved that bit. "That, Tooks," he said, poking me in the chest, "is what we must be like. One step ahead of the bloody generals."'

'That's rich coming from him. He won't be happy till he's Chief of the Defence Staff.'

'God help us, Lippy,' Tooks said, with real feeling. 'I'll bloody well pack it in if he gets that job.'

'Don't kid yourself it's not what he's after.'

'He might be after it, old son. But not even our brass is dumb enough to give it to him.'

Lippy had gone over to the wall, to look at the Falklands map. 'You think he's after a para drop?'

'Possible, Lippy, very possible.'

'That was binned before South G.'

'By JRM. And before *Sheffield* went down.'

Lippy did another very passable imitation of Hosier's voice, sounding quite a bit like Miss Jean Brodie. 'Then I think, Major Tooks, that Colonel Robertson-Macleod should be told.'

'So do I. Comply with the request, and then send a copy of Hosier's signal to *Fearless*.'

Neither man knew the half of it. The Special Forces were Thatcher's darlings, to her an extension of her own tough personality. Hosier might not have been around for the Embassy siege, but he knew how to milk it in a way that seemed to escape Luffenden. A stream of personal notes landing on the Downing Street doormat, little *billets doux* that kept the PM informed of any innovations the Regiment had made in the counterterrorist field. Because of this continuous contact, and the intimacy it fostered, the new Director could get to talk to her in a situation in which many of his superiors would struggle. He used the prestige of the position shamelessly the next time he saw her. They were not alone, so he wasn't daft enough to confront her with anything other than a hint. But that was good enough to let those he would talk to next see the hope in her eyes, so that when he put in his request to be allowed the same freedom to act as his inferiors, it would be granted with alacrity.

'Just what is it you're after, Corny?' asked the GSO2 over a drink in the mess at Special Forces' Headquarters.

'Victory would be nice.'

'It's actually not very pleasant when one is unsure if one is being guyed.'

General Robert Brotherton made that comment in a soft tone, his air of gentlemanly unconcern entirely intact. But Cornelius Hosier knew he'd just be pulled up short. This man was his senior, and could have a hand in his future promotion prospects. But then he might just be able to pull off a stunt that would make his position unassailable.

'The freedom to move another squadron, Bob, without having to clear it with Jamie Robertson-Macleod. Plus two dedicated C130s with crews to be placed at my, or rather Special Forces', disposal.'

'And am I, or the Old Man, to be granted an explanation for this?'

Hosier favoured the General with half a smile. 'Of course you are, Bob. You will have to clear my plan. But I'd rather like to see the PM before I go into details.'

'Not even a hint to liven up the mess tonight?'

'No. But I tell you the way my mind has been working. How would the Old Man like it if we could do a bit of business that would have the matelots, especially Radcliffe and Onslow, grovelling at his feet?'

Brotherton looked suspicious. He didn't entirely trust Cornelius Hosier, and for a second it showed. But he recovered himself quickly, the expression returning to one of bland enquiry.

'That would depend on the level of casualties.'

'They, I can assure you, would be acceptable, Bob. Very acceptable.'

'If you can give the Navy a black eye, Corny, the Old Man would kiss a gunner's arse, and you know it.'

The Iron Lady was clearly still affected by the loss of the *Sheffield*. But Cornelius Hosier wondered if she was laying it on a bit thick. He'd met her quite a few times, and had guessed from the very first that she was a master of the use of feminine wiles, the counterbalance to that no-nonsense brusqueness which her political colleagues found so hard to cope with. It appeared as soon as the ship was mentioned. The slight wetness of the eyes, the drop at the corners of the mouth and the mute appeal that someone act to save her were firmly in place.

It was, in large measure, genuine. For all her hard exterior she was extremely upset by the loss of life. And she was operating in an area where her dependence was acute. But there was also a strong dose of political nous at work. The knowledge that to lose in the South Atlantic would be to lose occupancy of the room they were now entering. Hosier reminded himself, as he stepped into the Cabinet room behind her, that behind that pleading look there was a rod of steel. If solutions were not forthcoming, the mute appeal wouldn't last long. Red hot tongs on bare flesh were not out of the question as far as this PM was concerned.

'Please take a seat, Brigadier Hosier.'

Corny Hosier was slow to oblige, looking around the Cabinet room with a sense of wonder. This was where it all happened, the hub of the nation's government. He couldn't help being impressed. Clearly Margaret Thatcher, not noted for her patience, was accustomed to this reaction, since she made no attempt to hurry him. Finally, pulling on the hem of his camouflage jacket, he sat down.

'It's good of you to see me, Prime Minister.'

58

'The Chief of Staff suggested it might be worthwhile.'

'Not true,' Hosier thought.

The old bugger had been very reluctant. Only the fact that he was Director Special Forces had wangled the meeting. The Chief knew that Corny Hosier saw the PM more often than most of his rank. He didn't want the DSF mentioning, at some future meeting, that he'd had a workable plan to deal with the Exocets, only to have it sat on.

'I need permission to go ashore on the Argentine mainland. Only the War Cabinet can give me that.'

There was no unnecessary question. She understood immediately what he was talking about.

'Go on.'

'I felt it best to approach you first.' That earned an almost imperceptible nod. 'I take it we are still unclear about the number of Exocet missiles the enemy possess.'

'Very unsure, Brigadier. And then there is the question of their range. The Air Staff tell me they have no extra fuel tanks at present. But we have no guarantee that will remain the case. I need hardly point out to you the effect they would have if they could stay in the air for a longer period.'

'Then my point is made. They must be neutralized, and there is only one way to do that. The Exocets must either be taken out on the ground, or the aircraft with the ability to deliver them need to be destroyed.'

He got no response, just the kind of hard look that melted senior Cabinet ministers.

'The Chief of Staff has made it plain to me that, while he is prepared to consider any suggestions I may put forward, this is a political decision that has already been considered and discarded.'

Again there was no use of superfluous words, no explanation of the difficulties that would entail, both at home and abroad. He had to admire the way she remained silent, forcing him to speak.

'It is exactly the kind of task Special Forces were created for. And though there are bound to be losses, they will be significantly less than those brought on by the sinking of a capital ship.'

'How many?'

Hosier coughed slightly. He had to cover his own need to think. There was no point in lying to her. Yet he knew, instinctively, that numbers were best avoided.

'I would commit an entire SAS squadron.' The shrug that followed was eloquent. 'Naturally they would be unsupported. But they would have surprise in their favour, and an escape route through an adjacent country, which is not unfriendly.'

He waited for her to provide the word he'd avoided. Chile! With nothing forthcoming, he was again obliged to keep talking. 'Whatever happened, I would expect that the job would be completed.'

He was trying to track her thinking, the weighing of the conflicting odds. The loss of fifty men set against the loss of a carrier; the possibility that the men who, at the Iranian Embassy, had done more for her reputation than any political decision she'd ever made, might actually pull it off. The Americans wouldn't be pleased, and neither would the UN. Could she cope with that?

'The very least we could do, Prime Minister, is impress upon the world, and particularly the Argentinians, our absolute determination to carry on, despite losses. And to retake the islands.'

'You will receive a minute from the War Cabinet.'

'So much for collective responsibility,' Hosier thought, as he replied, 'I need to get a programme of training set up as soon as I've cleared my plans with the Chief of Staff.'

'And this operation could go in before the Task Force has to land our troops?'

'I would expect so.'

Her voice had all that huskiness, emphasis and passion that had enthralled the nation as she concluded the meeting.

'Go, Brigadier, and do so with my blessing.'

You can always hear yourself think, even in the pitch-black cabin of a chopper. And you can feel your own anxieties, the tightening of the muscles, the fact that your jaw begins to ache from being clenched. Everything shaking made Blue wonder if he was doing some of the trembling, the reaction disguised by the vibrations of a wave-hopping Sea King, battling against powerful headwinds, a craft that had seen too much service and too little maintenance.

'That's good!'

Blue could almost hear the voice of Sam Clark inside his head, see the square, grinning face and bright brown eyes on either side of a well broken nose. Sam was now the B Squadron Quartermaster Sergeant. He'd been one of his instructors during selection, then his patrol DS on the jungle phase of his continuation training. Admiration was not something SAS troopers really indulged in. Yes, Blue would acknowledge that a guy was good in certain areas, keep quiet about it where he scored less well. But the bottom line was nothing to do with likes, dislikes or appreciation. If you'd earned the winged dagger, and were badged as a trooper, you had done selection. Every member of the Regiment knew how tough that was. So they all respected each other for having made it. Sam was different as far as Blue was concerned, a bit like the dad he'd always imagined but never seen.

'The adrenalin buzz from fear makes you really sharp. You see better, your hearing's right on, you can smell your own feet through your boots. No good performer ever goes on without stage fright. We're the same.'

Blue smiled. Sam was a huge film buff, and went on and on about badged troopers being like actors, joking about the way a guy's whole shape changed when he was dressed in his counterterrorist gear: tight black suit and balaclava, wearing body armour. And it was true. Blue had seen it and felt it. A screaming ego lived with you through thick and thin; filthy in the jungle, freezing in an icy river, or dressed like an unemployed dickhead on the Falls Road in Belfast. But when you got that CT kit on you felt like a king.

Not that you carried that out into the world. Being a grey man, invisible in a crowd, was as much a part of the job as shooting the bollocks off terrorists. Any berk could be a boastful loudmouth, and draw attention to himself; be a 'goldfish in a bowl'. An SAS trooper was careful about where he showed off, usually confining it to time spent with his own kind, and would never make his presence and skills known to strangers if it could be avoided.

Sam Clark was just like that. He'd led one of the teams into the Iranian Embassy, and Blue wasn't sure if he'd even told his wife. But when with his mates, talking about the Regiment, something he loved more than her and the kids, he would gesture with his hands, a big arc, centre to extremities, and mouth his mantra.

'We are the custodians of illusion!'

61

On ops you try not to think about anything that doesn't have a bearing on the mission. That's why you're badged. There have to be guys on selection fitter than you, and not even the biggest ego tripper could claim to be the cleverest. But to be fit, intelligent AND able to concentrate under extreme pressure was the key. The whole ethic of Special Forces was based on mental strength. The ability to react, when totally knackered, after running twenty Ks. Being given a map reference and ten seconds not only to choose your direction, but to work out a ground appreciation as well, so that you would choose a route that would get you to the next point in the prescribed time window.

That translated into every action, be it in jungle or on a glacier. There were as many jokers in the SAS as there were in any other military unit. But the joking, for most of the men, went on hold in the field. You had to be serious to avoid getting killed. Even worse, a lapse could slot someone else, a sure recipe for being seriously unpopular when you returned to base.

Sitting in a chopper that was less of a need. Blue wasn't driving, and if the guy at the controls was going to take them for a swim there was nothing he could do to stop it. So once he'd got over worrying whether the team had all they needed in the way of equipment, he let his mind drift. The past to him was not a happy picture, and that was nothing to do with being a Barnardo's boy. But he knew that, whatever he thought about that upbringing, it had coloured his entire life. You learn a lack of trust early, since some of the people who look after you don't merit any. And your fellow orphans, carrying the same emotional baggage, provide neither a crutch nor faith. Blue knew he was an individual who'd learned in life to present to the world the face his surroundings required. You could be nice to authority because the bastards never knew what was in your mind.

The Army had been a natural for a kid with some intelligence and a need for discipline, especially one who was already institutionalized. Blue, who'd gone through his younger years hating books, now read masses. It was a dream, but maybe, one day, he might write a book himself. All he had to do was learn to spell. The number of guys that seemed to have been inspired by a good teacher intrigued him, making him wonder what would have happened to him if he'd had the same chance. Younger, and looking at the more successful, he had put the blame squarely at the feet of the bog standard bums who'd bored him into academic failure. Either age or the Regiment had cured him of that. He now knew that the fault was entirely his.

The Green Jackets started the process, because in the Army they look for the kit you're carrying, not what you might have hidden away. He was easy to get on with, quite well liked by anyone who wasn't brain dead, and rarely a trouble to the Ruperts. Blue had made his stripes early, lapping up the courses that were available on the grounds that, if you're going to be a soldier, you might as well be a good one. Sport had always been an outlet, so he'd played football for the Regiment, ultimately going on to play for the Army.

Looking back, the map reading and weapons handling stuff that had earned him promotion seemed so damned easy. And the time he had dropped his first and only terrorist in Ulster, when he thought about it, made him wonder why he was still alive. It could only be because the INLA guy had been more scared than he had himself. He'd been cock-a-hoop, but the wheels came off on the very next patrol. He'd seen his best mate killed, caught by a booby trap that he, as patrol commander, should have anticipated. That's where the SAS came in! Back in barracks, sick and lonely, he'd imagined that the only people who were getting any retaliation in were the Special Forces nutballs. There and then he decided he was going to join them.

Sometimes he thought they were all misfits, the guys in the Regiment. Each had a personal style. Some craved danger yet also had a need for a stable home and family. Others needed no one, and were content with a solitary withdrawn existence. Then there was the rest, the mass of blokes who were into their second or third marriages, and could be seen down the Booth pub in Hereford still chasing tail. Concentration often didn't leave much room for the woman in your life; relaxation meant having a selfish good time. It didn't add up to much in the way of sense. But then life never had.

The change in the note of the engines, as the heli dropped slightly, brought him back to the present. It wasn't like a plane going into a descent, because they were so close to the water that was out of the question. A tap on the shoulder told him that they were coming in to land, the pilot using passive night goggles to pick his spot. Now everyone aboard was wide awake, pulling at Bergen straps and belt kits for one final check. Blue held up a piece of paper with a huge N drawn on it, the dispatcher reacting with a pointed jab to tell him which direction was north, so that he could work out their route.

A jarring through the frame of the helicopter signalled they'd hit land. Blue, with Digger right behind him, was out before that thud reached the tail rotor, two G Squadron troopers at their heels. He ran, nearly on his knees, being pressed under the downdraught, Armalite up and ready covering the left arc. Graunch and Luke got themselves, and the gear for the patrol, out on to the tussock grass. Within seconds they were running too, eager to get into position to set up an all round defence.

The pressure on Blue's head eased within ten seconds. The Sea King, clear of its burden, lifted straight back up into the night and headed back out to sea, leaving eight men and their equipment in a loose defensive ring, every gun aimed out, with one up the spout ready to fire. No one moved as the noise faded, or looked at the moonlit surface of the South Atlantic as it was flattened by the low-flying chopper.

Only the guns moved as the noise faded, sweeping back and through the arcs. SOP stated what was common sense. That noise from the rotors had to be well gone before you'd ever hear any threat. That at night your ears are your best weapons until the eyes are fully adjusted to the available ambient light. Threats? Half the fucking Argentine Army alerted by the noise of the chopper blades, moving in to surround and waste the group before they could tab on to a more secure position.

Blue Harding's adrenalin was working flat out now, so much so that he would have heard a maiden aunt's suppressed fart at half a mile. He was not alone. The hair was standing up on everyone's head. Every sense that eight men could muster was fully engaged. Yet not one of them so much as twitched until the signal was given to move. Digger was no more than a dim outline as he stood up, and another minute passed while the rest of the team eased themselves to their feet and moved out, searching for better cover.

'Right,' Blue said quietly, 'let's get sorted.'

The G Squadron guys were up as well, and they did a joint map and ground appreciation before moving out towards their designated grid reference. The task was to set up mutually supporting OPs round Goose Green and report back on Argie strength and deployment. It was get in close and sit still stuff, no patrolling, which had led to a real heavy raid on the Navy for the comforts of underground life. They were dug in by the time the British public knew that *Sheffield* had been hit, some of the only people engaged for whom the war hadn't changed.

CHAPTER FIVE

HM Ambassador at UN to Cabinet office: 12.00 hrs 5/5/82. Regret to inform you that Argentine Junta has refused to accept Peruvian Peace Plan. Await instructions.

Hosier smoothed his well-manicured hands across Jamie Robertson-Macleod's desk. He made no attempt to hide the fact that he loved sitting there, in the CO's office at Stirling Lines. It was a post he'd always wanted, but had been denied, he thought unfairly. Luffenden had been Director when the job became vacant, and whatever recommendations the short-arsed swine had made to the Army Command hadn't included him. That should have cut him off from the Director's job, no doubt another consideration in his predecessor's mind. No one had ever been granted the Director's job without first being Regimental CO. But Luffenden had underestimated Hosier's determination, as well as his ability to lobby those who made such decisions.

His first order issued was to make sure the men he needed were on the base. To his mind it was one of the laxities of the Regiment that they were allowed to accommodate themselves outside the camp regardless of their marital status. Given time, and a CO he would himself appoint, that would begin to change. Once he was sure they were assembled, he sent for Gerry Tooks and Lippy Grant.

'It has been decided to activate B Squadron. Archie Grosvenor will take over temporary command of the base. He and A Squadron will stay here, in Hereford, to look after Ulster and Counterterrorism duties.'

Gerry Tooks had been wondering why only he and Lippy had been called in to the office. Now he knew. Both men were too experienced to respond to Jock the Sock's enquiring look. But Tooks heard Lippy Grant suck in a deep breath. They knew if Hosier had something to add he would say it without prompting.

'Just to clear the decks, Gerry, I am taking over direct control of the two remaining squadrons. Until they are active in the operational theatre they are my responsibility.'

'Director,' he replied, formally, unblinkingly and without emphasis.

Hosier pulled out an envelope from his camouflage jacket and spun it across the table. 'That comes from the top table, and has already been copied to Jamie Robertson-Macleod so that he knows the score. Any comments?'

'Welcome aboard, boss,' Gerry Tooks replied.

He was fighting to keep the irony out of his voice. He was being relieved but he hadn't even moved to open the orders. That was because they were unnecessary. Cornelius Hosier was a Brigadier and Director of Special Forces. He was already in command. But such a move, the protection of his own back, was typical. He had a reputation of being a past master at the art of hogging success and shifting the blame for failure. And this had an added feature, being in some way part of the turf war between him and the Regimental CO.

What followed was a roundup of the intelligence picture. The problems of the Task Force now that they had to stay well to the east of the islands. The continuing arguments regarding landing sites, and the political unacceptability of heavy casualties, either at sea or on land. This was mixed with the knowledge, scary to the government, that having finally got 3 Commando Brigade on its way from Ascension, withdrawal was even less palatable. Most of this both his listeners could have gleaned from the *Daily Telegraph*, even down to the fact that the air-launched Exocets were the main worry.

'The intelligence on those is confusing. The French aren't being very helpful, and it appears that Argentine embassies all over the world have been ordered to send out buyers to scour the globe for more. And they may get some, despite the best efforts of MI5 to stop them, who can tell? Then there is the factor of range, which is a great concern to the PM. So, if we don't know for sure how many of the buggers we will be dealing with now, or in the future, or how far they can travel, we have to assume the worst.'

'Range is important, boss,' said Tooks. 'But they've only got so many planes to deliver them?'

'The reckoning is a maximum of five. But they must have more trained pilots than that, so flying double sorties could be a problem. Both elements of our fleet, carriers and escorts as well as transports, have to come well within their present range in daylight to execute and cover any landing. That's when they're vulnerable. And given the number of targets the enemy will be spoilt for choice. They can either go after the carriers or try to take out *Canberra*. You know how many men she is carrying. I need hardly tell you what tremors such a possibility engenders in the political breast.'

Lippy Grant cut in, his eyes boring into those of Jock the Sock. 'I'm betting there are one or two brass hats who're having trouble keeping their bottle when they look at this lot. They'll be shitting their pips.'

The look that produced on Hosier's face had Gerry speaking quickly. 'Any news on the UN front?'

'Hot air, Gerry. The Argies won't budge.'

'There's not much of an alternative to a Falklands landing if we're determined to take the islands back. That is where the enemy main force is concentrated.'

'Wrong! There is a very good alternative. One that will make the buggers reassess their aims. And we are just the chaps to pull it off. Follow me.'

Hosier led the way to the War Room. It was as new as the rest of the HQ section, a square uncluttered space, where the attached personnel, green slime, beavered away. The scaleys, non-operational, were in the adjoining signal room. They had direct comms links to *Fearless*, *Hermes*, Fleet HQ at Northwood and Ascension Island. The walls were covered with maps of the Falklands, one with blue flagged pins inserted to show where the G Squadron men on ground had set up the observation posts.

Another showed the results. Even after only a few days the main map was marked with a comprehensive outline of the Argentine positions, both in numbers and equipment: artillery, machine gun posts, bunkers, trench systems, minefields and troop concentrations. Most of the blue flagged pins covered the expanse of East Island, and a quick comparison showed many of them cheek by jowl with the Argentinian positions. It looked as though the enemy could hardly move a latrine bucket a hundred yards without it being logged.

Hosier allowed Gerry to take him through the scenario, nodding sagely as each fact was detailed. Tooks pointed out the pair blue/red flags around Goose Green, pointing out that these were the B Squadron men who'd first gone in off *Scylla*. But his favourite site was in the harbour of Port Stanley itself, where the SBS had set up a hide inside an abandoned wreck.

'Never thought they'd pull that one off. They can see the whole harbour and its approaches, as well as keep tabs on the airfield.'

'It just goes to show, Gerry, that the motto we live by is correct. "Who dares wins", what!'

There was something about the way Hosier said that which produced a funny feeling in Gerry Tooks' lower gut. It wasn't inspiring. It was scary. With Hosier leading they moved over to the opposite wall, to where a green slime bod was working out and taping a route that led over the South Atlantic. It went all the way from Ascension to Tierra del Fuego. Alongside each course change and refuelling point was a pencilled-in ETA, and when Gerry Tooks examined them he knew straight away that the times given were not for a fast, attacking fighter jet.

'C130s,' Lippy Grant murmured.

'That's right, Lippy,' Hosier replied, picking up a thick file. He jabbed a finger at the point where the tape ceased, the Rio Grande air base. 'And that is B Squadron's target. We've got to get in, get busy and cripple the Argentinian air offensive capacity. And gentlemen, we've not got to just surprise them, we have got to give the buggers the fright of their lives. Once they think the whole of their mainland is compromised, a landing might well be superfluous.'

'You're suggesting a direct assault on the Rio Grande airfield?'

'Correct.'

'Do we have any intelligence on the forces guarding the base?'

'Very little. But we can make an educated guess at the number of aircraft, which gives us aircrew and support staff. Then we just have to look at what we would assign to an airfield ourselves to get a profile of the defence.'

'I take it you've done that, boss?'

'I have, in a rough sort of way. I expect the number of personnel, from pilots to guard units, to be in the region of a thousand men. Not all of them will be capable of putting up a fight, of course. Aircraft mechanics are rarely commended for their battle skills.'

'In a HALO drop operation we won't be able to take enough kit,' Tooks said. 'And a low-level para drop will be picked up on radar. The Argies will know we're coming in, and judge by the aircraft numbers our available strength. I don't think fifty guys, however good, are going to give a thousand men the fright of their lives, however poor.'

Hosier had a cunning look in his eye, as well as half a smile on his lips.

'Who said anything about a parachute drop, Gerry, high altitude or low?' He spun round and pointed to the drawing he'd just laid out on a table. 'The flight times for C130 are accurate, subject to air currents, and it would obviously be preferable to have a tail wind close to target. Two Hercules transports, with half B Squadron in each, can carry as much equipment as they desire including vehicle-mounted gunnery. They can choose anti-tank weapons, explosives or machine guns, whichever seems the most appropriate.'

Gerry Tooks guessed what was coming, and didn't want to confirm it. But despite himself he couldn't help asking, since Hosier had paused.

'And what do we do then?'

'It's just like Entebbe. We land the buggers on the runway, before the Argies have even woken up to the fact of who they are. Then in four-man teams we destroy what aircraft they have, kill the pilots to a man, then find and neutralize their missile capacity.'

Hosier's finger was on the Rio Grande air base, and with his back to the two men he couldn't see their stunned expressions.

'Surprise, gentlemen, the key to war, the entire *raison d'être* of the Regiment. At one stroke we will have nullified half the air offensive capacity of the enemy. I need hardly tell you what a difference that will make to the proposed operations.'

'There were no real hostile ground forces at Entebbe,' said Gerry Tooks. 'At least none worth the title.'

'Would it have made any difference if there had been? By the time they'd have chosen to intervene the operation would have been complete.'

'Numbers don't tell us very much, boss. I grant you the mechanics, but do we know the quality of the troops charged with airfield defence?'

'We must assume they are good, Gerry, without being special. We, on the other hand, are just that. The very best there is, and that includes the Israelis. And since, like them, we are going to land inside their defences, most of those troops will actually be useless.'

'Always assuming we can get in.'

'We can, Gerry, and we must!'

'What about the radar pickup?'

'Four minutes is the best guess. Our intelligence indicates that the Argentines have nothing more sophisticated than that. And there are no air traffic control corridors that far south of Buenos Aires.'

'Ground to air?'

'Our intelligence is that they've shifted most of that to the Falklands. But I would assume they have retained some capacity to defend their main air bases.'

'Roland Two ground to air has a range of eighteen hundred metres, and the kind of multiple warheads that will trash a transport plane. And they will be at a high alert condition, set to fire. They'll take us out in about sixty seconds. And if they miss, there'll probably plenty of Oerlikons and Bofors.'

Gerry Tooks dropped his voice deliberately, so that no one in the room could hear. 'You're proposing to land.'

'Crash-land, Gerry,' Hosier interrupted, 'and in the type of aircraft the Argentinian air force use themselves. We will have to use counter-measures to confuse them. So they won't be sure who we are, and that will give us time.'

'OK. We've slipped the radar and the Rolands and have crash-landed. Now we've got two pranged Hercules on the runway. Our guys are inside, and might already have taken casualties. They will certainly be under fire as they debus and set out to destroy their designated targets.'

Gerry Tooks paused then, to see if his words were having any effect on the Brigadier: The sole response he received was a smug smile, which was in sharp contrast to that of SSM Grant. He was seething, his face growing redder and angrier by the second. His troop commander wasn't much better placed, and had to fight to keep his voice even.

'Does it occur to you they could be slaughtered?'

Hosier's nostrils flared. 'We will suffer losses certainly, Gerry. But the SAS, just because it is an elite unit, cannot evade the notion of taking casualties. Quite the reverse!'

'They'll take more than that,' Gerry Tooks replied, looking at the files Hosier had laid on the table. 'Is there an E&E plan there for when it all goes pear-shaped?'

'There's no plan there,' snapped Hosier, sidestepping the need to explain how the men engaged would get clear when the operation was over. 'That is your job. What I have given you is a whole-squadron task, one that has to be put into effect with speed. I need hardly remind you that our ships and men are in grave danger. And if we don't get our fingers out that will apply, in spades, to the chaps thrown in on the ground as well.'

'Can I ask one question?'

'I hope you will find it necessary to ask several.'

'You mentioned the top table. Just who has this operation been sanctioned by?'

Hosier was infuriatingly smug in his reply. 'I believe I also mentioned the War Cabinet and the PM. The idea of a Special Forces operation was given the green light at the highest level. The aim is to produce a speedy conclusion to the conflict at the minimum cost. To, if possible, obviate the need to land a main force at all. The detail of how we achieve that is down to the Regiment. Or, more specifically, to you, Gerry, as OC of B Squadron.'

'You're not asking for a plan, boss. You're asking me to come up with a sure-fire way of writing off my men. Damn the consequences, just go over the top.'

Hosier put his hand on Gerry Tooks' shoulder, in an act of such blistering insincerity, coupled with such a sugary tone of voice, that he nearly earned himself a full force butt from the Major's head.

'As I said, there will be losses, Gerry. Of that I am in no doubt. But you are, like me, an officer. And accepting that some men will die or be maimed is part of the responsibility of rank.'

Gerry Tooks heard the words, but doubted that it was actually him that said them.

'I won't do it!'

'What?'

He could feel the blood heating his reddening face as he continued, his passion so strong that his choice of words lacked any care. 'I'm not planning a massacre so that you can ponce about at Northwood playing the big cheese.'

'Me? Big cheese! What are you talking about man?'

'You know very well what I'm talking about,' Tooks said, his voice rising as he lifted up one of the files Hosier had laid out on the table.

'What if we don't even get down? What if the bastards lock on with their Rolands and just shoot us out of the sky? A Hercules has a limited ability to avoid those type of missiles. They're way too slow.'

'I can't recall saying this was an operation without risk.'

Lippy Grant, still seething in the background, finally exploded, speaking so rapidly that the words were garbled.

'Risk! It's not a fuckin' risk for you, ya useless, stuck up bastard.'

Hosier went bright red, and opened his mouth to deliver a rebuke. But Lippy, fists bunched, had pushed past Gerry Tooks, who grabbed his jacket in an effort to restrain him. Jock the Sock, wisely, took a couple of quick steps backwards.

'You'll be sittin' drinkin' whisky at Headquarters while we get our arses shot to hell. The best we can hope for is to get blown to bits without feeling any pain.'

'SSM Grant,' Hosier hissed, the shock for once making him forget regimental informality. 'I will, if you apologize, at once, for old times' sake, ignore your outburst.'

'Lippy!' said Gerry Tooks, still trying, only marginally successfully, to hold his SSM back.

'You useless, no good fucker, stick your old times' sake up your jacksy. You never were any bloody good. You're nothing but an arse-crawling bag of shite.'

Gerry turned to address the other men in the Ops room, fighting to keep himself from shouting. He ordered them out. Then in a forced, gentle tone, with Hosier moving discreetly away, he spoke to his sergeant.

'You can't talk to him like that, Lippy.'

The fight suddenly seemed to go out of Don Grant. The shoulders slumped and his voice had a pleading quality to replace that of his previous anger.

'You'll have to apologize.'

It was as if Lippy Grant couldn't hear him, and his voice rose as he continued, so that Hosier couldn't help but register what was being said.

'We all fuckin' hated him in the Gulf, except for a couple willing to kiss his arse. The bastard would be at home in the First World War. Never mind the body count as long I get another pip on my shoulder.'

'Major Tooks,' said Hosier, from several feet away. His voice was as tight as the skin on his face, evidence that he had heard what Lippy had said. And for once the use of Gerry Tooks' rank was appropriate, certainly to the words that followed. 'Please see that the SSM is removed. He is RTU'd forthwith. Only the good of the Regiment, and a desire to avoid washing our dirty linen in public, stops me from ordering a court martial.'

'Wait over by the door, Lippy,' said Tooks, pushing his SSM away. He waited till he was far enough distant, shaking his head and cursing both himself and Hosier. Then Gerry Tooks turned back to talk to the Brigadier, who was standing, feet apart, hands and swagger stick behind his back, and eyebrows raised. Even with all that had been going on, he'd had time to think of the consequences of the course he'd adopted.

'Well, Gerry?'

'I think Lippy is out of order. But he's been in the Regiment a long time.'

'That, Gerry, is history. We are here and we are now. You know very well the question I am asking.'

He couldn't answer right away. The consequences of the only reply he could give were reeling about in his brain. Everything he'd ever striven for falling apart in one brief moment. His voice had a hollow quality, inside his own head, as though it wasn't him who was speaking.

'I have no choice but to repeat what I said, Director.'

'Which is?'

The tone of stiff formality was a touch alien, but he knew he had to employ it. He had to sound like an officer.

'I said that I will not work on any plan that's going to achieve nothing but get the men it is my honour to command, killed. Some of the people I'm talking about served with me when I was a trooper.'

'Do you like service in the Regiment, Gerry?'

'You know I do!'

Gerry Tooks wanted to scream that it had been and was his life, but that would sound like pleading, a thing he was determined to avoid.

'Then you have a stark choice. Either do as I have ordered, or pack your kit and head for Platform Four.'

'That's a decision I would need to have confirmed by my CO.'

That earned Gerry Tooks a snort of derision. As if to underline that, as well as himself, the CO of the Regiment was an ambitious serving soldier. Hosier touched one of the red collar tabs.

'Don't get your hopes up on Jamie Robertson-Macleod. He knows what the Regiment is for, even if you do not. Why do you think we have such privileges and extra pay? To duck out when the going gets rough?'

'I can take the rough, Director. I have in the past. But there's such a thing as common sense, even in the Army.'

'I give you one more chance. I am ordering you, as your superior officer, to plan, train for and execute an assault on the Rio Grande airfield, forthwith.'

'No!'

'Then remove yourself as well, Major Tooks, and send me your second in command, Captain Lowry.'

It was like a knife in Major Tooks, a surgical cut that told him in no uncertain terms that he was no longer in the Regiment. He was back in the Green Army, with all the bullshit that implied.

'No threat of a court martial?'

Hosier half-turned, so he was no longer looking at Gerry Tooks. 'I will extend to you the same favour I gifted to Grant. You see, Tooks, I care deeply about the Regiment's reputation, something you clearly do not.'

'Bollocks,' Gerry replied, suddenly reverting to talking like a trooper. 'Maybe I'll ask for one, so we can have this pile of shit examined in open court.'

'Don't fool yourself that you'll ever succeed, laddie. Now get out of my sight. And you will oblige me by speaking to no one about what has happened here. That, in case you are in doubt, is a direct order that you will disobey at your peril.'

Gerry Tooks turned to leave, knowing what Lippy Grant had already discovered, and for which the Sergeant was still berating himself. That this might be the Regiment, the best fighting force in the world. But it was still the good old British Army, a place where shit floats and usually ends up telling you what to do.

David Lowry was too junior to take over the command himself. But the SAS usually had a ready supply of officers on various detached duties. His first task was to contact Major Vere Symington, who'd been Special Forces liaison officer in Washington. He'd returned when the Argentine invasion was confirmed and was, at present, in London. The offer to take temporary command of B Squadron was accepted with alacrity. Symington didn't even ask why it had come about; just told Lowry he'd be at Stirling Lines in three hours.

Hosier had the captain call all the men from B Squadron to the briefing room, his gentle question as to the whereabouts of his previous Troop Commander brushed aside by a clearly angry Brigadier. The men filed into the room, another part of the new building shaped like a small theatre. They entered with that lack of discipline in the face of a superior officer which they saw as a token of their special status. Not one of them was in a complete uniform, though several wore camouflage trousers and tee shirts. Many were smoking and some carried cans of soft drink. They too seemed curious about the missing men, gazing quizzically at the stage, as though something quite common was absent. To Hosier, standing at the front looking at them, they seemed to represent the kind of lineup the police might gather to stand with a particularly physically fit suspect.

'God!' he thought. 'If ever I'd got my hands on this unit, I would have changed all this.'

'OK, men, settle down,' he called, then waited till the fifty men in the room comported themselves, and exchanged jokes. Of the eyes that were on him, he suspected that several were ill disposed. But that didn't matter: he had to carry the bulk of the group. Do that, and those he'd had to put in their place in the past would fall into line. 'I know I risk the accusation of being over-dramatic. But what I am about to impart to you will be details of probably the most important operation ever undertaken by the Regiment since the Second World War.'

That got their attention. By the time he finished that teaser you could hear a pin drop. He took them through a situation report on the developments in the Falklands: how well the reconnaissance groups were performing, and listing some of the valuable information they were sending back.

'So far the Regiment has performed brilliantly. But that still leaves a problem. We have to land our troops in the face of an extremely potent threat to both our ships and our men, namely that of the Exocet missiles.'

He rehashed all the things that he had said to Tooks and Grant, realizing as he did so that they were slipping, losing their concentration, not listening because they'd heard all of this on the bloody news and endless discussion programmes which clogged the airwaves, as well as filling the newspapers. Every retired know-all was at it, coining appearance fees for just sitting talking balls. There was nothing the top brass knew which wasn't bloody common knowledge.

'I intend that you, B Squadron, will disabuse the Argentine forces of any notion that such technology will save their hides.'

That got them back again, and they were grinning now, sitting forward, and exchanging glances, eager once more to hear what he had to say. It gave Hosier a good feeling, and made him puff his chest out a little more.

'I dare say that of the four squadrons that make up the 22nd SAS Regiment, you think you're the best.'

The boots should have been stamping before his last words were out, accompanied by cries of 'too right, boss', and several whistles. That was the sort of thing that would happen in any normal line regiment. But it didn't here. All he got for his flattery was a few self-conscious grins. There were also silent unimpressed stares from the long-serving members of the Regiment, men whom no one could impress.

'Now is the time to prove it.'

Inside his head, Hosier was chanting to himself, 'Build them up, build them up.' He'd never admit it, but what had happened with Tooks and Grant had jarred him. He was determined there was to be no repeat.

'You know we're not interested in medals, or recognition. Princes Gate would have in some senses been more satisfying without a TV camera in sight.'

Several heads were nodding, including those of some of the troopers who'd done the Iranian Embassy siege, the thought that being seen on the box had exposed an organization supposed to be secret and discreet to the full glare of public adoration.

'But that has done nothing to alter our basic task, which is not just to infiltrate and report on enemy movements, but to take them on where we find them and give them a bloody nose.' Only half responded to that, the less experienced judging by their youth. 'And that is what we're going to do.'

He could feel the tingling in his fingertips as he outlined the operation, feel the eyes of over forty men boring into his own, some in quite evident disbelief. Beside him, David Lowry, the commander of Boat Troop, was sitting as stiff as a board, looking over the heads of the men, some of whom he would have to lead to Rio Grande.

'Our first task,' Hosier concluded, 'is to formulate a workable plan. Then we will institute a programme of training. I have already spoken to the Air Staff, though without going into details, and they are setting things up. We will start at 08.00 hours the day after tomorrow, which will give you time to sort out what kit you need. David here will inform you of your detailed tasks in that department. Vere Symington is on his way from London, and is, from this moment on, your squadron commander. That is all.'

Hosier came down off the platform and strode up the aisle, eyes front and ignoring everyone. He needn't have bothered. No one was looking at him; they were just staring ahead in stunned silence. Just as he reached the door a voice spoke.

'The cunt's mad. Stark staring fucking mad!'

The buzz of agreement, larded with expletives aimed both at him, Ruperts in general, and his orders, followed him out through the door, to be silenced as it swung shut. That also allowed him to pause and take a deep, very necessary breath.

CHAPTER SIX

Reuters News Bureau: London. 10.25 7/5/82: The British Government today extended the Total Exclusion Zone surrounding the Falkland Islands to 200 (two hundred) miles. This takes it to within 12 (twelve) miles of the Argentine mainland coast.

T he whole camp knew what had happened to Tooks and Lippy Grant within an hour. In fact, men from A Squadron, who'd gone home to their wives and kids, were suddenly around in abundance, not asking but looking curious. With over fifty men on the base who saw themselves as staring down the barrel of a gun, the nature of the proposed operation soon became common currency too.

Any SAS troop contained individuals who'd been in the Regiment for years. Men whose experience could be relied on. But it had, as well, troopers who'd just been badged and everything in between. The newcomers were the most eager to prove themselves. It mattered little. The squadron was in a ferment of speculation, the notion that they should follow the lead of the men who'd been dismissed gaining a strong following among the older, wiser heads.

In truth, there wasn't an inexperienced soldier amongst them. In terms of self-motivation and commitment they were the best the British Army had to offer. Quite a few had come from their regiments as senior NCOs, accepting the loss of their rank to serve with the SAS. These were men who'd already shown high commitment and leadership potential. The longer-serving troopers had seen action in Dofhar, during Operation Storm, fighting rebels in the desert. But most men who'd been badged for any length of time had seen action.

The Regiment operated worldwide, often in small teams, doing jobs that they discussed amongst themselves, but of which the wider public was unaware. There was hardly an insurrection or revolution that they had not been close to. Coming to the aid of the civil power was a commonplace, doing those things which regular police forces couldn't contemplate.

Of the newer recruits, many of them had served in Northern Ireland before doing selection, and had gained from that the one quality that made the Brits stand out as a fighting force, even amongst the world's Special Forces. They'd been through the pressure cooker of the Ulster proving ground. They had been on a station where the threat of death was a constant, a possibility so all-pervading that anyone who couldn't stand the heat soon got out of the Army, leaving behind men who could face the realities of a soldier's job.

Perhaps men less experienced would have been fooled by Hosier's flattery, and fallen for the 'Death or Glory' line. There were a few of those in B Squadron. But there were more whose intelligence made them question any orders, even if they never did so overtly. Men who were bright enough to see that the only place the Brigadier's plan was going to lead them was to a plot in the regimental cemetery, and a plaque on the clock in Stirling Lines.

Yet ingrained pride and the habit of obedience were strong. If you cared about dying you could never be a badged trooper. What made them disgruntled was the notion of useless sacrifice for what might be no more than a token, black-bordered headline and a couple of decorations for Ruperts. So when Lowry sent for Sergeant Sam Clark, there was no mystery about what the Captain wanted. Sam, true to his nature, breezed in, grin well to the fore and not a hint of a salute in sight.

'Sit down, Sam,' said Lowry, waving to a chair.

Sam Clark stared hard at the chair, which forced the question out of the officer.

'What's the matter?'

'I just wondered if I was going to sit myself in a pile of shit.'

'That's me, old son, at least till Symington arrives.'

Sam Clark liked David Lowry, which was not something he gifted to many Ruperts, though he liked Gerry Tooks as well. But Tooksy had been a trooper, just like he was now, and had gone for pips to up his pension rights. He'd never been one for the double handshake, or taken much part in the eternal backstabbing that most Ruperts seemed to revel in. Lowry was minor public school and an ex-Para, normally good grounds for the old arm's length. But there were exceptions to every rule. Sam was quite prepared to accept any Rupert who showed that he knew the score. That the British Army was run by the NCOs; that the best of them were badged SAS; and that the proper thing for a commissioned officer to do was stay out of the way of men who knew the job better than he did.

'Is this it?' he asked, tapping the top of a heap of files.

'Most of it. The maps are in the War Room.'

'Lippy Grant came to see me.'

'And told you all.'

'Fuckin' right, he did.'

'Shall I put him on a charge?'

It was a poor joke, wearily delivered, and the evidence that Sam Clark thought so was on his face long before he replied.

'That's not funny, Davey. His whole career's just gone up the Swannee. Twelve years in the Regiment and he's out on his arse because of a no good sod like Jock the Sock.'

'Tell me about it, Sam,' Lowry growled. 'I might be just about to join him.'

'You an' me both.'

'Hosier is spitting blood.'

'By the pint, I hope.'

'I know the first thing Symington is going to ask me. You're the SQMS, next in line. I wondered if you'd like to take on Lippy's job?'

'The flagon with the dragon is the vessel with the poison; the chalice from the palace has the brew that is true.'

'What?'

'*The Court Jester*, mate,' replied Sam Clark, an inveterate film buff. 'Starred Danny Kaye and Virginia Mayo.'

'Jester. Is that what that sod Hosier wants to be?'

'The job,' Sam insisted, bringing David Lowry back to the point. Much as he liked movies, this was no time to be discussing them.

'Yes,' Lowry responded.

'There's two probs.'

'Which are?'

'Lippy himself. We go back a long way. I'm not steppin' into his size elevens unless he OKs it.'

'And?'

Clark sat forward, suddenly very serious. 'Look, Davey, you're no different to Symington. You've both been shafted with making this work because you're Ruperts. Turn it down like Gerry Tooks and it's goodnight nurse.'

'This is one Rupert who'd kind of like to stay in the Army, Sam.'

That produced a lop-sided grin and a swift response. 'Quite right too. You're never goin' to get a job anywhere else, are you? It's a hard, cold world out there and unemployment is three million.'

Lowry looked at his watch. 'Our new boss will be here in less than half an hour. What's the second condition?'

'I need to talk with the boys. There's no point in doing anything if they won't buy it. Lippy and Tooksy doing what they did, well ...' The voice trailed off.

'What's the mood?'

'They're like pigs near an abattoir, as jumpy as fuck.'

'And you?'

'Jock the Sock is an arse, and this ops he's come up with is bollocks. I can just see him smooching round GHQ and Maggie Thatcher, promising the moon.'

'Do I detect a positive note here?'

'I was about to say we've got a reputation. We're the best there is, no contest. I didn't black up and leap around Princes Gate to let a cunt like Hosier bring us all down and make us look like wankers.'

The voice was rising as he spoke, Sam's index finger beginning to jab the air. 'I've been in this mob a full ten, and I've seen it change, Davey. We were good, but by fuck we're better now. And that didn't come about because of our fucking Ruperts. It came about because of the kind of people that pass selection—'

Lowry held up his hands, because, as usual when Sam Clark started on about the way the Regiment was run, he was becoming very, very passionate.

'I'm sold, remember.'

Sam tapped the files. 'You know that bastard Hosier mentioned Entebbe. He's a silly sod, always has been. But you never know, he might be right. Maybe, Davey my boy, we can pull it off.'

'One thing's for sure,' Lowry replied, grimly. 'If we can't do it, nobody can.'

'Damned right.'

The door flew open, to reveal the dishevelled figure of Major Vere Symington. He was wearing tracksuit bottoms and a torn Harlequins rugby shirt. He had both the height and the squashed features of a man who played rugby in the second row. Number four or five in the scrum was the place for real hardcases, or total dickheads, depending on your point of view. Those who didn't admire them wondered how they could spend their lives with their heads stuck up someone else's arse, getting punched by the opposition for their pains, and claim to enjoy it.

Symington would have said it was the only place to be, always in the thick of the action. His nose was flat from more than one break and his ears were like battered cauliflowers. But there was no doubting his air of authority, and the way he snapped his orders.

'My office, David, if you please.' The eyes shifted to Sam Clark, who met them with an even stare. 'And be so good as to get someone to round up the rest of the troop commanders.'

'Troop seniors as well, Vere?'

'Just the officers at present, David.'

Symington was gone as quickly as he'd appeared, the rubber soles of his trainers squeaking on the hall floor.

'Can I tell him you take the job, Sam?' said Lowry. 'It will make me look like a right arse if I can't recommend an SSM.'

'OK. But just as long as you know that I might give him the good news later. If the boys vote to bin this op, I'm not going to be the one standing out against them. It would be like fuckin' *High Noon*.'

'If it gets to that stage, we'll all be in the shit.'

Symington called his first planning meeting within the hour. Washed, combed and his sparse, sandy hair tidy, he still looked like a complete ruffian. But he was the kind of ruffian you just knew was a gentleman, and one out of the very top drawer. It was an impression his rich, deep voice only served to underline, as he addressed the men he'd assembled: four troop commanders, Sam Clark and the troop seniors, plus a green slime intelligence officer.

'Right chaps, we have a task. I will not refer now, or in the future, to my reasons for being given this command. I have it, and I shall exercise it with all the determination at my disposal. The mission is like Entebbe, with knobs on. To land at the Rio Grande air base on Tierra del Fuego, and destroy the capacity of the Argentines to threaten our Task Force ships. Method of entry, two Hercules! Weaponry, down to us! On the wall behind you are flight times for the C130s. First opinions?'

'Radar window?' asked David Lowry.

'Four minutes, I'm told,' Symington replied, with such languor the question had to be a prearranged plant.

'Size of garrison?'

'Unknown.'

'How do we know they will be on that airfield, and not at Comodoro Rivadavia?' asked Tommy Laidlaw, an Air Troop senior. 'That's where their main force is based.'

'That will be taken care of. The details of how don't matter.' That was a clear warning not to enquire, and was taken. 'Let's just stick to our own task.'

The questions flew round the room, answers less forthcoming. There was no intelligence on the ground in Argentina, outside of Buenos Aires. And even that was slim. The airport was marked on the map, stuck out in the middle of nowhere, one of those desolate spots that probably allowed the installation to spread in all directions without hindrance. That was partly a plus. The main centres of activity, built when the place was selected as an airfield site, would be bunched together. That would include admin blocks, aircraft and maintenance hangars, the control tower, any communications and the accommodation for officers, pilots and the garrison. The peripherals – fuel storage, along with ammo and missile bunkers – which would have to be manned or guarded, should be well spread out. Since they intended to land in the middle, as close as possible to the nerve centre of the place, that might cut down on the opposition they'd have to face.

At this stage the job was to identify the main targets and assign the necessary troops to take them out. Every man in the room knew about airfields. They'd spent a lot of time on them, mostly waiting around to either go on training or an operation. All very different. But they had shared characteristics in the buildings and installations they needed to operate. Vere Symington had also to set various parameters, one being the number of vehicles.

There was no point in the troops planning their individual tasks, only to be told that they couldn't take certain equipment. Weight slowed the aircraft, and added to fuel consumption: therefore it was agreed that a maximum of four Pinkies would be deployed. The Land Rovers would carry two co-axial-mounted GPMGs plus, stuffed in the back, Milan anti-tank missiles, which could be used to destroy aircraft or buildings. They could also penetrate the steel doors on missile bunkers.

'Any chance of a bit of aerial photography?' asked one of the troop sergeants.

'None,' the green slime officer replied. 'Only the Yanks have satellites and high-flying spy planes that can do the job from space, and they're not playing. If we overflight their bases at anything like low level we will only alert them to the possibility of a raid. We want the buggers as sleepy as possible.'

'Right,' said Symington, summing up. 'Boat Troop, infantry assault. Main targets admin blocks, guardhouse and control tower, particular attention to be paid to the pilots' accommodation. Mountain Troop, initial suppression of same targets, then covering fire for Boat Troop and destruction of peripheral installations. Air and Mobility Troops get the Pinkies. At least one must go after the Exocet missile storage. The rest, get about the place, destroy and distract, then provide covering fire for Boat and Mountain. Everybody to carry the means of aircraft destruction. Remember that time is a luxury. We have to lay down so much fire that we impose a sterile environment for as long as we need to do the job.'

'When do we start rehearsals?' asked Heering, one of the troop commanders.

'The Director had tomorrow in mind,' Lowry replied, seeing that his new OC had not thought that through.

'That strikes me as a touch ambitious,' said Symington quickly. 'Let's put a couple of days into planning, so we know we've got it right.'

The groups filed out, each to compile its own individual plan at troop level. These would then be brought back to the OC and thrown open to discussion. Overlaps were unavoidable. It was in the nature of the Regiment that troop commanders strove to achieve just that bit more than was possible. The OC had to adjudicate, adding to one troop's task while downgrading the ambitions of another. Only when Symington felt that the best combination had been achieved would he then call the men of B Squadron together, and brief them on the overall plan and their detailed orders.

Sam Clark entered into the planning with the same enthusiasm as the others. The notion that his fellow troopers might bin the whole enterprise was not a consideration at this stage. He and his fellow NCOs came to the same conclusion without discussion. The boys had to have something to look at, and it was as much their responsibility as that of the new OC to make sure that what they got was the best appreciation of the risks possible. But Sam did mention the one part of the operation everyone else avoided, which was 'E&E'. That earned him a glare from Symington, nods from the troop seniors and rather sheepish looks from the troop commanders.

'I'll deal with that one in the Interest Room.'

The atmosphere, the sense of anticipation and caution, when they filed into the Interest Room was so thick you could almost touch it. All the guys of B Squadron were there, in the place that was home to their collective memory. The walls were lined with photographs and mementos, the artifacts and snapshots of exploits that went all the way back to World War Two. There were the big group photos, whole-squadron shots taken on every training mission; the individuals and groups in Hereford and on operations. Pairs and foursomes grinning, either clean and drinking beer, or filthy and confined to water. Then there were the piss-taking shots, those magic moments when somebody fucked up on camera, his misdeeds mounted as a permanent memorial to his status as an arsehole.

A lot of the men in the photographs were retired, though they still lived for the reunions and spent as much time in the Interest Room, re-living their service, as they did in the regimental plot remembering their fallen comrades. Sam was wondering if Symington was wise to have his briefing here instead of the regimental theatre. If B Squadron had a collective soul, it was ingrained in these walls. Yet that might work in his favour. It might serve to remind the guys of what they needed to uphold. But the opposite might just be true. It could remind them of what they were being asked to sacrifice.

'Right,' called Symington. Every eye in the room was on him. There was no fidgeting or lounging now. This was the proper monty. 'As per, I will outline the mission first then brief you on the overall plan. The first thing you will observe is that we have no model to work on. The info on this target is so sparse that in my opinion such a layout, which could only be speculative at best, would do more to mislead than enlighten anyone. In this case, when we get down, it's use your eyes and your experience.'

It wasn't a good start, that admission that the whole operation was *ad hoc*. And it didn't get any better as Vere Symington continued. Every planned move was hedged with ifs and buts, evidence that some of the time they might be running around like headless chickens looking for targets. And that all went back to the first big question: could they get down at all? Because the state of the anti-aircraft defence was just as speculative as the rest.

Symington expected some form of missile – either Tigercats or Rolands – because the Green Slime told him that was the highest estimated level of Argie equipment. The intelligence guys got some hard looks for that, though it wasn't their fault that one of those systems, the Tigercat, was British. The French-built Rolands were more of a worry. First, they were a newer level of kit, and they had a range, 6,800 metres, which was a third greater than the Tigercat's.

'But both systems need time to lock on, and crucially someone has got to tell them to do it. No ordinary Joe is going to fire off a piece of kit worth a few thousand quid without express orders to do so.'

'What about rapid-fire anti-aircraft cannon?' asked a voice from the back.

'They have it, I'm sure. It would be foolish to pretend otherwise. But from what we know it's upgraded World War Two stuff, with an add-on control system. It represents a threat while we're still airborne. But again, no one will let fly without orders, and that equipment will be rendered useless once we're on the ground.'

'No it won't!'

That was said with such force that it turned a lot of heads. The speaker coloured slightly. Sam Clark registered the fact that it was the newest recruit to the squadron. Paul Hill, a member of Boat Troop so fresh he hadn't even got his feet wet.

'The guns can't depress enough to fire at ground target,' Symington insisted.

'They can!'

'That is not my information,' Symington paused, and half-turned to

David Lowry, dropping a cauliflower ear to pick up the whisper. Then he looked back at the speaker. 'Trooper Hill.'

'Then, boss, your information is wrong.'

Sam had to suppress a smile. The way Symington stiffened was, to him, a hoot. They could never get used to it, these Ruperts. Mind, at the same time he was impressed that Hill had spoken out so boldly. It wasn't common for new boys to raise their heads so early. But the most significant thing had to come next. Sam knew very little about Paul Hill. He'd been a croupier before doing selection, which was just about as unusual as you could get. But in his past he'd been in the RAF Regiment, and they were the blokes that manned airfield defences. He must know more than Symington about ack-ack gunnery. But the new OC was probably unaware of that. Would the Rupert put his foot in it by challenging him? Chest puffed out, it certainly looked like it.

'Hill's right,' said Serious Sid. 'Ever since the days of German 88 mils nearly every gun made has been geared to fire at ground targets. That goes for Bofors and Oerlikons, which is, according to *Jane's*, what the Argies are equipped with.'

Symington had already opened his mouth. But he shut it quickly enough when Sid Franklin spoke. The squadron bore, Serious Sid was one of those people who knew the details of everything. Most guys, handed a piece of kit, like a weapon, were only interested in what it could do. Not Sid! He had to know its weight, muzzle velocity, who designed it, where it was built and the name of the sire and mare. You didn't ask him a question unless you wanted a very heavy earhole-bashing. And when he said a gun could be depressed, then it could be taken as fact.

'If they're Bofors,' Sid continued, 'they fire a point nine six shell at one hundred and twenty rounds a minute. They have a slant range of three thousand metres and a surface to surface range of just under nine thousand metres.'

'Good,' said Symington, recovering himself, and cutting Serious Sid off before he got on to barrel length and ceiling. 'That's what this briefing is about. Making sure we have it right. The final plan will not be formulated until we are on Ascension. And that will be after we've done some very heavy training.'

'Second part, true,' thought Sam Clark, 'first part bollocks!'

The OC turned to the troop officers. 'We will have to look at that, and perhaps redeploy some of the heavy firepower to take out the AA guns.'

'If they concentrate on the planes, which they should do, we'll nail them,' added David Lowry, 'because the Pinkies will be well clear in seconds. Perhaps they should have that as a primary target.'

'Good thinking, David,' Symington replied.

'That four-minute radar window, boss?' asked another trooper. 'How sure are we of that?'

'That is solid information. The RAF sent in Vulcans as soon as the Argies invaded. They hauled out as soon as it locked on, marked the spot for future reference, and they haven't been back since. Our lot must think they're safe by now.'

There was something not quite solid about the way Symington said that – a lack of real assurance, as though there was another answer.

'If the Vulcans can get there, why don't we just nuke them?' demanded Serious Sid.

'Politically impossible.'

Sam piped up. 'Get the matelots to fit a conventional warhead to a Polaris. That would take out the runway.'

'I'm sure that all such options have been discussed, and if they've been discarded it is for a very good reason.'

'Like we need the permission of the Yanks to fire them,' called Robbie Knox.

'You been reading the *Guardian* again, Robbie?' asked Sid.

'Can we get on please?' said Symington, wearily.

Question and answer flowed again, as the SAS troopers exercised their right to grill the men who commanded them. Very few of the responses satisfied. Even Vere Symington, a positive thinker *par excellence*, must have guessed the mood was gloomy. The guys didn't like it and very few were making any pretence otherwise. It was Marty Roper, another Boat Troop member, who posed the killer – the same one Sam Clark had raised at the Command-level briefing.

'And once we've worked the oracle, boss, how do we E&E?'

'That again is an on-the-ground decision. Chile is not ill disposed to our dispute with Argentina. They've been at loggerheads for years over the very terrain we will cover. If there are vehicles to add to our own, we will motor out, and race for the Chilean border. If not, we will have to do it on foot, either as a fighting group or in smaller teams.'

'I'd like to be convinced there'll be enough men to make up a fighting group.'

That produced a growl from more than one throat, one which had the officers going stiff. Symington tried hard to control his voice, but he was clearly angry.

'We will undertake this operation if the orders are given that we should do so. That is our job as members of the Special Air Service Regiment.'

That set up some more growling. These guys knew who they were, and they didn't need some fuckin' Rupert to remind them. What they needed was an escape and evasion plan that gave those who got through the assault a chance to survive.

'Permission to speak to the men, boss?' asked Sam Clark, moving out to the centre. He looked Symington right in the eye. 'Without the officers being present.'

That was like a slap to every Rupert in the room, and Sam, with his hard look, made no attempt to soften the blow. The OC was glaring at him, part of the stare probably an attempt to make out which way the new SSM was inclined. Was he for the operation or against it? But it was also a request that couldn't be denied. This was the Interest Room. It belonged to the men, not the officers. Asked to leave, they had little option but to comply with as much grace as they could muster.

'How long?' demanded Symington.

'As long as it takes,' Sam replied. The delay in adding 'boss' was deliberate.

'There is a lot to do, Sam.'

'I know that.'

Sam Clark deliberately looked over his shoulder to the assembled troopers. Their eyes told him discussion was useless. The OC nodded, and led the Ruperts out of the room.

Sam Clark didn't mince his words. He put the alternatives plainly to the guys in front of him. Go in and get shot to fuck, or turn the whole operation down, which would mean handing it over to A Squadron, with every man in the room RTU'd. Even in normal times, any one of them could resign at a point of their own choosing and return to their original units. You came to the SAS as a volunteer, and you stayed that way. So he began by reminding them why they joined, and why they stayed. It wasn't just ego-tripping. With this, the whole ethic of the Regiment was at stake. That if they had to go to the wall, so what. The people paid them their wages for just such a risk!

'Then why did Lippy and Tooks turn it down?' asked Johnny 'Concorde' Tucker, a member of Boat Troop with a huge, pointy nose.

'They didn't turn down doing it, mate,' said Sam Clark. 'What they turned down was ordering us in.'

Robbie Knox wiped his flat, broken nose. 'Lippy always said that bastard Hosier would do for him one day.'

'He's about to do for the lot of us,' added Marty Roper. 'He's a paid up member in the widow-making fraternity.'

'I've got a wife and kids,' Sam Clark added, 'and I'm not the only one. But so have those poor bastards on the ships. Let's fuckin' get to the nitty of this. What happens if we blank it, they take a pasting, and the story gets out?'

He left them to think on that for a bit before continuing. 'You blokes know me. I'm no nutter, am I?'

'Except about bloody movies.'

Sam ignored that. 'I can't turn it down. I'm not going to let that cunt Hosier make me feel like a useless prick. But if anybody wants to take the same route as Lippy Grant, then I say they can walk without any comeback from the guys who stay.'

'Aw, fuck it,' came a voice from the back of the group. 'Who Dares Wins.'

'How about we talk it through, then decide?' asked another.

Dinger Bell called from the back, his Geordie accent thick. 'That could tak' all bloody night, man.'

Concorde turned round to argue. 'Well if you've got a better way of sorting this out without talking, I'd like to hear it. We're not fuckin' telepathic, you Tyneside berk!'

'Calm doon, ya daft bugger.'

'I make him right,' said Sam Clark. 'Let everybody have their say, then we either do it as a squadron, or blank it as a squadron.'

Dinger Bell was in like Flint. 'Tell me if'n a'm wrang, man, but have you just changed yer tune? Half a mo ago ye were on aboot us ahl making up our own minds.'

'I just had a thought, Dinger. That if we don't stick together, it will be the fuckin' Ruperts who have won.'

'Sam. Ah don't know where you've been all yer life, man. But the fuckin' Ruperts always win.'

CHAPTER SEVEN

Cabinet office to Officer Commanding 3 Bgde. 7/2/82: 08.00 hrs. Execute Operation Sutton forthwith.

S am sat forward in his chair, rubbing his hands as he talked, trying to aid his conversation. Some of what he said had emerged in the Command briefing and the troop planning groups. But to that was added his own thoughts and experience.

'You've got to figure that troops guarding an air base are low-grade, right?'

'OK,' Marty Roper replied. 'So you don't put good guys on sentry duty. Mind you, Sam, we don't know if they're air force or conscript jundies.'

'I can't see it matters. They've got to be low-grade, and bored shitless after a month of a possible war that's got fuck all to do with them. It's three hundred miles away and all they see is planes taking off sometimes. This operation isn't due to go down for at least a week. That can only improve things.'

'You've got nothing to back that up,' snapped Concorde Tucker, one finger tugging at a nostril. 'They could be the keenest cunts in South America.'

Sam wasn't actually bothered by that remark. Tucker was just doing a job – playing devil's advocate, making Sam justify himself. Half the guys in the room would have had that thought; he'd just voiced it. But he sounded harsh enough when he spoke.

'What's up with you? The Argies are a conscript army. That must go for footsloggers in the air force too. Very few of them are regulars. And if there were any, and I was Galtieri, with the murderous cunts he's got around him, I'd have the fuckers stuck right outside my bleeding bedroom.'

'All right!' said Tucker, making a gesture of surrender. 'They're crap.'

'So if they are low-grade, and we can take them by surprise, then they're not goin' to stand for too long against the kind of shit we can put down.'

'What about their officers?' asked Paul Hill. 'The pilots are reckoned to be the best thing about the buggers. Let's face it, Sam, they're the ones who're doin' the damage.'

'We get them first.'

'If we can find them,' Paul replied.

'Two seconds in the Regiment,' started Serious Sid, with a scoffing tone in his voice. But he got no chance to finish, since the new boy put him right in his place.

'That won't stop them fucking slotting me – or you.'

'They're all Brylcreem boys in the air force, especially the pilots.'

'KY jelly more like,' insisted Tony D'Ambrosio.

'Can we concentrate?' Sam called. 'This is not some joke. It's for fuckin' real.'

Tucker had to have the last word. 'Let's hope the pilots are heroes, and getting fucked senseless by the local crumpet every time they crook their little fingers.'

'The officers are not all pilots.'

'They're all South Americans,' said Sam. 'Maybe I've seen too many Zapata movies. But I bet they'd rather be getting pissed in town, or getting up some tart, than sitting around all night playing cards in the mess.'

'What are we?' asked Marty Roper. 'The Wild Bunch?'

'They got killed,' Sam replied, smiling.

'Thank Christ that only happens in films,' said Marty Roper, sarcastically.

'Getting the crates down is the problem. But I think if we can solve that we can do the business and get clear.'

'I buy the first bit, old son,' said Concorde Tucker, 'but I can't see the rest.'

'Right,' Sam replied, sitting even further forward. 'We're on the Hercules, a plane they might well recognize the signature on. There's a half-asleep Argie sitting on the radar, picking his toenails. It's a quiet night, not a lot happening. Then suddenly he gets a blip. "What the fuck is that," says he, and he fiddles with his console. Fifteen seconds, minimum, gone.'

'Somebody write that doon,' said Dinger Bell.

'Then he gets on his handset and makes a call. We don't reply so he repeats. Half a minute more gone. The third time we do respond. We have a Spanish speaker in the cockpit, putting out a load of guff about engine trouble and the need to make an emergency landing. It's all babble and panic stuff, like we're really in the shit. And we have to be able to string that out for a whole minute.'

'There's two planes.'

'We'll talk to the pilots.'

'That's a point,' said Marty Roper. 'Has anyone asked them if they want to do this shit?'

'Someone'll do it,' Paul Hill replied. 'Take my word for it, there's as many stupid cunts in the air force as any other unit.'

'There has to be a way to make it look like one profile,' Sam continued.

Tony D'Ambrosio cut in again. 'Two planes up each other's arse. That's goin' to take an awful lot of KY.'

Sam stuck two fingers up to him. 'We are flying at night?'

'Through what these guys think is friendly airspace,' added Paul Hill.

'Not convinced,' Tucker responded, 'but go on.'

'The guy will insist on a call sign, one that his own pilots use. We give him a bogey one, and then we shift the frequency so he gets nothing after that but interference. That's at least another minute used up before it clears.'

Tucker spoke again, doubt in his voice. 'You're now one and a half minutes from touchdown, in a plane they're not expecting. And this man is fuckin' suspicious.'

'So what does he do? He can't go ahead on his own and order a general alert.'

'So he needs an officer.'

'Right. And my guess is that he will have to send for one. Even if the guy is downstairs and stone cold sober it would take at least a minute to get him in and explain. He'll look at the screen himself. Who knows? He might even try to call us. And all the time our Spanish speaker is screaming down the radio about how much shit we're in.'

'By which time they can hear the engines.'

'C130s, which they'll all recognize.'

A few of the guys looked doubtful.

'Believe me, they'll know. Paul will confirm that. Air force guys like to show off just as much as anyone else. They do that by telling people like you and me what plane is flying overhead without looking up. And now we're over the end of the runway, and still they don't know if we're kosher. If anything the doubts are doubled. We're now so close any missiles they've got are useless. The warheads won't arm at short range. And I'll bet that the anti-aircraft cannon won't be permanently manned. So what does Galtieri junior do? He has an identifiable plane in aural, not visual contact, which claims to be his own. How does he make a decision about what action to take?'

It was Tony D'Ambrosio who answered, finally adding something constructive to the conversation. 'He illuminates the runway lights to take a look-see.'

'I never thought of that,' said Sam.

'Somebody write that down!' Marty Roper called, in an exaggerated way. 'It's a fuckin' first!'

Sam gave him two fingers as well. 'It makes no odds whether he does or he doesn't. By the time he reacts we are down on the tarmac. We can debus a Hercules in under a minute. We'll be shooting at the bastards in two minutes flat, and most of them will still be trying to find their underpants.'

'Have you ever thought about writing a movie?'

'Every night of my life.'

'Say this cunt does illuminate,' added Tony. 'Will your imagined Argie officer have the nous to do the obvious, and switch the bloody lights off again?'

'He will when the first Milan rocket lands on the top of his bonce, mate. But then it will be too late. Every one of our teams will have picked a target and be giving it the full monty. In the dark, if they're the kind of useless fuckers I think they are, they'd NEED a hundred to one to cope with us.'

'Let we's go through that again,' said Dinger. 'Just so as we're sure wahve got it right.'

'That's what happens when your brains are in your dick,' said Tucker, with feeling. 'You can't hear properly.'

'I thought you were supposed to go blind, wanking,' said Paul Hill. 'Not deaf.'

'Then a'm as safe as a hoose, man, cause' mah arms aren't long enough.'

Dinger said that with a note of real triumph. He had, by common consent, the biggest prick in B Squadron. He was definitely a man to avoid standing next to in a pissoir if you wanted to keep some self-respect. He did well down at the Black Bull, where a lot of the local talent went just to try their luck at fucking an SAS man.

But he was right, and they went over it again, adding points, refining options and getting heavily involved in a process they all enjoyed. Sam wasn't sure if subconsciously he'd planned it that way. That by getting the guys talking, and discussing the finer details, he would get them to accept the operation.

'E&E?' Marty Roper insisted.

'We don't clobber the vehicle park. In fact, since none of the trucks will be in use we leave it well alone.'

'Which side of the road do they drive on?' asked some wag.

'Who gives a fuck?' Sam replied, with a grin. He had a reputation as being a demon behind a wheel. 'We take out the planes, Super Etendards, but basically anything that's laying about the place. In short, boys, we blow the fuckin' lot.'

'And all those blokes sitting on their arses on the border?'

'Are forty to fifty miles away. That's two hours' travel in anybody's language, and that's always assuming they can shift. By the time they turn up we'll be long gone.'

'Has anybody got a rosary?' said Tony D'Ambrosio. 'I think I want to pray.'

Sam summed up for everybody, ruthlessly killing off any interruptions. In any Chinese parliament, there was a time for talking and a time for conclusions, and they'd done enough chatting. His job was to bring it all together.

'There's two ways to look at this op. In the positive, or the negative.'

The fact was that no one in their right mind would go. So it was best to look on the bright side. How could Sam say he had a good feeling about it? But he did! He knew in his boots that they could pull it off. Not without losses, but that was part of the job.

'It all hangs on that four-minute window.'

'Symington sounded to me as if he was fannying,' said Sam. 'Did anyone else pick that up?'

That caused a lot of heads to shake.

'The Green Slime said there's supposed to be a sub doing early-warning aircraft spotting off the Argie coast. Maybe they can do something.'

'How are they going to do that from the bleeding seabed?' asked Marty Roper.

'So what do I say to them?' asked Sam.

It was one of those occasions when nobody relished decision time. When no one person wanted to be the first to speak. Sam Clark stood up and walked out of the Interest Room, leaving his mates talking quietly behind him. He was back within five minutes.

'It's got be checked,' said Sam. 'Even Jock the Sock gave the nod to that. They are going to put in a request to the CO to ask if he's got the men to do a recce. Meanwhile, we train, yeah?'

The nod that Sam concluded with was answered by several more, some quick and determined, others slow and resigned. But he'd got what he wanted, and was pleased.

In Jamie Robertson-Macleod's sleeping cabin, he and his adjutant, Oliver Rabatt, were discussing the matter, well away from prying ears. Hosier, knowing he had a Satcom, had been on the blower, and asked for a private chat.

'I told him he'd have to find his own troopers. That I'm not downgrading Falklands ops to oblige him. Politely, of course. All my chaps committed, that sort of thing.'

'You don't like it do you?'

'Not a lot, Ollie. It's one of those chancy things that could go very well, or go completely pear-shaped and leave us all looking like total idiots.'

'You could insist that it be binned.'

'Not that simple. Given the threat those carriers face it doesn't have to be a very sound operation. If it had come from another source, I would be less stressed. But Hosier's making capital out of it in the right places, which does nothing for the Regiment's cause in our little battle for control.'

'You can't keep Jock the Sock in his drawer.'

'I'm not sure I really want to. But I do wish he'd just clear his stuff with me before he goes ahead and puts it out to the chaps for a detailed plan.'

'I wonder how they took it. B was a little pissed off that G got the Falkland travel permits.'

JRM looked surprised at that. The notion that the men would be anything other than gung-ho had never occurred to him.

'Vere will fire them up. He'll make it sound like a rugger match with bullets.'

'You still have no real explanation as to why he removed Tooks and Grant.'

That induced a silent, pregnant pause. Each man had his own thoughts on that, as well as slightly different agendas. The one thing you could never be sure of in the Army was that promotion routes would remain static. Nor who would be in the driving seat at the appropriate time. Jock the Sock might be a power in the land at some later stage. Certainly JRM could enquire about the dismissals, but it would have to be couched carefully, so that Hosier didn't see it as an attempt to rebuke him.

'He's such an awkward sod,' said Rabatt.

'Scotch?' said JRM, refusing to be drawn as he reached into a locker. 'Never say no to the CO.'

'Checking that radar time is essential,' said the JRM as he poured.

Rabatt took a sip. 'That's true. But surely any notion of going in without knowing about the troop strength the chaps are going to face is sheer tosh? The recce mission must include some kind of ground appreciation to give them a workable chance.'

'One thing's for sure. There'll be all hell let loose if any of them get picked up, Ollie. Old Al Haig is, according to the World Service, still chuntering at the Peruvians and the UN.'

'Perhaps we should impress on General Haig that it will jeopardize Hosier's chances of another promotion, for which the old bugger will NOT be grateful.'

'Sod him,' said JRM, finally coming off the fence. The expletive was accompanied by a lifting of the glass.

'Rather you than me, old boy,' said Rabatt. 'Do you really think he got the go-ahead from Maggie herself?'

'Yes I do. But I'm not sure he gave her all the facts. Surely, the last thing Thatcher wants is B Squadron splattered all over the Rio Grande tarmac, with survivors fighting off a whole load of Argie troops from the border?'

The first training mission was on for the following day. Chinooks lifted their kit to the air base and they took off as soon as they were loaded, heading for Manston in Kent. As an emergency strip it was not fully operational. It was also spread out over a huge area, and had the longest runway in the country. In fact the terrain was very like what they could expect in Tierra del Fuego. That made it a good place to start.

Flying high, a Hercules is noisy but, barring thermals, fairly level in flight. Low and wave-hopping it was like being in a blender. The frame rattled and the aircraft bucked and shuddered, picking up every variation in the air currents. This was not good for performance, since a lot of the guys were thinking about how to avoid puking, rather than the task ahead.

At the red light they were up and ready, the drivers, who would move out first, starting and gunning up the engines on the Pinkies, ignoring the way this filled the compartment with smoke. The tyres hit the tarmac with a screech, and the C130 immediately put on the air brakes. At the same time the tailgate started to drop on its hydraulics. It was all too slow, the plane stationary before anyone could de-buss. By the time everyone was on the ground it was over four minutes from first landing, a time that had to be cut by a very minimum of fifty per cent.

So it was do it again and again, beginning the opening of the tailgate before touchdown. That was progressed so that when the plane hit the runway there was no more than a few feet of clearance between it and the ground. That improved the timings, but not by enough. But Vere Symington was not disappointed. The men were re-learning their tasks, ironing out the gremlins that occurred regardless of competence. This operation had to be carried out in the dark, not daylight. So they would have to be able to do in blindfolds.

The men for the recce were pulled out, two from each troop. Concorde Tucker and Craig Walker, a Kiwi, were chosen from Boat Troop. Though not too much was said about their means of infiltration, it was generally accepted that when it came down to the wire, these eight guys and the officer who led them had the less hazardous mission.

The next week saw half the RAF stations in the country, especially those in Scotland, under attack, as B Squadron toiled to achieve perfection. It was circuits and bumps, then forty-odd guys screaming out the rear of the planes, Pinkies haring right and left. Task one for everyone was to choose a target from bases that differed enough to make it difficult. At least the Pinkies could race to theirs and pretend to shoot them up with some degree of reality. Not so Boat and Mountain. It was too risky to fire off even dummy rounds from grenade launchers on an active RAF base at targets several hundred feet away.

The Staff Sergeant of Mobility, after a conversation with Sam Clark that revolved around the film *The Italian Job*, asked for and got a flat-bedded truck and a spare Hercules tailgate. The engineers of RAF Maintenance provided some wheels from an old forklift so that he could experiment with running the Pinkies off while the planes were still moving. An air base was perfect for this, as the truck could get up the required speed. The maximum safe landing speed of a Hercules was just over a hundred knots, more than a truck could achieve. But that slowed rapidly to nearer seventy and they got it up to that before they rolled off the first Pinkie.

Killing people was not the aim, so the Land Rover went off, in reverse, with its wheel roped to either door. At that speed it didn't look too clever, the vehicle swerving and turning over almost as soon as it hit the ground. A quick examination of the dented vehicle showed that the ropes had snapped. If they couldn't hold, neither could a human being. Such force would both break the driver's arm and leave them with eight dead men and a loss of a quarter of their firepower.

They tried going forward at high speed, but that was even worse, so there was no alternative but to drop the pace. Four Land Rovers were in bits before they settled at thirty-five miles an hour, going backwards so that the plane would move away from the vehicle. The next stage was to get the RAF to attach the wheeled tailgate to a real plane so that, by taxiing, they could check out the effect of the Hercules' airstream. That wrecked another Pinkie, and it was decided that driving off forwards, at around thirty, was preferable. The slipstream of the fuselage kept the Pinkie on track, and they could use the Land Rover's own brakes to slow it down before they turned to seek a target. It also helped to load the vehicle with sandbags. That added protection for the men aboard, and the lowering of the centre of gravity helped to keep it stable in a fast turn.

Throughout, the whole squadron went through furious mood swings. Sometimes they were up for it, yelling and screaming as they fired off their personal weaponry. The motto was train hard, fight easy. But nothing could disguise the fact that they would still be operating in the dark, both physically and metaphorically, and even the most enthusiastic training day was followed by a black nocturnal mood.

The other exercises, carried out on a disused airfield on Salisbury Plain, went OK in daylight, but showed just what they were up against when it came to night time. Using old, parked vehicles to represent buildings, trucks that were constantly moved around, there was no hiding the fact that there was a huge discrepancy between theory and practice. Shooting the trucks up offered some relief, and in the final attempt the M203s and Milans could blast away. Seeing the actual targets go up lifted their spirits. But only until someone, over an after-action brew up, got negative.

The conclusion was stark. The fog of war was a fact for any soldier, regardless of his abilities. And as they went through the debus from another taxiing plane, exiting in pitch darkness, mistakes slowed them down. Half the gains that they'd made training on the C130s seemed to be lost on contact with the ground. There was not a man involved who didn't realize the truth: that even with the best available luck, they could expect to start taking casualties before they got close enough to engage. The only saver was that on the real operation, the pilots, if they weren't taken out by gunfire, would try to run them within close proximity of the main installations.

But much as they worried, and sometimes moaned, they still trained. If they were going to do the business, which was still up in the air, then that was the time to make a decision. After every session there was a debrief, and a search for improvements. Many were made, like firing flares from the C130s on the point of landing. Sam Clark admired the aircrew for agreeing to that, being proactive instead of just passive. Of course, the guys they were training with might not be the ones to actually fly them in. If they were taking off from Ascension then the pilots would come from an operational squadron. You had to wonder how they'd feel about firing off flares. They would be the main targets when the shit hit the fan. Every AA cannon on the base, if it were manned, would fire off at them, before they realized there were other opportunities. The thin-skinned Hercules would be shot to ribbons, quite possibly before the airmen got out. Still, it was a good idea. Maybe they could time the ignition of the flares with their de-bussing so they'd be engaging their targets with speed, drawing down the counter-fire that would otherwise be aimed at the planes.

There were some improvements that were impossible. But the OC had achieved his main aim. The squadron could de-buss the C130s in less than two minutes, and engage the enemy thirty seconds later. What he couldn't command was the growing knowledge that they were using up time and that soon the panto would stop, and they'd be down for the real thing.

'We're going to try a night training exercise in Lincolnshire,' said Vere Symington, to the assembled planning group. 'I won't say which base, because some of you might know it.'

They took off at twilight, and stayed in the air for a long time, this to add the feel of the flight they'd make from Ascension. Only when they were airborne did the news come through where they were going. Apart from the very top brass, they were not expected. The RAF was using this to test their own reactions. The lead Hercules pilot would, as on the real operation, pretend to be in trouble and seek an emergency landing. That would be granted, though no flares would be fired, since the field would be illuminated to help them in.

It might be a drill, but there was a growing suspicion that this was the last one. If the feeling was right, that meant that the decision had been made at the very top level to commit them to the operation. That in itself contributed to the way the men prepared. Even the pilot was doing it right, feathering his engine occasionally to change the tone, so that those on the ground would really believe that the C130 was in trouble. Only the guys in the control tower would know there were two, and they were not about to tell anyone.

The plane Boat Troop was on picked up speed, a sudden thrust of power to take them in to the ground, as the tailgate started to drop, filling the cargo bay with a deafening roar of wind that swirled the smoke from the Pinkie exhausts all over the place. It was so low that the thrust of the wheels followed within seconds. The tailgate was a few feet from the tarmac when the first driver gunned his engine and headed out. The second Pinkie was right behind, screaming down the ramp past the men who'd fight on foot. They were hanging on to their straps, fighting against the force of the braking Hercules, waiting for the moment when that would ease and they could run for the open air.

Then they were out, fanning right and left in the wake of the Pinkies, kneeling down as soon as they were clear to pick their targets. The crack of blank ammunition was audible above the screams of Boat Troop as, weapons up and ready, they raced across the tarmac, following David Lowry, who was directing them towards the main installations on the air base.

It would have been just right if they hadn't exited onto a brightly lit scene, full of flashing lights and fire appliances, and yelling their lungs out did nothing to alter that. They had got no more than fifty yards when the whistle went to halt them. They stopped running, and stopped yelling. An eerie silence followed, as the shocked good Samaritans of the RAF stared down the barrels of rifles, grenade launchers, the Gimpies on the backs of the vehicles, and into the dark cammed faces of B Squadron SAS.

'Don't anybody say fire,' said a voice, floating over the scene. 'Or the bastards might give us a right soaking.'

'05.00 hours tomorrow,' said Vere Symington. 'The operation is on go. We will have some time at Ascension, and I want it understood that we will be training from the minute we land to the hour before we depart.'

For the bachelors it was a night on the base, packing their personal kit. The married men went home, to do the same thing, and to say goodbye to their wives and children. Security about operations was tight, but it didn't take a genius to work out that with the prospect of the Falkland landings being discussed hourly on the box, the men were not going off to some picnic. And you can't live with someone for years and not have them notice how tense you are. Julie Clark was no exception.

But she helped Sam pack, and said nothing, trying to keep from the children the feeling she had that she was about to say goodbye to Sam for the last time. If she shed a tear, it was when her eyes were directed to the typed list of kit taped onto the back of the wardrobe door. The kids, ten-year-old twin girls, weren't fooled. They watched the TV too, and knew just as much about their Dad's moods as his wife.

Sam tried hard to lighten things, talking about a future he wasn't really certain existed. And he thought about the others, the men who would be going with him, all of them probably going through the same emotions as him and his family. It didn't matter how many times you did the parting thing; you never found an easy way. The jokes he tried just didn't come off, and he nearly lost it himself when it was time for his kids to go to bed. The sex they had was necessary and functional, rather than imbued with blistering passion, an act that might be part of a last memory.

In the car, at three o'clock on a cold spring morning, Julie was crying before they'd pulled out of the street of small terraced houses. Unable to contain herself any longer, she'd demanded to be told how bad it was. Sam couldn't bring himself to lie to her. The operational details were left out. But the risk was not. He had to get out of the car, when they reached the gate, with speed, lest he crack himself. The last sound he heard, after that of the slamming boot lid, and as he walked away, was his wife sobbing in the front seat.

Sam looked through the photocopy of his quick-move checklist, ticking off the items that remained to be packed. Over a hundred and twenty bits and pieces, and that didn't include stuff for operations in hot theatres. There were the basics, from holdalls to his Bergen. The medical kit: field and shell dressings, crêpe bandages, morphine syrettes and airway, and an artery clamp. That would be used for sure. The survival kit was less of a certainty. Some of the rest would stay on Ascension. He couldn't see PT singlet and shorts being much use to him on Tierra del Fuego. But it was cold down there, so he paid particular attention to packing the cold/wet theatre kit.

Socks Arctic, 3 pairs. Thermal underwear, 2 pairs. Mountain boots, gaiters, salopette trousers, duvet waistcoat and jacket, snow gaiters, sleeping bag, Arctic, mat and cover. The individual bivi tent, woollen balaclava and wristlets, gloves outer and over. He fingered the five magazines that would hold his ammo, dull and green. The enemy would have the same. When his kit was packed he took it to the Interest Room, a place full of quiet individuals. They didn't stay quiet long. Sam Clark nearly went through the roof of the old Nissen hut when he heard about the sovereigns.

'What fuckin' genius came up with that one?'

Sam Clark was standing in the doorway of the B Squadron commander's office, his square face puce with anger. But the man he wanted wasn't there. Instead, David Lowry sat at the desk, sorting through some papers.

'Where's Symington?'

'London. He's meeting us at Brize Norton.'

'Was it his idea to stop the issue of sovereigns?'

'No, Sam.'

'Then who?

'Actually, the order came from Archie Grosvenor.'

'What the fuck has it got to do with him?'

'Will you come in and shut the door, you berk. I don't mind you yelling at me, but not so the whole bloody building can hear.'

Sam's face relaxed at that, then went hard again in case Lowry thought he was soft. But he did take a step forward and shut the door.

'Look,' Lowry said. 'Grosvenor is now the acting CO. I asked about it, and Archie more or less admitted that the order came from Hosier himself.'

'I suppose he's fucked off to London as well!' Lowry nodded. 'Has either of them any idea of what this is going to do to the lads? The gold sovereigns are part of their standard kit. Sending them out without them is like saying goodbye. "You're goin' to get slotted, lads, so why waste money? You won't want to be looted for twenty gold coins."'

'It's not like that, Sam.'

'What are we supposed to do? Take pound notes?'

'I should take something, just in case we do make Chile.'

'Fat chance.'

'Thanks for cheering me up.'

Sam was aware that David Lowry was just as trapped as the rest of them. He'd chosen to make a career in the Army. If he ducked out of this he could kiss it goodbye, and that went for normal regimental duty as well. He'd be lucky to make major, never mind get a crack at Staff

College. The attempt to lighten the mood didn't work that well, but it at least established that the new SSM understood his predicament.

'I can just see it. Me walking up to an Argie and offering him a pound note for a night with his sister.'

'I hope you get the chance.'

'Have you got a credit card?'

'Diner's Club. Why?'

'Then I can ponce off you.'

Sam might have made a joke, but that was just his nature. He was far from being a happy man.

'You should have come and told me about this, Davey. The boys are jumpy enough as it is, without something like this happening. My arse was left hanging out to dry when I walked into the Interest Room.'

'OK, I'm sorry.'

'Don't worry, sir,' Sam said, with heavy irony. 'One day you'll learn how to be a proper soldier instead of a poxy Rupert.'

'Get out of here,' Lowry said wearily.

'I'm gone, boss.'

CHAPTER EIGHT

'Good evening. This is the World Service of the BBC. First the headlines. The liner Queen Elizabeth the Second, converted for use as a troopship, left Southampton today bound for the South Atlantic. . .'

The Goose Green settlement, along with the Argentine garrison and airfield, lay beneath the position Blue and his patrol had taken up, the observation position in a hide so well cammed that the Fijian, who revelled in camouflage work, hailed it as a work of art. It had taken them four days to get here, across the awful, wet, exposed terrain of the island, moving at night, Blue out in front well aware that he had no time to search ahead for booby traps or minefields. He had to keep moving over the uneven ground in pitch darkness and hope that he would survive.

The first day on site had been rough, lying in a shell scrape with only their personal cam nets to keep them hidden. The hill they were on was used by all the incoming traffic, both fixed wing and helis, as a navigational approach marker for landing. Some of the aircraft flew so low over their position that it felt as though they were going to set down on top of them, especially the choppers, whose rotor downdraught threatened to dislodge their flimsy coverings.

But when darkness fell they'd been able to work on it, improving the internal layout and the external appearance over several nights to the point that an Argentine patrol could have come within ten feet of the place and walked straight past. Wire netting supported hessian, covered with tussock grass to blend in with the surroundings on what was a bumpy, rocky hill. Not that they were in any way safe, with aircraft so close they could smell the exhaust fumes.

They counted the troops on the ground: 600 men, a whole battalion in strength, and being reinforced by the very same transports that over-flew them. They counted the planes and choppers, both stationed and ferrying, then morsed that back to the Headshed, another hazardous operation since it was well known that the Argies had direction-finding equipment. But there were patrols all over the island, ten in all, several close to Blue's, and the level of signal traffic must have caused confusion.

The first result of what they all sent in was a raid by four Harriers that blew up the shoreside fuel dumps and beat up on the garrison in their encampments around the airstrip. It was beautiful stuff to watch, as the planes swooped in over the flat sea of the inlet, the rocket trails clear in a blue sky, as they slotted their targets without once endangering any of the white-painted, red-roofed civilian properties dotted around on the flat peninsula. Smoke billowed up from the burning fuel, as well as the wrecked helicopters and wheeled vehicles. But they missed the planes, a couple of Pucara ground attack aircraft, which the enemy had sensibly camouflaged.

The damage slowed the air traffic for a while, and kept the enemy busy clearing up the mess. But they'd become more bustling, finally behaving as if there was a war on, and with good reason. They'd heard the news. The BBC World Service even told them in Spanish what the British were up to. And if they hadn't mentioned 3 Commando Brigade by name, heading south to take them on, they'd covered the departure of 5 Brigade from Southampton. If the Argies hadn't known things were serious before, they did so now.

Continually reinforced to two-battalion strength, they were digging in, each trench position and freshly arrived unit added to the map that, from information passed through the Skeds, covered the wall back at the Headshed. None of Blue's team could see it. But they all knew how many patrols were ashore, and how good they were. You had to doubt if any army had ever been so territorially compromised as the Argies. And because of the care the men watching them were taking, it was clear the enemy had no idea of their presence. It was going to be a real shock to them when they found out just how much the troops attacking them knew about their defences.

Eight days went by in an environment far short of comfort. The cold air meant they couldn't do much during the day, and the idea of animal interest meant they had to pass everything into a piss and shit bag. Food was cold, and washed down with carefully conserved water, though there was no shortage of that commodity in the Falklands. Indeed, if

112

they wanted any, all they had to do was put their heads down, since despite the plastic sheeting that lined the floor, water seeped through to form a puddle at the bottom of the hide deep enough to soak their boots.

And it was cold, a deep form of chill that seemed to seep through every fibre of the body. The Gonk bags were soaked, so that when sleeping the shivering sometimes became uncontrollable. SOP said that you stayed inside the hide day and night. But Blue Harding was a great believer in that old adage that rules were what wise men listened to and only fools lived by. So at night, after the end of the stand-to, they would emerge in pairs, one man standing stag while the other worked to get blood flowing into stiff and cold limbs. After stand-to Graunch would check out his antennae, and if the frequency had been changed, add or subtract the prescribed distance of wire for what was required. The Sked would go off morning and night, detailing news of what they had observed that day.

They logged locations, weapons equipment and dress; tried to assess relative strengths and capabilities; noted tactics, training, leadership and morale; and sought out the source of any potential reserves. It was also part of their task to survey the ground, and complete a sketch map that would hopefully identify the vital points for both defence and attack.

The routine was hard and demanding, but there was no moaning. This was what they had trained for. It was a matter of personal pride that they should endure discomfort without comment. There was no need for Blue Harding to issue any orders. Luke, Digger and Graunch could think for themselves. They could work out at what part of the day each trooper would undertake other duties, like light cleaning of his weapon. It was simple stuff: check the magazine, chamber and the face of the breech-block. A quick pull-through oiled the barrel. As they undertook the drill for the morning and evening stand-to, they checked their belt kits, grenades and emergency medical kits. Then it was eat, drink and pack the few items left outside into the Bergens, ready for a quick bug-out. Stood down, they took turns at sleeping through the hours of darkness, dawn heralding another day of quiet, rotated observation.

It wasn't quiet on the ninth day! There was little digging going on, and it seemed that the bulk of the Argies were out patrolling. Blue and Luke watched as they moved over the terrain beneath them, rifles up and swinging about as the point men searched the rises and dips, clearly looking for the very thing that the patrol was hiding in.

'Some fucker's woken them up,' whispered Luke.

Even concentrating hard, you can't help speculating. Blue was wondering what had happened. Had the Argies found just one hide on the island, and been alerted to the idea that there might be more? That would mean that some poor sod had been compromised. He just hoped if it was true that they'd got out alive.

On the other hand, it could mean that some of the guys from D had gone into action. Infiltration to gather intelligence was all very well. But that produced targets, some of which might be too tempting or mobile to leave alone. A flash of envy followed that thought, and in his mind he could see Grizzly and his mates going into action, guns blazing, grenades flying and Argies dying by the dozen. It was like an imagined movie, complete with a sound track by Vangelis, which made him smile. You had to be a bit of a big kid to do the job, and he was no exception.

But what the patrol had to worry about now was that they were in danger of being on the receiving end of that very thing themselves, and a decision had to be made. First, to go or stay! And, if the last, whether to hunker down in pitch darkness, hoping those searching would just pass them by, or keep watching through the thin gauze that fronted the hide, so that they could make a fight of it if their position was uncovered.

Imagination produces bad movies as well as good ones, and he hated the idea of being suddenly exposed. That might not happen anyway. If the Argies did find the hide, they might just drop a grenade in to pulp them, or blast away through the sod above their heads and waste them that way. Without relating his daydreams, Blue consulted the others.

'I'd rather go out standing upright, mate,' said Digger.

Serious as it was, Blue couldn't resist the joke. 'But would they notice, Dig?'

With Luke and Graunch, the answer was in the eyes.

'Double check we're secure.'

Each man went through his own mental list, the same one they'd done twice a day since arriving. The kit was ready, they knew the location of the emergency RV. The latest heli pickup point, with times, had come in that morning and been decoded. Blue checked that everyone knew it. Graunch, having got the codebook to where he could destroy it in a second, hauled in his antennae and secured the radio. Blue didn't open the piss and shit bag, but he did check the seal. Digger never took his eyes off the enemy.

There was no need to check the weapons. They were ready at all times. And they had enough with them to lay down some serious shit. The GPMG, even in a light role like this, could put down up to a thousand rounds a minute to an effective range of nearly 800 metres. Each man carried an M203, with eight mags containing thirty rounds. All the kit that wasn't in actual use was already packed in the bergens. They were ready to move with everything they owned at a moment's notice. This wasn't done in a rush, but methodically. Not one of the patrol even got warm from getting prepared. They sat still, weapons ready to fire, with grenades on the belts that were easy to get at, feet planted firmly in the water at the bottom of the hide.

If the days before had been long, this one was longer, the element of impending risk doing nothing to speed the daylight hours. Common sense made them abandon the use of binoculars. The risk of a reflective flash was small. But with the enemy coming ever closer it was too big to take and they could see anyway with their naked eyes just how much of a threat they were under. It was good to know they weren't alone. Not too far away, above and behind them and within a visible radius of their position, lay two G Squadron hides. The men in them would be at full alert as well, ready to back them up if they were so badly compromised they couldn't get clear.

They could see about four patrols, all under command of the first Argentinian officers they'd observed outside the trench lines, groups of ten nervous guys whose fear was almost visible, even from a distance. Everything they had seen of these people told them they were conscripts. The badly fitting, incomplete uniforms and the way they held themselves. Now, patrolling, they reacted to the slightest sound, most of which appeared to be coming from their own mates. As they made their way up the slope, what could be seen, in terms of numbers, diminished until there was only one group in their field of vision. No one spoke, but all four troopers knew that, should they try to break out, the other patrols, now lost to sight, would be on either side of them, causing as much anxiety probably to the other observation posts as the guys in front were causing them.

The gunshot took more than Blue's patrol by surprise. The Argies they could see panicked to a man, diving in all directions. They took a tighter grip on their own weapons. Only the guy who'd fired seemed unaffected, but that was probably because he was dazed. He stood looking at his rifle as if trying to figure out who had fired the negligent discharge. His officer, a real hero, who'd hit the grass as soon as the gun went off, got to his feet screaming abuse. He knew he'd been made to look like a wanker. The gun was still in the hands of the poor bastard who'd fired it, and the officer raised his own pistol, pointing it at the conscript's head and demanding in a high-pitched squeal that it be handed over.

Digger's lips didn't move as he hissed: 'That's what I call leadership. Typical fucking Rupertino.'

Blue was too busy worrying to respond with even a smile. He was thinking about the guys they couldn't see. Just because they'd worked straight up the hillside didn't mean they'd keep that up. They could, right now, be traversing across the slope, moving towards them. Then he relaxed. Even if they had been, that guy with the ND would have changed their minds. That was real ammo, and if they were anything like the ones he could see, they'd be traversing away from the hide and the gunshot, not towards it.

The officer was still yelling, and indistinct as the sound was they knew he was threatening the conscript. That must have been what triggered the reaction. His rifle still in his hands, the kid began to run, not down the hill towards the trenches, but up the hill, straight towards the hide.

'Go another way, you stupid cunt,' hissed Blue, squinting through his sights.

If the Argie officer was mad before, that reaction sent him loopy. Before he started off in pursuit, he fired a shot over the conscript's head, which was a dumb thing to do to a youngster who'd already panicked. The kid picked up pace, still heading straight for them, unaware that he was staggering into more danger than he faced to his rear. They were counting off the paces, trying to decide at which point to drop him, because in his present frame of mind, blind terror, the soldier could run straight over their position and not know he'd done so.

Even if there were four guns trained on him, it was Blue's call as patrol leader. The others would hold their fire as long as he did, which made him wonder if they shared some of his thoughts: that the guy was so terrified he himself presented no threat to them. If he uncovered their

116

hide it would be by pure fluke, which was a lousy way to die. Blue kept his trigger finger still, prepared to risk it, his gaze now fixed on a face so close he could see the terror in the eyes. That's when the officer started shooting. If he was taking aim he was a terrible shot, the bullets from his pistol thudding into the ground right and left of his running target, with one, which must have missed the kid by a millimetre, going right through the wire mesh just above their heads.

The kid then did, as far as Blue was concerned, the worst thing possible. No more than five metres from the front of the hide, he stopped dead in his tracks and stood, his shoulders pressed together as though by shrinking his body size he would cease to be a target, a trembling, gaunt figure in a uniform four sizes too big. Behind him, his officer was reloading his automatic pistol on the run, pulling out one magazine and replacing it with a fresh one.

The kid was crying. They could see the tears coursing down his thin cheeks, streaking across the grime that had accumulated since he set out that morning. Occasionally he sobbed loud enough for the sound to carry to the four troopers, and Blue heard Digger hiss, under his breath, 'Walk away son, walk away.' But he didn't even turn round as the officer caught up with him, grabbing his limp arm to pull him round, the pistol following through to whip the soldier round the ear.

That dropped him to his knees, using his rifle for support, the officer standing over him screaming abuse, jabbing at the boy with the pistol barrel. Digger was cursing under his breath, his emotions shared by all four troopers judging by the tightness of their breathing. The desire to slot the Rupertino was almost overwhelming, as the conscript sunk lower and lower under the weight of the blows. It was a mistake for the kid to lift his rifle. Blue could see what he was doing, trying to either show why it had discharged or to hand it over completely so that he was no longer responsible.

His officer saw it very differently. Typical of the coward he was, he couldn't face the muzzle. He jumped back, raised his pistol and fired in what was clearly panic. The bullet took the kid in the side of the head, jerking as it entered, spewing forth a great lump of blood and brains as it exited from the other side. Four trigger fingers closed a fraction. But training kept them from the pull they so wanted to execute, stopped them from putting in the Argentine Rupert's head a four-for-one payback for what he'd done to an innocent kid.

The officer stood rigid as the body slowly fell over. They could see his features too, observe the shock in his own eyes at what he had done. He started shouting and cursing again just as his victim's body hit the wet grass, where it twitched once before becoming still. To the rear, the rest of the patrol were moving forward, not at a run and not in line, their weapons no threat to anyone as they concentrated their gaze on the body of their dead comrade. Their rifles stayed that way as they gathered round, unaware that the first one to look up the hill could very likely join him. In fact, Blue Harding knew that not one of them would still be alive ten seconds after a firefight started.

But that hadn't happened yet, and even in a situation this dangerous Blue still hung on to the belief that it could stay that way. You sort of stop breathing when the enemy gets close enough, and you hope that your body, which you know smells like shit, suspends excreting oil through the pores for just a few minutes. They could see their breath misting as the scrawny conscripts exhaled, see the drawn, tense faces of men tired from a day spent marching, a day that had ended in an informal execution. But Blue could also see the lack of real interest on the soldier's faces. It was as if their officer was more shocked at what he had done than they were.

The concentration inside the hide was immense, every sense alert to a sudden twitch of movement that would mean discovery. Being on the inside, you had an opinion, not a view, of what it now looked like from the outside. Luke had hailed it as perfect, but there was no guarantee it had stayed that way. All it took was for something to seem slightly out of place to make any one of the Argies look a bit harder. They could be ten dumb fucks but it only took one with sharp eyes to do the trick! They wouldn't shout and point. Conscripts they might be, but there would be enough of a feeling of self-preservation to stop anyone who spotted the hide from reacting. No cunt in his right mind would do that. It was a sure way to get slotted by the first shot!

Was Blue alone in praying that they'd fail? Seeing that kid gunned down had affected him. The officer apart, he had no desire to kill the rest of these kids. And to be compromised would count as a defeat, even if they got away intact and left the whole Argentine unit dead. This was a non-aggressive patrol. It was a real pisser, when you'd gone to all the trouble of creating an observation post, and staying there for a week, to be flushed out. And the biggest bummer was, if they found one, they'd put out a maximum effort to find all the others.

A whistle blew. A long blast but distant. That seemed to concentrate the officer's mind. He holstered his pistol then ordered two of his men to pass over their rifles. They took hold of the boots of their dead comrade, dragging him back down the hill, his broken head leaving a trail of blood and gore in the long wet grass as it bounced over the tussocks. His comrades seemed determined to look anywhere but into the sightless eyes. But the officer was marching with his shoulders square, like a man who'd won some kind of victory, unaware that there were four weapons pointing to a spot right in the middle of that arrogant back.

The training intensified once B Squadron were on Ascension. Hosier was in the background, harrying Vere Symington to ever greater efforts. By now the squadron could do the whole debus procedure blindfold, and deploy in a dozen different ways to meet endless unknown scenarios. He must have known that they had to keep the men busy, known that if they had a chance to sit and talk to each other for any length of time he might well have a mutiny on his hands. Not that there wasn't open dissent. Every time he came close negative remarks were aired in a way that he couldn't fail to hear.

But the Director of Special Forces seemed immune, and just stared at some distant object, like his field marshal's baton. But not even he, with his well-known ability to avoid dangerous responsibility, could leave the Squadron Commander to do the final briefing. As he stood up to address B Squadron, he could almost physically feel the animosity emanating from the men before him. There was a table in front of him, with various bits and pieces on it, models of buildings and hangars that would have made up a diorama. That is, if anyone had known where to put them.

'Right, pay attention!'

It was unnecessary, and treated as such by a totally silent response from the men facing him.

'Our recce patrol is in place, and will be going ashore from *Hermes* as soon as it is dark. The method of entry is by Sea King, and they are carrying with them not only one of the new Satcom radio telephones,

119

but a hand-held radar detection device that will tell us precisely how long our window of opportunity is. They have to fly a long way, so the ship has been stripped down to the very bare essentials to allow for extra fuel. As soon as they are on the ground, and have confirmed our window, we will lift off for the target. Any other information they provide will be signalled through to both aircraft on RAF comms, up to the point at which it threatens to compromise the security of the operation.'

'Surprise, gentlemen,' he added, after taking a deep breath. 'The element that makes what we do successful.'

'I certainly got one when this was dreamt up, boss,' said Marty Roper. Sitting on the aisle seat, it was obvious who had spoken. Nor was it a secret that Marty was one of the most negative troopers on the payroll. Symington glared, but Hosier ignored him.

'We must balance risk against gain,' Hosier continued loftily.

'All risk, chancy gain.'

'It can be put like that. But it is my nature, and I believe the ethic of Special Forces, to accentuate the positive. It is my job to get you to the runway without incurring initial casualties that might jeopardize the whole attack. I believe that, once our recce patrol has reported back, I will be able to do that.'

None of them was happy, and part of his being could understand why. The job they were being asked to perform was a bugger. All he knew was that it was necessary, and that if he had been in their shoes, he might have shown the same doubts. But crucially, he would never have given the impression that he was reluctant to go. In recalling the two men he had dismissed, and in repeating something he had said to them, Hosier knew he was taking a calculated risk. But these men had to be made to understand.

'Gentlemen, I had occasion to say this to two EX-members of the Regiment who should be with us now. I will repeat it to you! The SAS cannot be seen to be in the position of not taking casualties, when other elements of the British Army are. We are the elite, and that implies responsibilities as well as benefits. I know that what is proposed is dangerous. But that is our job. All told, adding it all up, I say the odds of getting you in will be fairly good.'

A voice from the back called out. 'Is there a William Hill about? I'd like to put on an ante post bet.'

The laughter, even if it was gallows humour, lightened the atmosphere.

'I know, men, that once you get in, you will, as usual, excel yourselves.'

Hosier looked at his watch, in an elaborate gesture that was typical. 'Shall we say 16.00 hours? I want everyone, and their equipment, loaded onto the trucks by 18.00 hours. Vere, I will be over at RAF HQ confirming the flight arrangements, if you need me.'

Symington didn't blink at that; didn't let on what only he and Hosier knew. That the RAF aircrews were just as nervous about this op as the men in the briefing room. One navigator had already refused point blank to go, and had been stood down and replaced. At all costs that had to be kept from his men, since it would only add to their reluctance. But he had to know if matters had improved or deteriorated.

'I'll walk part way with you, if I may,' he said.

Hosier nodded to him, and they departed, leaving a buzz of unfriendly conversation in their wake.

'I don't flaming well believe him!' said Lowry. He was talking to Sam Clark as he watched the retreating backs, the Director's head bent in deep conversation with Vere Symington. 'The SAS must be seen to be taking casualties!'

The voice suddenly became very hard, the expletive unusual from a man who, normally, didn't swear. 'He's not fucking going, is he?'

'He would, though, Davey,' Sam replied grimly. 'Ours is not to reason why.'

'Am I letting them down, Sam?' he asked, a pained expression on his face. 'Should I do the same as Gerry Tooks? Would another officer refusing orders make them see sense?'

Sam patted him on the shoulder. 'That's the great thing about the Regiment, Davey, there's nobody to make up your mind for you.'

The timing of the operation meant that the squadron had to be ready to go the minute the patrol radioed back on the radar window. The signal would come from Hereford, since that was where the Satcom patched through to, then passed on to Ascension. The routine was established and followed. Everything was checked, both personal and unit weapons and loads. Plans were re-hashed, with targets and timing repeated so that every man knew his place and task. The operation was a secret, so no loading would take place until the signal to go was confirmed. Fast loading had been trained for as well, so that they could be aboard the Hercules and airborne before anyone knew what the aircraft were carrying.

Each man had an individual way of expressing it, but they were fantastically keyed up for action. Never mind that they'd have to spend hours in flight. Even the troopers who wondered if they should be here at all were buzzing. It was what they had trained for. They had written their last letters home, enclosing whatever instructions they wished to leave behind should they be killed. That was like detaching yourself from the reality of normal life, a cutting off point that once you'd crossed made you a whole different being.

Some laughed at silly jokes, and took the piss out of each other. A few prayed, while most ran over in their minds the list of scenarios that they'd practised, determined to do well. Even if they hated the idea of going, not one of the men sitting in the trucks or Pinkies wanted to let himself down. True, there was the Regiment and its reputation to think of as well. But push come to shove it was a man's feelings about his own behaviour that counted. So nothing was worse than, having got so wound up, to be told to stand down, get some kip, and then be ready to do another training exercise that afternoon.

It was hard to appreciate, running around sweating buckets in the benign climate of Ascension, what was holding matters up. They didn't know that, down in the South Atlantic, it was blowing a gale, a westerly headwind that would so slow the Sea King it might not make its landfall. The radio told them that no more ships had been hit by Exocets, and that General Al Haig was in a place that John Cole, the BBC reporter with the thick Ulster accent, called 'Burrnos Airs'. It didn't tell them, and neither did their own superiors, that D Squadron had just hit Pebble Island.

They went through the same routine a second night, packing Bergens and going over plans, before climbing aboard again to sit throughout the hours of darkness, waiting. The signal came again after midnight. Operation postponed!

The same the next night, with some of the guys praying it would be third time lucky; that they'd bin the whole operation. Sam Clark wavered back and forth. He was Mr Positive during the day – not because he was absolutely sure it was going to be that way, but because of the need to maintain morale. Never mind the moaners; they were going in. Any guy that had wanted to pull out would have done so in the UK. Even if they were still miserable, it was an expression of feeling, not a prelude to resignation.

But it was hard, sitting in the dark with nothing else to do, to avoid examining the worst-case scenario: that they would take incoming Roland missiles while they were still short of the field; that one of the eighty-five small warheads that Serious Sid had told him about would come blasting through the thin aluminium skin. In that case, all you could hope was that death would be quick, that the bugger would explode right underneath your arse.

He could hear the others talking quietly. Sam got a slight lump in his throat occasionally, as he thought of the people he was with, how much he respected all of them. And what he'd said to Lowry was right. Hosier would have come if he had been at Tooksy's rank. There would have been no stopping him. The mad cunt would have been first off the plane.

CHAPTER NINE

Sitrep A: 12/5/82 17.30 hrs: B: Delta Two Four: C: Pebble Island installation not, repeat not radar: D: aircraft facility offensive: E: Support troops battalion plus.

The recce team from B Squadron were parachuted into the sea, picked up by Rigid Raiders from a patrolling frigate, which immediately closed on *Hermes*. What followed was really hairy, being winched over a heaving sea, singly, by crossdeck jackstay. It didn't matter what the Chief Petty Officer strapping them in said: there was no way anyone felt safe suspended between two heaving ships on a single cable.

Once aboard the command carrier, they were given another briefing. Not that it added much to the sum of knowledge. The Green Slime officer from *Fearless* was waiting with some pretty indistinct aerial shots of the place they were slated to land.

The task had already been discussed, both in Hereford and on the way down, with only the method of entry left to be decided. So the actual final briefing was short. Above their heads, on the top deck, explosives were being packed into the floor of a Sea King, stripped of everything that was superfluous to save weight. They had their transport. The only problem was the weather.

This was a one-way trip. The heli didn't have the range to get to the mainland and back again. So any heavy headwind cut into their ability to run the distance. The patrol was tasked to go in on the ground, collect the information that the rest of the squadron needed about the Rio Grande air base, Satcom it back to Hereford and then be there to assist when the assault went in. They were under no circumstances to be captured. And if the Sea King looked as though it might fall into enemy hands, it was to be destroyed. Thinking about that, as they sat around waiting for two days, did nothing to engender a jolly mood. But there were other factors to add extra worries.

The officer leading them, the Air Troop commander Captain Ralph

Heering, was not the most popular Rupert in the world. For a start he was Blues and Royals, the Household cavalry: skinny, elegant and as stiff as a board. He wasn't a talker, easy communication being beyond him. And he had an annoying habit of looking at anyone who asked him a question as though the speaker had committed some terrible mistake. His answer, when it came, only reinforced this. It was delivered in a voice that sounded as though he was straining at the arse.

The sergeant for the operation was Lofty Glynn, a six-foot-four bruiser from the slums of Salford, who never stopped asking Ruperts what they were up to, on the very good grounds that he suspected they rarely knew. Lofty had won a DCM in Dofhar, which he thought gave him great moral authority. What it did give him was battle experience. His main interest was in gardening. Not the Kew variety, which might have interested Heering, but in the produce from his allotment. The combination looked like chalk and cheese.

Concorde Tucker was there, with the other Boat Troop member Craig Walker, moaning that the mix was a less than brilliant idea. OK, so they'd shared the risks out amongst the four troops. And all SAS men were trained to work together. But he would have been happier with his own mates around him, the guys he knew and trusted enough to get pissed with. For all of the men it was an odd feeling. Having been at the briefing for the air assault, they half-figured that this operation was a bit of a lifesaver. But when you stood back and looked at what they were about to do, no one was quite so sure.

The wind dropped finally, leaving one of those long brilliant sunsets that made you forget how bad the weather had been. The last of the twilight was fading as, muffled up in full Arctic clothing, they boarded the chopper. Carrying extra fuel and loaded with nine men plus crew, there was a very serious discussion about takeoff. None of the troopers were left in any doubt that it was going to be hairy, that they ran the risk of going for a swim. The pilot revved up the engines to maximum power, which only managed to get them about two feet off the deck. He took them forward, more like a fixed wing than a heli, then hauled on his stick to take them out over the side.

'Jesus, Holy Mother of Christ!' yelled Concorde as the heli dropped.

It was like the worst kind of stomach-churning fairground ride, except you would drown in a thousand fathoms at the bottom. Most of the guys

126

had their eyes tight shut, and a silent prayer in their heads. Tucker didn't. If he was going to die he wanted to see it coming. So did Heering, sitting next to him, although the expression on his face was unconcerned. He was staring straight ahead, his slightly bulging blue eyes calm and indifferent, no doubt thinking that they wouldn't have the damned cheek to even wet the feet of someone as well bred as him.

The nose hauled up, seemingly just a few feet from the waves. The pilot skimming the black surface so close that he was throwing up heavy spray. Slowly the Sea King lifted, and began to achieve a bit of forward motion, the nose being hauled round on to the heading for Tierra del Fuego. As it gathered speed, the heli lifted slowly clear of the water, until it was flying high enough to relax the passengers. Not that they were comfortable. The cabin lacked any doors or heaters, having had them removed to save weight. It filled with a freezing, howling gale more than strong enough to penetrate the clothing they were wearing.

There was nothing that could be done about it. All the men could do was huddle down in their Arctic suits and think about what lay ahead. The plan was to run in over the coast, just out of radar range. The pilots would set the chopper down outside that, where its landing and takeoff could not be observed. Then the troopers would do a recce with the hand-held alarm that would confirm the radar window. Once they'd got the information back to the Headshed, the next task was to infiltrate close enough to the Rio Grande air base and gather some intelligence regarding the numbers and readiness of the defenders, this to be relayed to the rest of the squadron in the air. Then it was pick a target of opportunity, like a Roland battery or an AA gun site, and slam the bastard when the planes arrived.

Concorde Tucker sat right behind the pilot and co-pilot, a hand-held radar detection device on his lap. Even though they were a long way from contact it was set, ready to ping if the mainland air defences picked up the Sea King. Not that they expected them to! Their job was to stay just outside it. Given that arc of safety, the time it would take a C130 to close the same distance could be determined. Headwinds or tailwinds were not part of the chopper party's job. That was for the Hercules pilots to deal with. Westerlies were the prevailing winds in these parts, and a strong one could slow the close-in time for the squadron attack by as much as a minute. He was fairly relaxed, although frozen as the hours went by. They were still over water, heading east at full speed, daydreaming, thinking about the FA cup, when the loud ping filled the helicopter cabin.

'Fuck!'

'That's not supposed to be there!' shouted the pilot.

The remark was directed at Heering, who just stared back at the Navy officer. It was Lofty Glynn who answered, his voice rough, grim and loud. 'You're telling me, mate.'

'They must have coastal radar as well.'

'Then it's new,' Heering responded, uselessly.

'Do we go on or bail out?' shouted Lofty.

'We can't bail out now,' the pilot called back as he dropped even closer to the water. He gestured for both Heering and Lofty to lean towards him so that he could talk in a near-normal voice. Tucker was so close he heard every word.

'We've come in too far to turn back. We can't even stooge about with the fuel we've still got. The biggest problem is that if they've locked on to us this early, they can scramble night fighters. They might pick us up on their own sets, and come low to take us out over the sea.'

'So?' Heering asked after what seemed, given the circumstances, a very long pause.

The pilot waved an impatient hand, and holding his in-flight radio mouthpiece close to his mouth, started an animated conversation with his oppo. The pilot then leant back to talk to the troopers.

'Our best bet is to carry on. Get in close to the land and stay low. Jets will never pick us up against a solid background. If we can get down into a fold of hills and out of the radar picture we can figure out what to do next.'

'Will they know it's a chopper?'

'Yep.'

Lofty spoke while Heering thought on that. 'We have to get a signal off about the radar, boss. That at least will give the guys coming in the true picture.'

'Of course.'

'Then you might as well tell them that we've decided to take our annual leave.'

'Coast,' the pilot shouted, pointing towards the black line of solid earth, barely visible ahead.

His co-pilot was already taking the ship down. He put on his PNG kit. Once he had it in place, he took back the controls, and dropped even further. It's hairy being in a helicopter, close enough to look out the front screen, and not be able to see a fucking thing as the craft swoops over the terrain. Tucker went back to his detection set, so that he could tell them when they were below the electronic horizon. It wasn't looking good. They'd known the place was pretty flat, but not this barren. And it was a contingency for which they hadn't reckoned. They'd assumed they'd be able to set down at their chosen location near the coast and carry out their task.

'We're going to get clobbered if we put down around here. We might as well send them an official invite.'

'Try it?' suggested Lofty, looking to Heering for confirmation, which was given with a sharp nod.

The pilot didn't argue, didn't tell Sergeant Lofty Glynn that this was his chopper and he'd make the decisions. When it came to survival he was with the experts. He was happy to take instructions from a guy who was nominally his inferior. The Sea King floated down and hit turf, with Lofty spinning round to look at Concorde Tucker. He didn't need to ask him anything: the detection light was still on, glowing bright orange. The guys at the controls were looking at Lofty, not Heering, waiting for him to say what to do next. He held up one finger, to tell them that he wanted one minute to think it through. There wasn't a lot of choice. They were in flat terrain with no place to hide north and south. The Andes were right to the west, in Chile, and the foothills of those might give them a chance to at least stop and consolidate.

'Go west,' said Heering, a newly decisive note in his voice. 'Full throttle.'

The ship, lighter now that it had used up most of its fuel, was moving forward before the words were out of his mouth, while Heering and Lofty, heads together, tried to work out the next bit of the problem. The guy sitting at the console watching them would be able to tell where they were going, and pinpoint the exact location at which they'd hit the Argentine/Chile border. That was not good news. They had to sow some confusion.

Heering lent forward again to shout in the pilot's ear. 'We're going to have to put down from time to time, just to keep them guessing. Then when we lift off again we need a few changes of course until we can find some cover. I need a location to call my HQ and ask for instructions.'

'They might put choppers up too. But we will soon be beyond the base so they will be chasing us. Stripped down as we are we should have the edge. The only way to stay ahead of them is to go for it.'

'How long do you reckon we have before the ground changes?'

'Twenty minutes at least.'

'And they can't catch us in that time?'

'No way!'

'OK. Let's give them a run for their money.'

The pilot raised his thumb.

'What's it like out there?' Heering asked.

'Put it this way. The PNG kit is unnecessary. I can't even see a bloody tree.'

Lofty had gone back and got everybody's head close to his, so he could tell them the plan. Not that it was one – just a series of not very good alternatives. Nobody talked back or asked how the fuck they'd got in this mess, they just listened to Lofty as he talked loudly over the thudding noise of the rotor blades.

'The Headshed have got to give us the good news on this. Let's hope we get the time. If we're compromised we try to evade. If we have to we fight. The chopper is our base, and when the main man lands us the first thing we do is fan out to protect it. We need to establish an east-facing perimeter wide enough to keep it secure. We need a way of calling everybody back in to either defend or bug out. The Argies might be using choppers too. If one gets too close to us for comfort, take it out.'

That was easier said than done. For what was a fast recce patrol, nobody had brought anything heavier than a single GPMG. The Sea King, before it had been stripped, was rigged for lift, search, rescue and Special Forces duties, not as a gunship. All the armament she might have carried had been taken out to increase the load capacity and airtime.

'Even if we can't shoot the bastards down, we'll make them want to be somewhere else.'

'Just like us,' said Concorde Tucker.

'Ground changing,' shouted Heering, who was still close to the pilot.

'Concorde, get on that set and tell us the second we're out of the headlights. The rest of you get by the doors and take up firing positions.'

The Sea King started to weave as the pilot sought dead ground. It wasn't as simple as finding some and setting down. They had to find enough to make the Argies doubt their actual location. Dodging in and out of the radar picture was better than nothing. But it wasn't really what was needed. The ground was still too flat. Certainly there were folds now, shallow valleys. But they only lasted for seconds, and following the contours was slowing them down. The co-pilot was concentrating on the radar, waiting for the telltale ping that would say they had a tail. If that happened they were in deep shit, because a following helicopter could pursue them and would still have them on screen as they tried to touch down.

The pilot made a decision without consulting Heering. Nobody could see jack shit, but the man at the controls could. They'd trusted him to get them here; it was time to trust him to get them out. Tucker was still bent over his glowing detector. Everyone else was jammed in a position that would keep them aboard but allow the use of their weapons, glancing occasionally at both Heering and Lofty Glynn, who were talking, trying to figure out the tactics.

Was it better to send the guys out light, or to tell them to take their Bergens? In an emergency, where one trooper was too far away to be brought in without compromising the group, they would have to lift off without them. That would leave them stranded without any kit at all. But moving around in a Bergen, in a situation where everybody might have to leg it for the chopper at maximum speed, caused problems too. It didn't only slow the runner down: it hampered the loading procedure.

'No Bergens,' Heering yelled, having made his decision. 'Leave them on the heli. If we have to lift off and leave, we'll chuck one out.'

'I hope nobody ain't left their dirty socks in,' shouted a disembodied voice, in a strong Cockney accent.

Lofty Glynn spun round as the chopper's speed slowed again, grabbing hold of a strap as the pilot began to weave. The light went out on the radar detector, then came back on again after about thirty seconds. The co-pilot was watching it, talking to the man at the controls through his mouthpiece, as the light blinked on and off. Concorde Tucker found himself holding his breath as it stayed off for a whole minute. The

131

helicopter was bucking and weaving, over now-broken terrain; the only man who knew what they were skirting was the pilot. Suddenly he killed the forward speed, and settled the chopper down. Then he turned and yelled back to Heering.

'We're in good dead ground here, out of view. Do I kill the engines?'

'Not yet,' said Heering, edging towards the exit. 'But keep them as quiet as possible.'

They were out and in a defensive ring within seconds. There was no panic, no looking for instructions. Everybody knew what to do. It was SOP and had been discussed during the patrol briefing as the routine for their original drop. Heering moved faster than anybody had ever seen him do before, signalling to the radio operator to follow him towards some higher ground that would give him a good comms point. Lofty Glynn took charge of the search for a better defensive position, the soft swish of the idling rotor blades in the background.

The noise they made provided a good mark for the perimeter. The guys could move out in a defensive ring until it faded. That meant the enemy couldn't hear it either. The question was how to call them in if a patrol suddenly turned up searching for them. They had to be able to stay still for a while, to take the certainty out of the search and send back to the Headshed for orders. That wasn't all. The Argies and the Chileans had been arguing about territory for years, and they both probably had some good kit on the border. The enemy must have shifted some of it because of the Falklands invasion. But the Argies didn't trust their neighbours, and there was no way they were going to denude Tierra del Fuego of troops and equipment in case they were stabbed in the back.

What did that mean? Good air defence systems to discourage overflights. Perhaps even missile batteries – though they were not too much of a problem since the Sea King would stay low. Artillery, yes – though it should be long-range stuff. Trench systems, perhaps not manned, but minefields would be a certainty. That didn't matter if they weren't walking. Fencing did. Mobile radar? In broken country that would be mounted on hilltops. If they had radio detection gear they could fiddle with it forever and never pick up the Satcom transmissions. There was only a risk in telling base they were safe and evading if they used the normal high frequency. PNG was unlikely, since only the big powers carried that kit up to now. Soldiers? Troops to hold the border.

Quality unknown! Quantity? Lots, but it was a fucking long border. So mobility had to be good. The way to hold the line was a concentration of troops in strategic points, men who could be deployed rapidly over a wide area.

'We have to keep that chopper whole, sunshine,' whispered Lofty Glynn to Tucker, 'or we'll have a fuck of a job getting out of here.'

'We was goin' to have that anyway,' Concorde replied.

The Satcom operator had calibrated the kit and Heering was busy giving Hereford a real-time sitrep, adding a request for instructions. The reply, which he'd been told to wait for, wasn't long in coming. The Captain, after a quick talk with the heli pilot and his navigator, called everybody back for a briefing. When they arrived, the first thing they noticed was that the rotor blades were still and silent.

'Our orders are to try and continue the operation from here.' Heering stopped, waiting for the objections. None came. 'Two patrols. Sergeant Glynn and I will lead, using the PNG goggles to search for the opposition. This is our main LUP, and our ERV in case of trouble. The Sea King crew will stay here, ready to evade on their own or blow the ship if they are compromised. Should that happen, I am assured there is enough explosives in the flooring to guarantee that we know about it. We have to cover a lot of ground. It is very unlikely that we can do so without some form of contact, and I anticipate that we will need to set up temporary LUPs before we can recce the Rio Grande air base.'

Concorde Tucker was looking at Lofty Glynn as Heering spoke. The Sergeant said nothing to check the officer's orders. But the eyes, bright orbs in a blackened face, spoke volumes. Basically, even if he wasn't saying so, Lofty thought the whole notion crap. What foxed Tucker was the fact that a man not noted for keeping silent wasn't saying so. He was proved right quick enough. They didn't cover even a third of the ground between the LUP and Rio Grande. In fact they spotted the searching Argies within an hour and a half, on their third listening halt.

Once they looked hard it got worse. There were lights ahead and behind them, criss-crossing the edge of the Andean foothills. That meant troops on their way to the target and more on the ground on their route out. Those guys to the west didn't have to move. Just wait until the pursuit pushing out from Rio Grande flushed them out, and drove them like gamebirds into the waiting line. Concorde Tucker was trying to think what he'd do if he was in command of the Argie border force. Take the last known sighting, draw an arc of evasion from that, then place my counter-measures accordingly. Troops in the centre, the heaviest weaponry and any mobile AA stuff on the edges. They must have guessed by now that they were Brits, and already be anticipating the medals that would be flying about if they could be captured.

'D'you think they'll believe us, Craig, if we say we were aiming for the Falklands and just got lost?'

'They will if they try you at map reading.'

'Cheeky bastard.'

Craig Walker looked over his shoulder to where Heering and Lofty Glynn were crouching. The tall Sergeant was animated, the officer less so. 'I don't think our leaders are in agreement.'

'That's not surprising. Heering'll be thinking about his VC and Lofty will be on about getting back to his runner beans.'

Whatever else, they agreed that the patrol should stay still. The ground they'd covered had brought them to the edge of the foothills. In front was a flat, featureless plain, not something to move across in daylight. That came slowly, the passive night goggles, which had proved of limited use, being replaced by binoculars, and each man took a look at what they faced. There were hundreds of Argies spread out in long lines, tramping across the flat terrain, weapons up and looking very professional. Off to the right lay a road, with the flickering red taillights of trucks moving west to east. That had to mean troops dropping off to the south, and even if they couldn't see them they could well be to the north as well.

They'd moved fast, getting troops from the border area behind their last known position, so that they could sweep forward into what they assumed was a cul-de-sac. Heering watched them for another twenty minutes, trying to assess their abilities. They kept station on each other and their guns up and sweeping, so that anyone taking on one was going to get a lot of fire put down as soon as they opened up. You can tell a great deal from just watching soldiers. It's in the body language. These guys had to be afraid – they'd be fools not to, edging forward with nothing but a bit of early morning light to see by. But they were doing their job, and doing it well enough to make the conclusion obvious.

Heering had another animated discussion with Lofty Glynn, before the patrol commander finally did the obvious.

'Set up the Satcom again,' he said. 'Let's tell them what we're up against.'

Tucker reckoned Heering didn't want to make the decision. He wanted the Headshed to make it. So he told them about the flat terrain, no cover and an alert enemy. Yet those that overheard his conversation knew he was being circumspect. The Blues and Royals Captain was going to be the last to admit on an open line the plain truth: that the whole-squadron operation had been a no-hoper from the minute that radar detector lit up. They were being asked to recce a target that the boys on Ascension couldn't attack. The choice was either to get out by heli or evade on foot. There was no point in going forward. The Argies were too numerous. They couldn't even stay where they were and wait the day out.

They didn't run, but they moved faster than the pursuit, which had to be cautious. And no helicopter was a real bonus. Even with one of them the Argies could have covered half the landscape. The whole patrol was back in the ERV in an hour, with Heering quizzing the Sea King pilot.

'Do we have a route?' the flyer asked

It was Lofty Glynn who replied. 'Stay in the hills, out of radar profile, and go like shit for the border.'

'These hills are getting steeper. It could be dangerous.'

'So is taking incoming,' said Heering. 'And I don't think we're going to get over the ground without somebody shooting at us. And the really worrying part is some of them might be Chilean.'

'All aboard,' quipped the co-pilot.

Suddenly the valley they were in was full of sound. There was a procedure for this – a hairy one but something the pilots had trained for. And the guys hadn't wasted their time chewing the fat while the patrol had been away. They'd had a good look round to pick a safe route out of the drop point, one that they could hit at speed knowing there was no wall of rock in the way.

The heli weaved and spun through the increasingly broken terrain, twisting and turning, sometimes practically on its side as the pilot flew it through narrow gorges. The silver thread of river shone in a valley, and the pilot took the Sea King down to within twenty feet of the surface. It was a shrewd move. Any river here had to be running west to east from the high Andes. They drew fire all right, a short burst of automatic with tracer, responding through the door with little prospect of hitting anything, but just trying to disrupt the men on the ground. But with the Sea King going full tilt at 138 knots, the deflection required to hit it was beyond the Argies on the ground. The co-pilot turned round and whooped, pointing first to his map, then to the snow-capped mountains to the north.

'Welcome to Chile.'

'Find a place to get this crate down,' Heering shouted.

They were on soft green grass, beside seawater, lapping the shore of a deep inlet, everything from their Bergens spread out on the ground. Heering had talked to Hereford again and given their position, as well as agreeing his intentions.

'No ammo, no guns, not even a knife. We're tourists now.'

'What about the Satcom?' asked the patrol signaller, unhappily.

'Sling it in.'

Everybody had a bit of moan: they all had things they wanted to hang on to. But it was just that. There was never any doubt that they'd off-load all their compromising kit, because there was no way they'd get across the border without the Chileans knowing about it. The people looking for them now might be less dangerous, but that could change if they were found to be armed.

Finally, with everything stacked in the middle of the cabin, Heering turned to the pilot, then pointed to the switch that would arm the timer on the explosives.

'Do you want to do this?'

'Bollocks,' the pilot said. 'You Special Forces prats are the spoilt ones. If I do it they might ask me to pay for the damned thing.'

Heering smiled, his face grey and stubbled in the morning light. 'You're right old boy, we are spoilt.'

They were all well away when it went off. The boom of the first explosion was followed by all the others, as every grenade in the pile detonated, that followed by a whoosh as the vapour from the practically empty fuel caught light. They stayed only long enough to make sure it was truly torched, before donning lightened Bergens and heading north, looking for the road that would take them to Porvenir and the ferry to Punta Arenas.

Their contact found them as they sat at a pavement café in Punta Arenas. Nine unshaven men, with such an air of self-assurance they'd made the owner of the small cantina very nervous, even when Heering politely ordered tea. The man who approached was like a character from a novel by Graham Greene, a deeply tanned individual dressed in a white suit and a Panama hat that had some kind of club insignia round the rim.

'Good morning,' he said. Every one of the troopers had stiffened, except Heering, who was stiff already. 'I wonder if you'd mind if I joined you.'

'Be our guest,' Heering replied, indicating a free chair at another table. It was a measure of their interloper's self-confidence that he stood still until one of the men fetched it for him. Then he sat down, and smiled.

'There are some nasty rumours of explosions on the border. The local military are quite up in arms about the whole thing. In fact some of them are watching you at this very moment. I doubt that they are fooled by the way you've reversed your own clothing to make it look less like that of fighting men.'

'Who are you?' asked Heering.

'Your guide, Captain.'

That made Heering even more rigid. How did the man know his rank?

'I have come to take you to safety.'

'And the guys across the road?' demanded Lofty Glynn, his Mancunian voice rough and uncompromising.

'They are your escort.' The smile that followed was thin, the shake of the head that of an individual who cannot comprehend what he's witnessed. 'Believe me, the local commander is incensed about what has happened. Bombs going off, burning helicopters, frightened farmers. But he's prepared to turn a blind eye as long as we get you out quickly. I am therefore charged to offer you a lift to Santiago. There you can not only be comfortable but debrief us on all your exploits.'

'How do you know it's not a trap?'

'If you think the Chilean commander is unhappy, you should hear his Argentine opposite number. The way he feels will earn you nothing but undying gratitude in this country.'

137

Three range rovers slid up beside them. Their interloper stood up and gestured. Heering, whose decision it was, made the right choice and nodded. It made no difference what their reception was: they couldn't start anything in Chile. As they moved towards the door, a couple of jeeps appeared, the men in them relaxed, unarmed, but clearly soldiers.

'You are a cavalryman, Captain.' It was a statement, not a question.

'I'm a simple tourist.'

'I am a member of the Santiago Polo Club. I know that you will enjoy it when I take you there.'

'What about me?' asked Concorde Tucker.

Their self-possessed escort looked him up and down. The smile didn't fade but the eyes changed to a mixture of sadness and rejection.

'I think not. You would only be embarrassed.'

'We're safe, boys,' Tucker said. 'It's just like fuckin' home.'

'We calculated the time at nine minutes, minimum,' said David Lowry. 'They've obviously moved some air defence missiles to very near the actual coast. That more than doubles the risk to the C130s.'

Cornelius Hosier didn't respond; he just stared at the map Lowry was pointing to, as if willing him to continue. The preference that he should say something positive was palpable. But there was nothing the Captain could add that would alter such a bleak assessment. The team had been sent in to find out this very information, and they had reported back what they'd discovered. No amount of wishful thinking would change that. Vere Symington, just as glum, added his view.

'We've got to assume that the radar contact was a missile battery. We wouldn't even get the C130s to within ten miles of the end of the runway. They'd be blown out of the sky halfway between there and the coast.'

'All right, dammit!' snapped Hosier, leaving David Lowry to wonder what had happened to the gentle appellation 'Vere, old chap' which had been so frequent on the Brigadier's lips these last ten days. 'I think I have the picture. What I don't have is an answer to a very pressing question, one that I have to provide when the PM asks.'

That was another expression that had been on Jock the Sock's lips since he'd come in from the UK. It was PM this and PM that. It was as though Hosier had become her most intimate adviser, and could read the lady's innermost thoughts. David Lowry didn't know what the man had said, but he'd obviously promised something spectacular. The expression on Hosier's face said it all.

'We must wait to find out what Heering discovers on his recce.'

'With respect,' Lowry said. 'They will not even reach that for at least another twenty-four hours. And what information they give us will only serve to confirm the negatives. The whole base must be on alert by now.'

'All information is of value. There is a patrol in on the ground. It would be folly not to use it. Who knows? Despite the difficulties, we may still have to risk it.'

It was now Lowry's turn to snap. 'Risk it?'

Vere Symington went rigid as Hosier's voice took on an unctuous tone, as if he was addressing a nice but dim nephew. The prospect that the Major might be faced with the same fate as Gerry Tooks must have suddenly occurred to him.

'We still have capital ships out there, and they are still at risk. Perhaps even more so now than they were before. The Argentines must have concluded by now that the landings are only days away. If our troops get ashore they are going to realize that, despite their numerical superiority, they stand to lose. If 5 Brigade gets ashore as well, it will quadruple the odds against them. That introduces the need for a desperate counter-stroke, and the only one which will even remotely achieve anything is to take out one of our carriers.'

'They are very rarely in range,' said Symington, his voice no longer loud and confident.

'That all depends on whether the pilot wishes to come back.' Hosier sat forward, his voice slightly desperate. 'Just because they look vulnerable on the ground, we must not assume that they have no one in their air force brave enough to make the ultimate sacrifice.'

David Lowry listened to Vere Symington put the knife in with consummate ease. Perhaps it was fear that made him so calm. If not that, it was the fact that he'd found a very good escape route from what could be an exceedingly tricky situation.

'Well, Director. The only thing to do is put it up to the Defence Staff. Should they order us in, regardless, I have no doubt that B Squadron will go.'

Hosier suddenly looked tired. He was certainly glum. There was no point in putting such a plan up to the Army Command. They would throw it out. And he, in the process, would be made to look like a fool for making the suggestion. On top of that, he risked a full-scale mutiny if he put this to the men. They would suffer for it certainly. But so could he, in the way it would blight his prospects.

The signal, relayed through Hereford, about what Heering and his patrol faced in the way of Argentine opposition, came in, casting further gloom. No one spoke as the Director mulled over the alternatives. But at some point Lowry sensed that he'd made a decision. The curious thing was that doing so seemed to lift his spirits, not depress them.

'Rio Grande is cancelled,' he announced, standing up. 'But I want the men back on training tomorrow, Vere. If you need me, I will be in the comms centre.'

The approaching footsteps had the same quality as those of the two previous nights. There was no pace in them. The voices from the lead truck had spoken in the same urgent tones that had been used before. Sam Clark knew they were being stood down again before David Lowry spoke. But he wasn't prepared for what he heard.

'Scrubbed!'

'Yes. The operation is off. Our recce patrol hit a signal nine minutes out. Coastal radar or a missile battery that we didn't know was there. That definitely made it suicide to go in.'

Sam didn't know whether to laugh or cry. That wasn't something that the others troopers felt. The subdued mood evaporated in seconds, to be replaced by quiet grins and reassuring nods. They were off the hook. Why didn't matter.

'Did our boys get out?'

'I don't know, Sam. What they do next is being handled from Hereford.'

They knew the next day, by the time they'd finished training. What they were not sure of, with Rio Grande binned, was what they were doing rushing around carrying out the same drills that they'd performed for the last two weeks.

CHAPTER TEN

Cabinet office to Flag Officer, South Atlantic: 17/5/82: Confirm receipt of final plans for Operation Surrey. War Cabinet will consider and advise.

For Blue's patrol the next few days were like going through a revolving door. The signal on the morning Sked gave them their orders, plus the location of the pickup. They would be lifted out by heli and transported to *Fearless*. They spent the day doing the same as they'd done for the last ten, watching their enemy, then stood to as usual before nightfall. Having bugged out from the OP, they tabbed the ten Ks to the helicopter pickup point over a hairy two days. That meant moving in a situation where remaining secure was a hope not a certainty, at a pace faster than that which they'd used coming in. The patrol arrived in darkness, well before the agreed time, knowing there were going to be other troopers there, four of them, waiting for the same lift.

The approach to the RV was made with great caution, each man on edge because they knew how dangerous this part of the operation was. You always have to work on the principle that the enemy is improving, and just because you pulled off a stunt with ease before, you should never assume that you can do so again. There could be any number of ways to make life hard. Better radio intelligence might tell them more than they should know about Task Force operations. Or maybe, having sussed that the British Special Forces were operating, they would try to emulate some of their methods to catch the guys out. The impression everybody had was of an army poorly led and demoralized. But it only took one good officer, in the right place at the right time, with two or three keen soldiers, to bring on a rush of efficiency.

The other patrol had arrived first, and it was their job to sponsor the RV. That meant that their patrol leader decided on the defensive position, and whoever led that group was the main man when it came to decisions. Headshed had laid down the approach procedure, and it was Blue who went forward, both hands and his weapon above his head, so that those already in position knew he was friendly. Once identified he called in the others, and they took up positions on the extended defence perimeter.

No one talked as they lay in the long grass overlooking the silent South Atlantic. The SSM from G Squadron waited till the RV time. Then, using a torch with an infra-red filter, he started flashing a signal out to sea. This the heli pilot could pick up on his passive night goggles. The Sea King would not come in without the signal, it being too valuable to risk in a trap. It would be down to radio skeds to rearrange the RV. If the men who were supposed to be lifted out didn't make contact, then another group might have to be sent in by boat to find out what had happened.

Everyone was ready, Bergens on and kit tight for what had to be a very swift bug-out. With some moonlight, they saw the silhouette of the heli not long after they heard the thudding of the blades. It was coming in so low over the water that it seemed to be floating. The pilot didn't fuck about. He came straight in, hitting the grassy surface with a thud that was no good for the paintwork. Even if the troopers ran, it was done with discipline, having been worked out before, so that only two guys arrived at the doorway at one time. They didn't clamber aboard, they jumped, sliding along the rough surface of the cabin floor so as to leave the entry free for the next pair.

Graunch and Digger were second last, too slow for the Woodentop Sergeant and his patrol signaller, bringing up the rear. He gave them the good news for being slow arseholes, Chelsea Barracks fashion. They would have heard the bastard in Buenos Aires if the Sea King hadn't lifted while his feet were still outside. The dispatcher had already signalled to depart, and Luke Tuikabe had to grab and haul him in. As strong as an ox, he threw him behind them into the well of the cabin, an act that earned him not a hint of a thank you. But it did produce a pleasing 'fuck' that sounded like reaction to pain.

'Typical fuckin' B Squadron,' he yelled, as he sat up. 'Flash bastards on a fucking dance floor, greedy bastards at a scoff, but no fucking good anywhere else.'

'Who's got the swear box?' shouted Digger. 'This arsehole has just bought a regimental round.'

There was no laughter that Blue could hear to that remark. Why would there be? Digger was slagging off a leading light of the non-humorous tendency. The rest of the flight was made in silence, if you can give a name like that to the constant thud of the rotors. All of the guys, who'd been out like his for ten days sitting in the same kind of hole in the ground, were knackered, their heads lolling forward as they dozed. His boys were about to do likewise, but Blue nudged them to stay awake, then signalled that they should edge towards the door. Whatever question each of them wanted to ask, they knew better than to phrase them. If the patrol commander had a reason to be close to the door, that was good enough for them.

Fearless put on some navigation lights to guide the chopper in. Blue got to his knees, Luke, Graunch and Digger doing likewise, still mystified but prepared to follow. As soon as the Sea King hit the deck, and before the suspension springs had hit the bottom of their travel, Blue Harding was out, his patrol at his heels running across the top deck for the companionway that led below. Within seconds they were dodging through corridors and bulkhead doors, Bergens slamming off the ship's plating.

'Where's the bloody fire?' shouted Digger, as he slid, two hands on the metal rails, down a companion ladder.

'Let's get to the debrief first. And make sure you take the chairs nearest the doors.'

'What the fuck for?'

'I'm not waiting till we get to *Hermes* to have a cleanup,' Blue yelled. 'And neither will the Woodentops. How many showers do you think they've got set aside for us on this tub? I want out of that debrief the second it's over. I want to get to the hot water first. There's no way I'm standing outside waiting for those dirty bastards behind us to get sluiced down.'

The Headshed was waiting for them, slightly put off their stride by the way the B Squadron guys charged in then sat at the back of the room. The Woodentops arrived a good two minutes later, giving an innocent-looking Blue a hard look, before making a point of sitting as close to the Ruperts as possible. When it came to questions, Green Slime led the charge, eager to put even more marks and lines on his maps. There didn't look to be too much left in the way of space!

The Headshed had a list of their signals, and that formed the basis of the questions, as they sought to expand from the necessarily brief information they'd been given on the radio, and turn it into something with three dimensions. Neither patrol had much trouble in obliging. They'd been looking at the same piece of cold, wet terrain for over a week. The questions included tactical appreciations too, each trooper encouraged to speak out if he had any theories of how the defences could be neutralized.

A briefing winds down before it ends. You know the third time you're asked a reasonably basic question that it's getting near the time to quit. Blue began fingering his Bergen straps, a signal that was picked up by the others. Jamie Robertson-Macleod had barely begun to say, 'Right, chaps, I think that will be all,' before the back markers were shoving their way out the door. Shouted requests to sailors were met by jabbing fingers, and they found the crew showers within a couple of minutes.

All four went straight in, in their kit, except boots and weapons. The water was running good and hot before any of the G Squadron contingent made it. Happily they listened to the loud cursing and bad-mouthing as they washed their kit first, and their bodies second, the delicious feeling of clean water and soap on their bodies marred by the pain in their festering feet.

'What are they on about, Blue?' called Digger. 'I can't hear them over the sound of this nice hot water.'

'I think they want to have a cleanup, mate.'

'Woodentops don't wash do they?'

'No, mate. They just blanco the cunts up, doll them up in a furry hat and a bum-freezing red coat, then stick them in a box outside Buck House.'

It would have been nice to leave their boots off. Every one of them was suffering from feet kept wet for a week on end. And when they got back aboard *Hermes*, having been choppered over at first light, they soon discovered they weren't the only ones. Graunch charged straight off to the medics to get them all some dry powder, only to discover when he got there that it was in very short supply.

Lew Stradler was aboard, looking very sleek. Obviously life on board ship suited him. Any questions regarding events in their absence had to wait until he and Digger had completed a long discussion about the chance of Spurs winning the Cup Final. The most pressing problem was whether their side, simply the best team in the world, could play Ricky Villa, the Argentine World Cup star. The rest brought this to an end by taking their boots off.

'Trench foot!' exclaimed Lew, fingers up to pinch his nose. 'Who'd fuckin' believe it in 1982?'

'You would, you no good arsehole,' snapped Digger, all fellow feeling gone, 'if you ever got out of your poxy slippers and got your feet wet.'

'You should have kissed more arse, Digger, then you could have had my job.'

'Is that how you get to be in signals then?'

'Digger, you're naïve. It's how you get anything.'

'Are we ever going to find out what's been happening, Lew?' demanded Blue.

'Eight of your boys came through, Concorde Tucker and Craig Walker from Boat Troop. They were held up for three days. You only just missed them.'

'What's the story here?' Digger protested. 'Are we arriving at this war in drips?'

'Were they doing anything interesting?' asked Luke.

Lew dropped his voice. 'They're on the mainland.'

'Fuckin' Ada,' said Digger.

'Hey! From what I've heard they're not going to be alone. No details, but that cunt Hosier put B up for an Entebbe on one of the Argie air bases. Your guys, nine of them for Christ's sake, were supposed to recce it before the C130s went in.'

'Nine men? Was there a Rupert?'

'Heering.'

'God fuckin' help them,' Digger moaned.

'Lofty Glynn was there too.'

'What a combination,' said Blue. 'Happy families do not immediately spring to mind.'

'What else is happening?' asked Luke.

'The good news is you've got the day off.'

'And the bad?'

'You'll probably be going on a squadron operation with D.'

145

'I want to go home,' said Digger.

'Don't let me get in your way. In fact, if you can take me with you I'll buy your Cup Final ticket.'

Graunch returned, nose wrinkling, bearing the scrapings of foot powder that he'd cadged off some of the other sufferers. He sat down heavily. 'Whatever you do, don't go near Grizzly Cook.'

'They've been out to play?' added Lew.

'Had a great time,' Graunch continued. 'While we've been sitting up to our arse in water, they've been charging around like boy scouts blasting every target the infiltration teams have marked.'

'Over the moon are they?'

'Like roosters who've just rogered the flock.'

There could only be one reason for that, but Blue asked anyway. 'Have they done a bit of special?'

'Took out a satellite airstrip, then they hit an Argie airfield on Pebble Island.'

'Is the name the size?' asked Digger. 'Like where the fuck is this place?'

'Somebody told me it was in the Falkland Islands,' Graunch replied. 'But a berk like you couldn't be expected to know that.'

'Why don't you two get married?' snapped Blue, finally tired of their sniping.

'You sound just like my Mum and Dad,' added Luke.

'We've got to be better looking,' said Digger, his face adopting an innocent look. 'Did you have parents, Graunch, or did they put you together with the left over bits in the ward?'

That nearly earned Digger a clip on the jaw, and he knew it because he weaved backwards in his chair. But Graunch, after making a feint, just grinned. It was one of his saving graces. He was an ugly bastard but at least he knew it.

'So what happened at this Pebble Island?' asked Blue.

'One for the regimental book. The flyboys thought there was a radar station there so they sent in Boat Troop D to have a look-see. What did the bastards find? Not a radar station but a fuckin' airfield with guys just waiting for our mob to land so that they could blast them, short range.'

'That ain't fucking fair,' said Digger, his mouth now full of bread and jam.

'So they laid on the full monty. Boat Troop to guide them in, landing site holding party, and assault teams.'

'Half the silly bastards got lost, I heard,' added Graunch.

'Typical D,' Digger said, spitting out crumbs.

'Anyway. Turns out the fuckin' place had a five-hundred-strong garrison. Useless sods who woke up to find our guys happily torching the planes. They got eleven all told, Pucaras and Skyvans.'

'Argies not pleased?' Blue grinned.

'Very upset. Our guys are doin' the biz, and just getting out, when the cunts set off command-wired mines.'

'How many?' asked Blue, seriously.

'Would you believe it, only one of the bastards got a wound and that was in his foot.'

The slagging off was like a round robin, every oar in. But there was a wee bit of envy too – that added to genuine relief that none of the Ds had been slotted. Then it was sort out your kit time. They were going on an op, and if they left that bit to the last minute, it was always a bastard. It was the same as before: clean the weapons, check the ammo and grenades, ensure the right number of trauma kits, draw rations and part-pack your Bergen. Then you could go to a briefing, and at the end, you didn't have to stub out your fag in a rush. You could watch all the other tossers legging it, and puff away happily.

JRM had choppered over to do this one personally, having pulled most of the teams off the island for the purpose. Long pointer in his hand, swaying as the ship rose and fell in a really heavy swell, he looked like a man who was enjoying himself. And so he should. So far his men had performed brilliantly. And in the only hitch so far, on the Fortuna Glacier in South Georgia, they had been in a place no other troops in the world would have tried to go. He was an ambitious soldier who craved higher rank. But that didn't bother his troopers, since he was very open about it.

'Right, fellas, the landing of 3 Commando Brigade is on.' Robertson-Macleod threw back a blanket, which had been covering a map, jabbing with his pointer. 'They are going to sail the whole shebang, *Canberra*, *Norland* and half the bloody fleet into the Falkland Sound at dawn on the twenty-first, and put the boys ashore in San Carlos Bay. We have a job to

147

do, and that is to make the Argies think that, even if they spot it, it's a diversion.'

That first map was flicked back to reveal another, showing the targets the Headshed had chosen for Special Forces. 'So, we go in sixteen-man teams, attack our selected enemy positions, and hit them hard and LOUD.'

That shout got everyone sitting forward. 'We want to make them think that they are the ones. That the whole bloody British Army has decided to slot them. That means we take plenty of ammo, plenty of grenades, plenty of mortar and anti-tank shells, and we don't bring them back. This is deafen yourselves time.'

Robertson-Macleod paused, then called off the names of the unit commanders. 'I will brief you; you will allot detailed tasks to your teams. We chopper over to the assault ship *Intrepid* at 14.00 hours, and we take all our kit with us. She will take us into our landing spots and we go ashore in Rigid Raiders or Geminis. Our job is simple. I don't even want the Argies to think about shifting out of their trenches, never mind the idea that they might move to the beachhead at San Carlos.'

The rest of the morning was a blur, since they'd learned the Regiment was leaving *Hermes* and very likely not coming back. That meant taking along gear that was not meant for this job, but had to be handy enough to get hold of for follow-up operations. The rest would follow later. One thing you can say about the Regiment, you're never stinted for kit. They will give you as much gear as you want, and never ask for an invoice. But no trooper in his right mind indulges in waste, because you've got to carry every pound you draw on your back, and that's a bummer.

So it was the usual trade-off between weight, food and firepower, only this time they were being ordered to carry more ammo than usual, spread between sixteen guys. Blue and his team, assigned to the same group as Grizzly, worked hard to make sure the divisions were equal. Not that Grizzly was trying to top them up. They were no good to the rest if they were knackered. But he couldn't resist the wind-up, and there was no end of slagging and blagging going on, as the B Squadron's Bergens grew so heavy that even the giant Luke Tuikabe would have struggled to lift them.

As they came on deck, late in the afternoon, humping masses of gear, it was obvious that the swell had increased and so had the wind. The sky was unrelieved grey, low clouds that swirled and chased across the leaden sky. The chopper pilots sat in their machines, the masters of cool, like this was a good day out for them, sunny and warm, totally unfazed by the way *Hermes* was pitching and rolling, occasionally staggering and jarring through its whole superstructure as it hit a wave. Grizzly, as well prepared as Blue had been, got them on the first and second lift, so that they cross-decked to *Intrepid* in time to nick what little accommodation had been left free by the men of 3 Commando.

If *Hermes* had been rolling and pitching, then *Intrepid*, a fifth of her size, was bouncing about like a cork, the bows heaving thirty feet in the air before crashing down to send up a huge cloud of spume. And being an assault ship, hollow in the middle, she added a corkscrew motion to that which was seriously uncomfortable. You couldn't take a step unless you were holding on to something, and half the gear they tried to stow dropped right back on their heads.

'Fuck this,' said Blue, 'leave it on the poxy floor.'

'You feeling a little green, mate?' asked Digger.

Blue hated the first hour on a new boat. He was never actually sick, but he couldn't rid himself of the notion that he was going to be. That made his stomach churn in anticipation, with his jaw clenched as well. The guys always spotted it, and always took the piss.

'Let's go back up on deck for bit.'

Intrepid was a twin-funnelled boat with troopship accommodation and a storage deck that could be flooded to let the landing craft float out. It was no longer like those old World War Two movies, with marines using rope netting to get into their bobbing and unstable landing craft. Now they loaded under cover, and moved out for the assault under their own power. There seemed to be less tension on board – hardly surprising, since it was less of a primary target. Also, the carrier had been in the forefront of the battle, a busy component in the Task Force operations, with constant comings and goings, the noise of repairs and aircraft maintenance added to the din of planes and choppers taking off and landing.

The sailors, too, had the relaxed air of men well used to having visitors on board, working aboard a vessel in much better nick than the old stalwart, *Hermes*. Some of them actually smiled. For all the tossing and battering from the heavy seas, *Intrepid* was quieter below decks, better at absorbing the hammering waves, riding them rather than ploughing in. On deck it felt much the same, the superstructure streaked with salt, the grey warship paint showing signs of serious wear.

The fresh air and strong blustery wind helped settle Blue, along with a sky and sea that were such a uniform shade of grey, little or no horizon showed. The waves were large and rolling, miles across, showing almost nothing in the way of spume until they hit a ship's bows. Then they broke with a vengeance, throwing up great clouds of white water that was caught and carried away at an angle by the half-gale that seemed a permanent feature of life in these waters. It was fascinating in an elemental way, a scene that the men lining the lee rail seemed content to watch for hours.

The choppers were cross-decking away throughout the short afternoon, as first twilight came then night fell, dropping off the teams and the masses of gear on the after deck before scurrying back to the mother ship for another load. A lot of guys obviously felt a bit like Blue, and had decided to stay topside. They were hanging on to the rail as *Intrepid* went through her corkscrew gyrations. You had to admire the pilots for the way they were able to judge the rise, fall and pitch of the deck so accurately that, even with only floodlights to work with, they could have landed with eggs on their wheels without cracking a shell. Blue, still watching, now accustomed to his environment, saw one of the pilots make a sign to the landing controller that there would be one last trip, before he lifted off and headed back to the carrier.

Hermes was floodlit too, and at no more than half a mile apart, Blue could just make out the tiny figures scurrying like ants around the chopper. He watched it lift off and head out over the black sea, its navigation and floodlights bright. There's always a split second between something going wrong and noticing it, and Blue thought that when the heli's lights jerked it had just been taken by the wind. But as soon as it spun and began to drop he knew it was in trouble. Suddenly the deck was full of guys shouting and pointing, as the Sea King dipped sideways and, from a height of four hundred feet, dropped into the water.

A chopper on the deck immediately revved up and took off, scooting at wavetop height towards the crash site. The Navy had a lifeboat in the water so fast that Blue hadn't seen them launch it, and that roared through the huge swell, almost jumping clear of the wavetops as it sought maximum speed.

'Holy fuck!' said Digger, in what was his only form of prayer.

It was agonizing to watch. *Hermes* had launched boats too. But they, like *Intrepid*'s, were having a hell of a time keeping upright as they circled the site underneath the chopper's lamps. They'd got some of the guys inboard, but the way they were continuing to search didn't bode well. None of the troopers trans-shipping had bothered with survival suits for such a short journey, and there was no reason to suppose that the final party had either. The water they'd landed in was icy, and in normal clothing, which would weigh them down anyway, the time they could last was short.

The Navy was brilliant, and the helicopter crewmen even better, dropping from their Sea Kings into the water time and again to search for survivors. Initial success kept them at it, but there came a time when it was only bodies that could be found. Blue, just like everybody else, was down by the side ready to haul the men who'd made it out of the returning lifeboats. They too had bodies to lift out. The final toll, which included attached personnel, only came much later, to a subdued and silent audience, as they were informed that, of the thirty-one men from the Regiment who'd clambered aboard, only ten had survived. The rest had drowned, along with the pilot and co-pilot of the heli.

Digger's head dropped when they read out Lew Stradler's name, a silent tribute to a man he had had something in common with. There'd be no 'Spurs Win The Cup Final' for Lew. Not that he was indifferent to the rest, mostly the guys who'd hit Pebble Island. There wasn't a man listening who wasn't thinking 'there but for the grace of God . . .' Natural warriors they might be, but they all wanted to 'beat the clock', to be the people who mourned those names on the metal plaques that adorned the time-keeping obelisk in Stirling Lines, rather than one of their number.

Loss was always hard to take. This time the sheer number compounded the misery of a disaster greater than any they'd ever suffered in combat. But every man knew that the Regiment lost troopers. On exercises mostly, especially river crossings; in Ulster sometimes, and very occasionally on dodgy foreign ops that suddenly went pear-shaped. The only thing you could do was say a prayer in your own head, then get on with the job. There would be a service at the regimental plot in Hereford, and a piper to lead the funeral parade. Maybe, if one of the dead was a good mate, you'd get pissed that night and, maudlin drunk, shed tears for the loss.

Two days with little to do didn't help. Going over attack scenarios only reminded everyone aboard of who was missing. They'd lost a good portion of the squadron in the cold South Atlantic water, so it was with great relief, mixed with natural anxiety, that they made for the boats and the helis to start going ashore. The rumour was that a big bird might have brought down the Sea King. It should have survived that, but it was just carrying too much kit and too many men.

'You can stop looking at the sky now, Digger,' said Blue, as the Sea King began its shallow descent.

The Cockney had kept his gun pointed upwards, and his eyes, all the way from the ship, determined to shoot any bird that came within a mile of the blades. How he planned to do that in pitch darkness he never explained.

'I was just communing with God.'

'Don't tell me he effs and blinds too,' scoffed Graunch.

'He does, mate,' Digger replied. 'He swears to me that you are a no good bastard. And since he's dressed in a black and white football strip I believe him.'

'Can it, girls,' said Blue.

That wasn't necessary: both men knew what they had to do, which was get out and secure the landing site. The routine was the same: quick in, quick out for the heli, with each man tasked to either get out and cover the arcs, or throw the kit out of the helicopter, in seconds. A long silence followed, before the Rupert in charge called for them to close up. The tasks were re-hashed, maps checked, then they formed up and moved out. Positions, stop times and signals had all been worked out on the ship, so they tabbed out from the LS quickly, each man having to come to terms with his own very heavy pack.

With such a weight, it would have been nice to drop closer to the target, but since half the idea was to make the Argies think they were under a main assault, taking the choppers too close might have alerted them to the actual numbers they were facing. They de-bussed at an unmarked location, the first task to orientate themselves and establish their position. It was a cold night, with that nip and dampness in the air that promised snow. The sixteen-man troop, spread across eighty metres, plodded on, backs straight despite the 130-pound weight they were carrying, eyes now adjusted to the dark and peeled for the least sign of danger.

It's a great feeling, when you have mastery. You know where your enemy is and he doesn't. You're sure that when you hit him he is going to be useless for anything up to half a minute. The guys they were going to give the good news would be mainly asleep, the sentries so used to nothing happening after weeks on the island that they would be looking for a spot out of the wind rather than incoming danger. And it was coming, in spades, from some of the very people who'd been watching this position for a whole week. The B Squadron team knew the layout like their own backyard.

And what they didn't know they got from the other patrols who'd overlooked this spot, like the fact that the Argie HQ commanding the Darwin/Goose Green garrison was in the triangular schoolhouse at Darwin. That the trench systems radiated from that with the primary positions in an arc, with re-entries and fire zones that ran from one part of the shore to the other with the Darwin Harbour at their rear. The whole was effective if the attackers got close, and tried to cover the mined and barbed wired approaches, since they had good fields of fire. But to the men on the hills, hidden from view, staying out of the arc of the machine guns, they were no threat at all.

Grizzly Cook had been given charge of the heavy stuff, 81mm mortars with a range of over three miles. That was the central position from which firing would commence. It was also the RV that everyone could fall back on, being in a good defensive position should things go pear-shaped and the Argentines come out to fight. The other hot factor about the 81mm mortar, and the reason they'd transported such a heavy weapon, was its accuracy. It had a well-engineered barrel, plus a plastic ring to seal in the propellant gases. Getting them here, given their weight, had been tough. But the shells would land where Grizzly wanted them, well away from the settlement buildings. There were civilians in those, they supposed, and there was no way that they could be brought into danger.

The rest of the patrol had crawled forward, closer to the Argentine defence line but still outside the entrapment zone. Blue's section was carrying a GPMG as well as M203s with underslung grenade launchers. They were tasked to pepper the trench system at will, speed of delivery the primary object, rather than accuracy. The same went for the section with the lighter, forward-based 51mm mortars and those with the general purpose machine guns. Dead Argies were a bonus. Scaring them shitless was the real intention. Plenty of HE and phosphorus around their positions; flares fired low so that they lit the trench system without exposing the size of the attacking force; bullets and tracer whizzing past, and every indication of a major assault in the offing.

Blue lay flat, watching as the hand moved inexorably towards the number six, and as soon as it touched he was on his knees and firing. The guys to the south, carrying Milans with which they targeted on the vehicle park, beat them to the first explosion, which brought a curse from Digger. Suddenly there was stuff going off all over the place, the odd screams and shouts of the defenders drowned out by the sudden whoosh of the mortars. The whole Argentine line was under attack, the machine guns firing in strictly controlled arcs of fire, the lines of tracer bullets scything through the black sky.

Mortar-fired flares exploded to the rear, illuminating the chaos that the SAS troopers were imposing. Orange and red explosions mushroomed up as the mortar HE shells struck a target. Grizzly Cook had a grid reference provided by the patrols who'd overlooked this very spot, and with a good fix on his own position and an accurate weapon he wreaked havoc on the Argentine defence system, aiming particularly for those pressure points where trenches crossed. In the ethereal blue light cast by the numerous flares they could see the enemy running from one place to the next, trying to avoid death, achieving nothing but to sow confusion on their own side.

'Eat your fucking heart out, Guy Fawkes!' yelled Digger. That was followed by a whoop from Luke Tuikabe.

Blue kept his eye on the Fijian, who'd stood up, cradling the Gimpy in his massive arms, stepping forward as he did so until Blue leapt forward to restrain him. They were some of the best guys in the Regiment; strong and cheerful, men who, in battle, would never say die. Laba, who'd died at Mirbat, was a regimental icon. But they could also get excited, and Luke was no exception. With all this mayhem going on it would be just like him to stand up and charge the enemy trenches, sure he could end the whole fucking war on his own.

He might be right. Standing up it was obvious the Argies were in total panic, firing off wildly, the tracer evidence that they were more danger to their own than to the attackers. It encouraged him to move in a bit closer, right to the edge of the wire, to create the idea that ground troops were coming in. He knew there was a defence position close to the shoreline, a small redoubt that showed just as a shadow against the silver of the still inlet water.

Without yelling he directed all his patrol fire onto that, chucking in phosphorus to light up the target. A sandbagged position, it would have been a tough nut in the hands of a determined defender. But these were the same kind of kids as that conscript the officer had shot near the lip of the OP. The idea that his type might be around fired Blue up, and regardless of what other casualties they were inflicting he took a savage interest in watching as the HE grenades exploded close enough to begin to demolish the redoubt.

They totally suppressed any form of response. Luke sprayed the Gimpy fire across a line of the firing slots, while Graunch, Blue and Digger vied with each other to land the grenade on the installation which would blow it wide open, no easy task with a weapon that fired its projectile horizontally. All three had L2 grenades on their belt kit, and a deep desire to go in and lob a few. But that was not the job.

It couldn't last. Panic-stricken as they were, the enemy held good positions and a hundred-to-one superiority in numbers. Surprise was a finite weapon, which pushed beyond the limit could get you killed. The SAS trained for that as well. You had to know when to pull out as well as when to go in. There was a time on this operation just like any other, and when they reached it Blue shouted to his guys to fire off their last grenades and withdraw, before the enemy could put down any concentrated fire on a four-man patrol that was well within range.

CHAPTER ELEVEN

Top Secret: Operation Surrey: Commander Task Group 317.0 19N 02.20 hrs. 19/5/82: A: Ships pass to embarked forces: B: D-Day 21 May 82: C: H-Hour 06.39: D: Break down and issue first use ammunition: E: Act immediately.

Sam Clark, when he heard Hosier commence the briefing, found himself searching for those two French words he'd once heard a Rupert use to describe seeing the same thing twice. All the squadron officers were lined up, sitting behind the Director. Not one of them looked cheerful – not even Symington. But at least Sam now knew why they'd continued training. It was like a carbon copy of the Rio Grande operation, only much more dangerous. This time there were no unknowns. Every risk and every threat was as clear as a bell, all laid out in a diorama on a blanket-covered table.

'This operation will coincide with the main 3 Commando Brigade landings. It is, in its original concept, a diversionary attack to pin down the enemy forces. But it is my belief that we can considerably expand on that. It is not beyond our ability to so damage them in Port Stanley that, in conjunction with what is taking place elsewhere, we will contribute to, or even engineer, a general enemy collapse. The task, gentlemen, is to land on Port Stanley airfield, in exactly the same manner as was proposed for Rio Grande, and to sow confusion as to the intentions of the overall strategy.'

Hosier's eyes shone as he added the next point.

'But, and this is crucial, we must look to do more than just destroy. We must look to take and hold ground.'

Hosier talked on, outlining the aims of the task, again seemingly oblivious to the feelings in the room. These, summed up, would have been two questions. Why was he trying to use a force designed for either raiding or penetration to do a Green Army job? Second, and of more immediate interest to his audience: why was he so determined to get B Squadron, a unit he'd served with in the past, written off?

Sam Clark wondered if it was the nickname Jock the Sock, earned in the jungle, and gifted to him on behalf of the squadron by Lippy Grant. The tale was famous, as much for Hosier's stupidity as for the solution arrived at by one of his troopers, which just served to show how much better the troopers were at tactics and the appreciation of risk than the Ruperts.

He had to drag himself back from thinking about that to what Hosier was saying, as he stood over the table outlining the squadron's tasks. The layout of Port Stanley airport was no mystery. Having occupied it as a quasi-military base before the invasion, the Ministry of Defence had maps listing every installation and building right down to the smallest bog and the flagpole. The intelligence from the infiltration teams had been grafted on, so every rusting tractor, disused water tower or old petrol tank was marked. The Argies, who should have cleared their fields of fire, had failed to do so.

The recce patrols had listed all the trench defence systems, including numbers of occupants, the anti-aircraft gun emplacements, and the location of missile batteries, with the scale of manning and a schedule of sentry changes. The guardroom numbers and routines were there, along with the best guess they could make at the haphazardly timed perimeter patrols. Unlike Rio Grande, they knew the precise location of every target, as well as the interior layout of every room in every building. But there were no fighter-bomber planes this time, or messes full of highly trained pilots. Port Stanley was not an aggressive base, and even the satellite runways, which had held fast attacking aircraft, had already been destroyed along with the planes and helicopters that used them.

They might use the same method as Rio Grande. But the aim was to destroy troop concentrations, and to take and hold what Hosier insisted was vital ground. The task was not to avoid contact with the defenders, but to seek them out. The main garrison's tent encampment was outside that fence, and that was listed as the primary target for the assaulting force. So was the causeway leading to the main island and Port Stanley settlement.

'The Argentines are using C130s to re-supply their garrison. They've realized that the fleet steams away from the islands in darkness and returns at first light, which gives them a long enough supply window to bring in transports from the mainland. They're flying them in on a shuttle basis, arriving during the hours around dawn, with escorts of Skyhawk fighters to take them into the zone of protection provided by the garrison's own anti-aircraft. So, the men who are on the Port Stanley base are well accustomed to the arrival of such birds.'

He paused to let that fact sink in before continuing.

'Right now, we are painting up a pair of our own with the appropriate markings, and it is those you will use. The landing will be carried out as if it was genuine, although there will be a degree of confusion. The pilots, once on the ground and seemingly clear of danger, will be instructed to taxi as close as possible to the main troop concentration areas so that you can attack at once.

'The danger!' Hosier continued. 'In the past, the demand on the limited number of Harriers has meant that such supply flights have been left in relative peace. What they bring in is not enough to sustain the garrison and we do control access by sea. But on the day of the landing it will be a maximum effort. Since we will be going in ahead of 3 Commando, we get first crack.'

Hosier pointed to a map, which showed the flight route from the mainland.

'The enemy will be coming in through exactly the air corridor our aircraft have to secure to provide cover for the landings. The Argentines have no reason to suspect that they will be there. So, combat air patrols will be up early, and will intercept. They will, of course, try to scare off the Skyhawks, and what experience the pilots have enjoyed so far leads us to believe they will succeed. But they will also harry the transports, and it is our guess that as soon as they are under attack they will seek to evade. They will certainly crowd the airwaves with talk. The job of the Harriers is not to down them. It is to delay them, and turn them round so that our two C130s can replace them.'

'That's the best-defended airspace in the whole island,' remarked Paul Hill. 'It's not just the airport that's got AA. Port Stanley has it too. Its anti-aircraft guns and missiles can also provide cover from the other side of the causeway.'

'We can suppress some of that with air attacks.'

Serious Sid piped up. 'Not on Port Stanley. You can't mount sustained

159

attacks on that without losses, and we ain't got the planes. The Harriers won't come within Roland range. They've seen too many downed already, even in fast, low flying sweeps. The RAF isn't daft. They will stay well out of the way.'

'They will be doing the job we have requested on those transports. And we can keep them with ours long enough to make the threat look credible.'

Serious Sid persisted. 'If there's thick cloud cover they'll be invisible.'

'Not to radar,' Hosier responded smugly. 'And with signal traffic saying their own planes are the fighters' target, it is our belief that they will seek to protect the incoming Hercules, rather than fire on them, even if their targets are out of range.'

'But the whole airport will still be on full alert as we come in,' said Sam Clark.

'I believe that you can get on to the runway without the enemy even suspecting the real cargo. Once there, I have no doubt that you can do more than just bloody the defender's nose. We are, if you like, a Trojan Horse.'

'What is this,' came an angry voice from the back, 'a bloody Boy Scout jamboree?'

'What's the garrison?' asked Serious Sid.

'Six hundred men. But our observers tell us they are fairly low-grade.'

'That's still odds of fifteen-to-one.'

'Special Forces have faced worse, and triumphed.'

'And around Port Stanley?' Sid insisted.

'Our intelligence leads us to believe that there are in excess of eleven thousand troops. But they are dispersed to defend from a land attack, with a substantial garrison on the West Island. As for those on East Island and around Port Stanley, rest assured, a high proportion of our infiltration patrols will become active and seek to aid the assault and pin them in place.'

'And what's the E&E plan this time if it goes pear-shaped?' asked Sam. 'There's no convenient friendly border a few miles away to run for, is there?'

Hosier looked at Clark, his wary brown eyes narrowing. 'There's a heavy job to do when you do get down, I acknowledge that. You must take with you, in equipment, anything you think might come in handy, and I don't care if that includes a Challenger.'

Meant as a joke, this was as excessively heavy as the main battle tank Hosier referred to, and got an appropriate response.

'The E&E plan, boss?' Sam asked again, his voice hard and uncompromising. 'What is it?'

Hosier was looking over his head, to the men in rows behind. 'You will, naturally, want to take a very close look at the layout before formulating your individual troop plans. I suggest that be done one at a time.'

Sam didn't raise his voice, though David Lowry did raise his eyes. 'How do we escape and evade if we are getting clobbered?'

Hosier acted as if Sam Clark hadn't spoken. 'I know it's not my place to intervene in actual operational detail, but I would suggest that one whole troop be assigned to the task of taking the causeway. They may have to fight on two fronts for a spell, but if the rest of you can do your job, that will ensure the primary target is secured. You can then engage the main enemy force as they try to dislodge you, thus preventing them from moving out to reinforce the beachhead 3 Commando will, by then, have established.'

Sam's voice, loud enough for a Guards RSM, echoed off the roof of the hangar.

'Brigadier Hosier, would you please answer my question. On the Rio Grande operation we were given an escape route through Chile, which was well on the way to being a fairy tale. Here, we will have our backs to the sea. What plans do we have to evade from Port Stanley airfield if we are in danger of being overwhelmed?'

Sam always described what Hosier did then as the upside down trick. It was just like an upended winged dagger, the symbol of the Regiment, as Hosier spread his hands and stretched his arms down, before adding an eloquent shrug of the shoulders. Basically it meant that, if the powers that be had thought about it, they'd concluded that evasion was impossible.

'Vere,' Hosier said, turning to Symington. 'Unlike Rio Grande we have here defined targets. Therefore we have a chance to plan properly. Please collate the conclusions of each troop and let me look over them before

161

giving approval. I have promised the Army chiefs of staff a full operational briefing.'

'Director!' The rugger playing Major replied, trying to keep the doubts out of his own voice.

'As is normal for Special Forces, we do not have the luxury of time. 3 Commando Brigade will be going ashore in less than thirty-six hours from now.'

Sam Clark's voice was bitter. He hated Hosier, and he made no effort to hide it. 'Don't bother giving us any sovereigns this time either. Since we're not going to be alive to need them it would be a bloody waste.'

David Lowry was no more modest than the next man, but he had kept some of his extended connections hidden. From a family that had been in the upper echelons of the professional classes for more than a century, the number of people he knew that occupied positions of power was limited. But when it came to influence, it was different. Politics was not a family trade, but the Civil Service was. An uncle once removed was, he knew, a permanent secretary at the Ministry of Defence.

During the planning of the operation he had listened with growing despair to the odds they had to face. There was no disguising the feelings of the planning groups either, both at command level and once the tasks had been put in detail to the troopers. Six hundred airport defenders, on full alert, were bad enough. But how could they cope with the thousands of Argentine troops around Port Stanley, the main enemy concentration? That was a position not even 3 Commando Brigade, backed up by the Task Force, had been prepared to attack. Yet Vere Symington was being tasked to do it with less than fifty men.

He had practically stopped speaking, lest by doing so he give away the fact that he thought the whole operation sheer madness. Like the good second row forward he was, he'd shoved his head up someone else's arse and would push when told to do so. And Symington was right. That was what it was. Pointless! Offensively the airfield had become useless. Closing it down to incoming re-supply traffic could be done by a pair of Harriers. The only reasons that David Lowry could think of for mounting it was that either the Army command wanted in on what was a Navy-sponsored invasion, or that Hosier was so determined to shine, he'd contemplate anything. Whichever, the top brass seemed happy to write off over fifty men in a useless gesture.

He could count on one hand the conversations that he had had with his uncle, George Forgeham-Lowry – brief snatches at the odd family wedding or funeral. But Uncle George, like most Lowrys, had been a pupil at David's old school, Wraysbury. So even if family matters were not enough to sustain a conversation, the old school anecdotes had been dragged up to oblige.

What he did was strictly against the rules: a court martial offence in spades, enough to get him hanged, drawn and quartered in the Tower. If Hosier ever found out, he'd be out of the Army before his feet touched the ground. And he had to examine his own motives before he acted. Even to a career soldier on an SAS tour, who'd glorified in getting his para wings, and relished the hard training of his own regiment, there was still a gremlin of doubt. Was what he was planning to do brought about by cowardice?

A stranger in the officers' mess, he was left alone to debate both the act and its consequences, harried by the knowledge that if he was going to do something it had to be done quickly. Right now his men were putting together the weapons, ammo, medical equipment and explosives they would need to destroy Stanley airport. He had already committed one cardinal sin. He'd given Vere Symington a plan to pass on to Hosier that both he and Sam Clark had concocted just to please the bastard. They'd worked out an entirely different and more limited one with which to start team briefings, a plan that had the more manageable objective of causing maximum destruction before consolidating their position at a pre-determined location.

Then, Sam had insisted, and only then, could they decide what to do next. If the idea of taking the causeway was feasible, they would do it, and they would hold it if at all possible. But if it looked like the whole squadron was going to be overrun, common sense dictated they cease to fight. Otherwise men would die for no other reason than their own pride in themselves and the Regiment. Indeed, one of the hardest things Lowry'd have to do was to insist that, if he gave the order, he expected it to be obeyed.

Access to a phone was unrestricted for an officer, and he had no reason to suspect that calls were being monitored. But getting through to someone as elevated as George Forgeham-Lowry, when the nation was at war, was no simple matter. He watched the clock tick down to the start time with steadily increasing frustration. Eventually he was run to ground in his St James's club, where he was, as he put it, 'partaking of an early dinner'.

'Dear boy,' said his uncle, in that plummy voice, one which David knew had ripened as he rose in the Civil Service, to the point that it now seemed like part of a *Yes Minister* caricature.

Uncle George talked a lot, and wasn't too good at listening, a trait he no doubt picked up from dealing with ministers. So David Lowry had to let him ramble on for a bit before he took over, ruthlessly suppressing his relative's desire to continually interrupt. He outlined the operation to a man who held the Official Secrets Act to be sacrosanct. But Uncle George didn't check him, no doubt feeling that the family could be trusted. Nor did nephew David harp on about the fact that he might be killed. Instead he talked in terms his uncle would comprehend: of the political fallout from such an operation should the worst happen, with particular reference to who would get the blame.

'The men will go, Uncle George,' he insisted, 'and they will do what is required of them.'

He talked about Rio Grande as well, asking his uncle to grasp the truth. That if an officer of such vast experience as Major Tooks, faced with a similar operation, objected so strongly as to risk his entire military career, then there must be some serious doubts about the efficacy of such madcap schemes.

'But you've just told me your chap Hosier had that one sanctioned by the War Cabinet. And the Army staff must have passed this one, otherwise he wouldn't be allowed to even brief you, am I right?'

'Surely you would know, Uncle George?'

'ME! Know?' his uncle snapped. 'Don't be foolish boy! No one tells me ANYTHING!'

'I just wondered if you think our political masters have thought it through.'

'Dear boy, if they have, it will be a first. There's not a decent brain amongst them.'

'It will make a damned bad headline, if the landings are a success but the entire squadron's wiped out.'

That silenced Uncle George. He knew who was leading a goodly part of the entire damned squadron, just as he knew the orders were coming from a man who wasn't going. He'd met Hosier, and thought him a decent sort for an Army man, though not great shakes at the intellectual side of things. But his opinion was plummeting by the millisecond as he contemplated that the Director might contrive to get his own nephew killed.

'They'll blame Nott, probably,' added David Lowry, driving home the final nail. 'He'll have to do a Carrington, and resign.'

Uncle George was suddenly brisk, the foppish quality gone. 'I can't promise anything, David. But I think the minister should know just what burden he's being asked to bear.'

'Will he listen to you, Uncle George?'

'No, David, he will not. Politicians never do. But there is an inner voice, one to which he will pay heed. One that says, "I'm damned if I'm carrying the can for this lot." That he will harken to.'

'Thanks.'

There was a slight catch in his uncle's voice as he said his final words. 'If I can't do anything, boy, look after yourself. I don't want to see your name on the school memorial plaque the next time I go to an Old Boys' do.'

'Don't worry about me, Uncle George. I'm surrounded by the best soldiers in the world. All we've got to do is attack and overwhelm two hundred times our number. As my SSM would say, no sweat.'

David Lowry heard his uncle demanding 'his car immediately!' before the phone hit the cradle.

'All I'm asking you to do is run it past me verbally, Corny,' said the GSO2. 'To check if what you've sent in by signal is accurate. There seems to be a bit of a stretch on the objectives. I'm not, in any way, trying to interfere.'

'Like hell,' thought Hosier, clenching his jaw tight to stop himself from saying so.

'The Old Man spotted it right off. And he will, I'm afraid, with him being in no mood to be patient, demand that explanation. He's got a lot on his plate at the moment. Not least, he's fighting off the Navy's attempts to decimate 5 Brigade on some bloody Falklands rock face.'

Hosier was damning the old man for being like a weather vane. The whole idea of this operation, on which he'd seemed quite keen, was to restore some kind of equilibrium between the services; to dent some of that superiority which, adopted by the Kennel Club, had so offended his superiors. But he was wondering what it was that had changed his mind. It couldn't be the idea of casualties, because he'd already accepted the possible levels of those.

'What are they suggesting now?' asked Hosier, prevaricating.

'We need to leave that aside, Corny, for another conversation. Let me tell you that Nott has been on the blower asking for details of men committed, objectives and potential casualties. That's what made us look twice. You've got to remember that there's a political angle, as well as a military one, to everything we do.'

'I cleared this with the politicians. And I'm sure you know who I mean.'

'You cleared something, old chap. But I'm not quite sure that when you buttered her up, this was what she had in mind. War-winning escapades often appeal to non-professionals, who have no real idea of the risks involved.'

It's always difficult on a phone to catch all the nuances of another's speech. But there was no doubting that expression 'buttered her up'. There was anger there, and if not quite that, definite resentment. He was being reminded that going to the PM on his own – even if it had been reluctantly sanctioned – was neither forgiven nor forgotten.

'Bob. We can't fight a war with one hand tied behind our back.'

There was no mistaking the anger now. 'Should you ever get to sit where I am sitting now, Corny, which is looking increasingly unlikely, I may say, you will realize that you do everything with one hand tied behind your back. Now while I have to take that from my political masters, I do not have to take it from officers who are considerably my junior.'

'The idea is to give the Argies such a bloody nose that …'

'We are in some danger, according to your outline operational plan, of doing that to ourselves. Since when did taking on the whole main force come into the equation?'

'That is a follow-up to our main task, to be undertaken only when and only if that has been achieved.'

'We have discussed acceptable casualty levels. Given what the squadron will suffer, I doubt they'll be in a fit condition for secondary tasks.'

'That's an assumption I would question. There are any number of factors that point to our success. And if you wish I shall be happy to enumerate them.'

'Don't equivocate, Corny, there's a good chap. Just confirm my question then tell me what your time margin is.'

'Non-existent.'

'An hour, two hours?' Bob Brotherton insisted.

'Two maximum. If we don't go then, we will have to delay twenty-four hours and the landing will be in. I would also add that the chaps are already at the airfield, in the trucks waiting to take them to the planes, and so keyed up for the off I can hardly restrain them. After the cancellation of Rio Grande, any more delay cannot be good for morale.'

'I hear what you are saying.'

Hosier spoke hurriedly. 'Can I say, sir, that conditions over the target are perfect.'

The GSO2 ran quickly over his plan again, demanding confirmation of each main point. Timings, forces engaged, objectives primary and secondary, engendering increasing frustration as he spoke slowly. Then Hosier cottoned on. The other staff officers were in the room, perhaps even the Old Man himself. The entire senior command structure had been listening to him plead his case, which was nothing short of bloody bad manners.

'Stay by the blower,' the GSO2 snapped. 'I'll be back to you in half an hour.'

Sam was back in the truck again, along with Boat Troop, Bergens fully packed and loaded weapons clutched in every hand. Even here on Ascension Island, every trooper held on to his gun. That was the first tool of the job, and you never let it go. You ate with it, slept with it, and even kept it in your free hand when you took out your cock for a piss. Getting the guys to buy this job had been harder than Rio Grande. And it was only the fact that they'd been up for that, had in some sense accepted being written off, which had swung the balance against refusal. He was wondering what kind of cunts could sit in their carpeted offices and sanction such a trip.

'The last time this happened to me I was going to Torremolinos for a holiday. Me and the wife and kids were stuck at Gatwick airport for two days.'

'Thank fuck for survival skills.'

Sam grinned. The voices were in the dark, but he knew the speakers. He heard the crunch of boots on the tarmac, and there was just enough light by the tailgate to see David Lowry.

'A word, Sam.'

That meant in private, so Sam Clark jumped down and moved away from both trucks. They were parked on an airfield apron, well away from anybody and anything; the two planes the guys would be loaded into would be wheeled out close to the take off point before they would load, so that no one could see them going.

'Vere Symington had a message from Hosier.'

'And?' asked Sam.

'A slight delay, and an injunction to keep up the spirits.'

'You'll keep them up if you serve some,' Sam joked.

'I've got something I want to tell you. It's really quite important.'

'If you're a poof that's your business.'

'Will you be serious?'

'That isn't?'

'It would be right enough.'

David Lowry then told him about the call he'd made. Sam listened in silence until he'd finished.

'Did you say anything about the fact that the lads nearly refused to go?'

'No. But I want you to know so that if the shit hits the fan, and I get carpeted, that ...'

'That what?' demanded Sam as Lowry's voice trailed off.

'I was going to say that I did it for the right reasons. But I'm not sure even now if I did.'

'Frankly, my dear,' Sam replied, in his best Rhett Butler impersonation, 'I don't givadamn.'

'You think I was right?'

'Are you fuckin' kidding?'

'Thanks.'

A plane was taking off in the background, its propellers roaring as it lifted into the sky.

'This reminds me of *Casablanca*.'

'Is everything a movie with you?' asked Lowry.

'I like movies. People don't really get killed.'

'But the baddie always does. Who was that German who got slotted?'

'Conrad Veidt. Now at this point Mr Rains, you and I are supposed to walk off into the desert.'

'Why do you get to play Humphrey Bogart?'

'I'm sexier than you.'

Every man in the control tower heard Brigadier Cornelius Hosier swearing, not hard since he was shouting out loud as soon as he slammed the phone down. And what really rankled was that it was he who was going to have to go down on to the tarmac and tell B Squadron that, once more, the operation had been binned. But by the time he came out of the office he'd been using he'd reasserted some self-control, and he strode across the control room as though he hadn't a care in the world.

Back in London, George Forgeham-Lowry was in his panelled office, on the phone.

'I think you've come to the right conclusion, General Brotherton, and it's not just politics. It does the entire Army establishment no good to go throwing men's lives away on the speculative chance of success. If you agree, I will not minute any of our conversations.'

He paused, while the voice at the other end spoke. 'No. We have committed nothing to paper, and I strongly advise the same for you. I'm sure Brigadier Hosier will be extremely grateful for that.'

Another pause, before he concluded. 'A fine officer, I agree. Should go far.'

CHAPTER TWELVE

Associated Press: 21/2/82: 10.25 GMT: The UK Government spokes-man announced that Marines and Paras from the Falklands Task Force have secured a beachhead in San Carlos Bay, Falkland Sound: Losses, in men and materiel, to follow.

BSquadron were lined up on either side of the equipment they were taking in, bum numb and stiff after a flight from Ascension which had taken thirteen hours. To Sam Clark it didn't matter how many para drops you did: there was always a knot of tension to live with, and going into the sea just added an extra dimension of risk to that. Nor could you forget it throughout the tedium of the flight, with a dry suit on over your normal kit that made you feel like the Michelin man.

Conversation was difficult. A Hercules, cruising at about 350 mph, was bad enough when adapted to carry passengers. Rigged for an air drop of men and equipment, when it came to noise, it was just like the inside of a wind tunnel. And it rattled like what it was, an air force workhorse that was hardly ever out of the sky. So talking to the next guy in the stack was a case of a brief shout, usually responded to with no more than a nod.

The relief when the red light came on was tangible, and the troopers stood up, running fingers over their equipment for a last check, making sure that none of the lines that held it were tangled. The roar of the slipstream suddenly increased as the tailgate on the C130 began to drop. At the same time the nose of the Hercules lifted slightly to ensure ease of exit. With the ramp in its locked-low position the troopers at the front released the bindings on the equipment pallets and pushed. On well-greased runners they shot forward, B Squadron men on either side, kit and soldiers exiting behind. If it had been noisy in the plane there was a moment during which it grew to a terrifying roar as each man was wildly buffeted. Then there was the abrupt shift to complete silence, followed quickly by the crack of the opening parachutes.

The heavy pallets dropped at a much faster rate than the men who

171

accompanied them, disappearing into the blackness below. They would be in the water long before their minders, well away from the ship that had been designated to pick them up, the port and starboard lights of which were just becoming visible. Clear now, each man pulled at the clips that held his Bergen, allowing it to drop below his feet so that it wouldn't do any harm on entry.

With little moonlight, Sam knew he must steer his chute to close with the destroyer, so that the boats the Navy had put out to pick them up could get them out of the freezing South Atlantic at speed. But he was heading too close, on a track that might well slam him into the superstructure. He hauled on the straps overhead to change his course – not a wild jerk, but one which, in the circumstances, made it difficult to judge distance. All he knew was that he was moving away from the ship. Perhaps too far, but he could see the lights clearly.

What the matelots on the destroyer saw was more thrilling, like a slow-motion fireworks display, as each parachuting trooper's cyalume lit up. Forty-odd pinpricks of light in the night sky that had the Royal Marines in the Rigid Raiders racing to the anticipated pickup points at which the men would land. The whole of B Squadron SAS, half of whom were coming in now, was going to war at last, not into some suicidal trap, but tasked to reinforce their fellow troopers already in action. This section was under the command of Sam Clark, with not a Rupert in sight. All the squadron officers had put themselves in the second Hercules, being dropped at another location.

Sam hit the water seconds after his kit, the chute billowing forward to float on the water. He pulled at the quick-release gear so that he was free, then took a quick look round. The lights from the destroyer were still visible, faint but reassuring in the distance, so he did what was necessary. He lay back, keeping his exposed hands and his face clear of the freezing ocean, and waited to be picked up.

Dinger Bell was the first one up the ship's ladder, so the count fell to him, the job of making sure that every man was aboard, and that all the equipment had been recovered. That was always an anxious time. The Regiment didn't need disasters cross-decking in Sea Kings. They always lost more men to water than any other element, and the troopers had a more than healthy respect for the sea. Parachutes not opening were a rarity. But even the best-trained man could make a mess of his entry into the water, injuring himself just enough to pass out. In these waters that could easily be fatal! Pickup times were tight, and anybody left for an hour, even with the protection of a full dry suit, would succumb to hypothermia.

Half an hour passed before Dinger was sure that there were some vital components missing: SSM Sam Clark, and a pallet containing half the squadron's kit. Even though there were men who'd come out alongside one and right behind the other, there was no accurate way to tell where either would have landed. And once in the water the swell ensured that sighting the cyalumes was difficult. Every boat was out looking for them, the finding of the man much more important to those already aboard than the search for the equipment. On deck, still in their dry suits, the rest of the squadron lined the rail, searching the black sea for any sign of a light.

In many ways this had become his squadron. He was the man who'd stood up to both Symington and Jock the Sock. He'd left the Brigadier in no doubt that he knew they were being readied for suicide missions. But he was also the man who had worked hard to persuade them to go. He'd reminded them of how good they were. That their own pride was what they cared for, not some high-ranking Rupert's reputation. The voice from the approaching boat, a sailor calling to say they'd found him, made them all feel better. That didn't last much longer than the SSM's arrival on the deck.

'Fuck me, I was getting cold,' he said, as Paul Hill and Dinger Bell grabbed his arms to haul him the last few steps. 'But it was just like waiting for a bleedin' bus. You swim for ages with every bugger ignoring you and then three boats arrive at once.'

'You'se is the last man, Sam,' said Dinger. 'But we's still light on a pallet.'

'Did you put a priority on the search for me?' Sam Clark demanded, in a harsh voice.

Dinger was totally unfazed. 'You're bloody right I did an' all, you stupid arse.'

'Then you're a useless cunt,' Sam added, without any trace of anger. 'That kit is much more important than me.'

'I hope you're not going to stand aroond waiting for an argument aboot that,' scoffed Dinger.

'Is that what you were telling yourself when your nose was about to drop off?' asked Paul Hill, who hadn't picked up on the fact that they were piss-taking.

'The boats are still out there searching,' said Marty Roper. 'They'll find it.'

'They should do, an' all,' quipped Dinger. 'It's only half the size of Sam's bloody heid.'

It was Sam who realized that there was a naval officer standing beside them, a half-smile of amusement on his face. He introduced himself quickly to what turned out to be the Executive Officer, a full Commander, and the man who was 2 i/c of the ship.

'Now that you're all aboard, you'd be better off below decks with something warm inside.'

A voice from the back piped up, as camp as hell, and very Scottish. 'Well you Navy chappies certainly know how to go about making a girl welcome.'

'That pallet,' said Sam.

There was a pause while the officer waited in vain for a 'sir'. It didn't come and he was forced to respond. 'We'll find it.'

The whole group went below, though Sam Clark only stayed long enough to get out of his dry suit. Then he was back on deck, staring anxiously over the side to no purpose whatsoever. Every so often a boat would come back in, engine roaring, to report no sighting. The EO wasn't quite so calm and amused now. In fact he kept looking at his watch, the furrows of worry deepening at each glance.

'I think we're going to have to give this one away.'

'I'm sorry. That's not possible.'

The Commander was taken aback at that. It had been a long time since anyone of inferior rank had checked him. And the tone of the SAS trooper's voice had contained no hint of suggestion. The EO felt as though he'd just been given an order. Yet he set himself to be emollient, without quite knowing why. He even signalled that the deck party waiting for the pallet to arrive move away, so they would not hear him put this cheeky sod in his place.

'Sergeant-Major. I cannot expect you to be aware of the difficulties we face in these waters. But I assure you they do exist. At dawn we cannot risk being here and damn near stationary. We will be at action stations, and steaming to take you and your men into Falkland Sound. After that, we must resume our required position in the defensive ring that protects the Task Force.'

'And we have to have that pallet, even if it takes you all day tomorrow to find it.'

'I realize you've had a trying experience, Sergeant-Major. An hour in the waters round here is bound to affect you.'

Sam's response was harsh and uncompromising. 'I'll have an even more trying one if you can't find our kit.'

'Can I advise you to remember my rank?'

'You can. But it won't do any good.'

Another ship's boat roared in then, the message again negative. The sailor in charge got the tongue lashing that the EO wanted to give to the cheeky bastard before him.

'Damn you man, just get out there and find it.' Then he turned to Sam. 'I will allow one more sweep by the boats. Then if it's still missing I will order that we get up full steam.'

They could have done without the pallet. It was an inconvenience, not a disaster. Who would need half their personal kit in the dump they were going to? The whole of the island was awash with replacement gear, so as a check on the squadron becoming immediately operational it was limited in effect. Sam was just being stubborn, without being sure why. Perhaps, he thought to himself, he'd just had enough of fuckin' Ruperts, be they in coats coloured khaki or blue.

'Is it possible to speak to the Captain?'

'No Sergeant-Major, it is not.'

'If you won't do what I want, I have to see him.'

The EO shouted then. 'Who the hell do you think you're talking to, man?'

Sam's voice was calm, infuriatingly so. He had dealt with non-SAS officers plenty of times, showing a decent amount of respect if they returned the compliment to him. If they didn't, Sam was well prepared to take them on. And if any of them complained, including the guy in front of him, whoever held the job of CO would listen politely, before informing the officer of just how special that winged dagger was.

'I'm talking to someone who either won't, or can't give me what I

175

need. That pallet is vital. Without it you might as well just call back the Hercules and chuck us all back up in the air.'

'It's not worth risking the ship for.'

'How would you know?' Sam demanded.

The EO couldn't speak, and nor could he clap this SAS trooper in the brig. Even he felt feeble as he fell back on that well-known officer's standby.

'Don't think I won't report this.'

Sam didn't flinch for this naval commander any more than he would have done for Hosier. 'You can report what you like, cock. But if the only man aboard who can keep this ship here is the Captain, you better take me to him.'

Sam had noticed well before. But it was only now that the EO realized that some of his men had been inching closer, attracted by the increasing anger in their officer's voice. The EO had a problem, more to do with his own authority on the ship than dealing with a man who wouldn't budge. He must have known that Sam Clark wouldn't back down, even if it meant undermining the man before him in front of his crew. What he said next clearly hurt, but he said it nevertheless.

'Follow me!' Then he turned and shouted to a well-wrapped-up petty officer. 'Take over here, Dicks, and continue the search.'

The Captain had the air of authority that went with his rank, equivalent to a brigadier in the Army. A small, compact man with thinning black hair, he'd made it in a service that was harder to survive in than any other. AND he had command of a ship at war. So when he and Sam Clark locked stares, it was a battle between two people who were very sure of themselves.

'We are not a taxi, Sergeant-Major, to be told where to go at the whim of a customer.'

'But you're no different to us, sir, I'm sure. You like to do your job right.'

Most of the people on board never came up before the Captain, his authority saved for the most serious offences. Those who did were likely to tremble. Yet here was a man, no more than equal to a chief petty officer, talking to him without being invited to do so, and treating him as though he was a nobody.

176

'I don't know how you go about acknowledging rank in the SAS. It is, I believe, rather lax. But I would remind you that you are on my ship. I decide what happens. You obey!'

Sam fought to keep his voice level. 'I'm not going to plead with you, Captain. But I'll just tell you that the equipment in the water is just as important as either of us. Without it we will struggle to become quickly operational. I don't suppose that will please my officers. And if it all comes on top, somebody is going to have to carry the can.'

'Is that a threat?'

'It's a statement, Captain. I am being honest with you, and if that offends your idea of rank then it can't be helped.'

The Captain didn't look at his EO as he replied. 'Find the damn thing, and fast.'

They did, though it was more by luck than judgement, cutting away the pallet itself, which was left to sink, and towing in the buoyant cargo. Sam didn't care, and refused to respond when his men asked how far he would have taken it. He had what he needed, and as they closed with the islands and the dawn came up, they entered the Falkland Sound: he had his first glimpse of the place. At least here there was some elevation on either side of the water. It reminded him of the Scottish lochs Boat Troop often trained in. The guys were lined up ready to go over the side as the destroyer anchored, they and their gear transferring to the landing craft ship *Sir Lancelot*. There were few troopers aboard, but the ones who were there gave them welcoming whistles, the loudest coming from Luke Tuikabe. Blue Harding, Graunch Powell and Digger Patterson were more muted.

'Thank fuck you're here,' said Digger, who was wearing a pair of soft oriental slippers. 'I was beginning to think we'd been deliberately abandoned.'

'We did our best to get rid of you, Digs,' said Sam. 'But they flew us down here just because D and G are so fucked off with you and your jokes. Now tell me all.'

It was an exchange. Blue and his boys filled in their mates on what had been happening down south, while Sam gave them the good news about the shenanigans they'd missed in Hereford and Ascension, that interspersed with Digger moaning about the Cup Final ending in a draw. The landings, now three days old, had been a qualified success and the beachhead seemed secure. The invasion fleet had taken losses, on the first two days, in both men and ships. But the Argentine air force had really suffered, losing seventeen aircraft the first day and seven the next. The waters they were in now were still subject to air attack, but with the Rapier surface-to-air missiles beginning to work well, any sortie by the enemy was a very hairy proposition.

'So we're safe?' asked Dinger.

'Safer than you were before you got here, sounds like,' said Graunch.

'That Hosier was always a no good cunt,' said Blue.

'Are the Headshed on this tub?' asked Sam.

It was Digger who answered. 'No way, mate. It's a Rupert-free zone, and a real good billet. For a start there's a galley, with Chinky cooks. The scoff is brilliant.'

'What's wrang with yer plates, Digger?' asked Dinger Bell, looking at the borrowed slippers.

'Trench foot.'

'You're that old.'

'You can take the piss, Dinger. But it's so fucking wet here, with that well-known weapon you've got stuffed in your crotch, you're going to have trench fuckin' prick.'

'Sam Clark,' a voice called down the companionway.

'Here.'

'There's a boat alongside to take you to *Fearless*.'

'Just when I thought it was safe to go in the water.'

'Welcome to the war, Sam,' said Jamie Robertson-Macleod, indicating that his visitor should sit down.

'Boss.'

They were alone. Even if JRM was careful, he was obviously fishing for info about what had happened up north. Sam would love to have opened up, to have kept nothing back, including his own doubts and fears about the aborted air assaults. But he confined himself to saying nice things about Gerry Tooks and Lippy Grant, without once mentioning the stand they took. When it came to Hosier he was non-committal, neither praising nor damning. JRM's face was like a poker player's, held blank so that no emotion showed, but his voice was designed to encourage full confession.

But Sam could handle it. The man was a Rupert. Not the same as Hosier, certainly, but with a loyalty to the Director and the corps of officers that would supersede any he felt to Sam Clark. He was therefore not to be trusted. Finally the CO got frustrated and posed a direct enquiry instead of an oblique one.

'Look, Sam. While I respect your loyalty to your fellow troopers, I know there have been problems. Ops that the chaps felt were a trifle over-ambitious. What I need to know, for the good of the Regiment, is how close were we to an actual turn-down.'

'Why don't you call it a mutiny?'

'Because I don't like the word.'

'It was never on the cards,' Sam lied. JRM would find out from others what had happened. But he'd never hear it from Sam's lips. 'Our own pride in ourselves is too important.'

'And our Regiment, of course.'

'It's not your regiment,' was the reply he wanted to give. It would also have been nice to add that it certainly wasn't loyalty to the officers. Most troopers considered them to be visitors, not members, more interested in enhancing their own career prospects than those of the men or the unit. But he just smiled and nodded.

'We'll be having a briefing later today, as soon as the second warship brings in the other group. Then, thank Christ, B Squadron will be operational.'

Blue, Graunch and Digger were in the sick bay, having their trench foot attended to by a naval orderly, with Digger keeping up a stream of filthy anecdotes and insults, most of it aimed at the other squadrons. Luke Tuikabe, whose thick-soled Fijian feet had survived the exposure, had just come along out of curiosity.

'I thought you were supposed to be one big happy family,' said the medical orderly, who had a rather high light voice and an over-graceful manner. But he also had a light touch, so that men whose feet were very tender were content.

'We are, mate,' Digger said. 'It's just that we hate each other.'

The orderly gave a thin-lipped and prim smile. 'That sounds awfully familiar.'

'D's all right,' Digger continued. 'A I can take or leave. It's those bastards from G nobody can stand. That squadron is sponsored by the Brigade of Guards, and everybody knows what army barmy cunts they are.'

'Oh I don't know. I've met some quite nice Guardsmen in my time.'

'I bet you have,' said Blue. 'But sidling up to them in a West End boozer is not the same as meeting them on a barrack square.'

'You ain't never seen a black one,' Luke added.

'I can just see you in that bearskin,' said Digger. 'You'd look like a fucking jam label.'

'You could fit inside the fuckin' bearskin,' added Graunch.

Blue saw Digger begin to sit up, and carried on quickly. 'They're the first bastards you see when you join the Army: dickheads who are only good for putting squaddies through basic training.'

'They're lunatics,' Digger added, adopting a voice nearly as light as the medic's. 'Always shouting and bawling and stamping their huge, noisy feet.'

'Don't you go stamping your feet, Mr Australia, or you'll undo all my work.'

'I'm not fuckin' Australian.'

'Then why are you called Digger?'

'It's a long story,' Digger replied wearily.

Luke Tuikabe spoke up. 'The first Woodentops in didn't do selection, and nobody is ever goin' to forgive them for that. They were just the dross of Guards Para, which was disbanded.'

'Selection sounds awful,' the orderly said, as he massaged some cream between Blue's toes. 'I met a marine who'd tried it.'

That wasn't the half of it. Blue could remember, vividly, his own selection ordeals, every blister he'd had on the feet now being cared for. The snow that had made life ten times worse. Constant running, thinking, concentrating, map reading, then more running. The exhaustion at night, the troubled, dream-filled sleep, the terror of failure. Then came survival.

'That's when you really learn to hate the Woodentops,' he continued. 'The training wing sent me out in old Army boots, scraggy old clothes, and with no money. Then they sent the fuckin' Brigade of Guards after me in trucks and jeeps. Now those are not nice guys. They're just looking to give anyone they catch the good news with a very long piece of four by two.'

'It's you lot that's mad, not them. At least they get to ride around in trucks.'

Blue just lay back. He knew it was too hard to explain. That you respected someone for getting through selection but you couldn't respect someone you thought had cheated. And the good old Guards had done just that. Frightened because some of their best men were being siphoned off by the SAS, and with what they saw as their best unit being disbanded, they'd lobbied to set up a squadron of their own. The older hands reckoned it had ruined the Regiment. It wasn't true, but old lags were like that. Blue was often tempted to tell the old buggers that they'd never get through selection now either.

One of the scaleys popped his head round the door. 'Your Ruperts are in. The Headshed's coming aboard with them for a briefing. So it's full kit and carpet slippers, on the double.'

'Tell him I'm having a fuckin' pedicure,' said Digger. But he got up anyway.

If Blue Harding and his guys looked slightly bored, it was only because they'd been through this kind of briefing already. The rest were really on the ball, leaning forward, listening hard. They were going in as replacements for existing patrols, but not just as observers. The battle was reaching a point where action was more likely every day. The need for static information gathering was giving way to a proper fight, in which the SAS would take its full part.

The maps they were shown were so detailed it practically included the number of Argentine toothbrushes. It was obvious that G Squadron and the SBS teams had done a brilliant job, and just as obvious from what the Green Slime was telling them that they'd done it under bloody awful conditions. The Regiment had, like everyone else who got their feet on the Falkland Islands, proved themselves.

None of the Headshed briefers actually told them that there was a major battle planned, but they could see for themselves that the British troops needed to break out from what was now a secure bridgehead. And it didn't take a genius to figure out that 5 Brigade must be close. All you had to do was listen to the BBC. No one said it, but it looked as though they'd got into things just in time. JRM concluded the meeting.

'We stay on the defensive for twenty-four hours. This is because tomorrow is Argentina's national day. There is the possibility, faint but present, that they may choose that as an excuse to mount some kind of counter-attack.'

'B Squadron can throw them a party, if you like, boss.'

JRM responded with a tight grin, one that underlined the fact that he not only didn't like the joke, but he hated to be interrupted. Most people in the cramped cabin thought that was precisely why Digger had done it.

'That will give you a day to get yourselves sorted, and allow ample time for the men you will be replacing to pull out. Plans on your troop commanders' desks by 18.00 hours. That will be all.'

The piss-taking suggestion that they celebrate Argentina's national day with a party came to be seen as a very bad joke by the time that twenty-four hours had passed. The soldiers didn't move. But the Argie air force pilots did their country proud. The sinking of the *Coventry* was bad enough. But the loss of the *Atlantic Conveyor* to an Exocet was a disaster. The Army immediately lost seventy-five per cent of its heavy lift capacity when the Chinook helicopters went down with the ship, and those big choppers were, apparently, a vital part of the battle plan.

To the Navy, the loss of such a vessel, so like a carrier in radar profile, was terrifying. The small crew of the *Conveyor* had suffered nine casualties. But in the Task Force commander's imagination, it was not difficult to translate that into either the *Invincible* or the *Hermes*. The nightmare scenario of having to cope with the evacuation of nearly fourteen hundred men from a carrier haunted not only him.

Suddenly the air threat was back at the top of the agenda. And it wasn't the troops they'd put in on the ground that were in trouble: it was the entire fleet.

CHAPTER THIRTEEN

Cabinet office to Commander 3 Bgde: 11.30 hrs 26/5/82: Confusion re. delay in expanding bridgehead. Please respond to War Cabinet immediate.

'We can't have a heli lift,' said JRM. 'All the Sea Kings are now tasked to troop movement and re-supply to try and make up for the loss of the Chinooks. There are none to spare.'

He didn't even mention an air drop. There was no way that could be made from the actual war zone. The only airport was at Port Stanley, and that was in enemy hands. David Lowry, as he listened, was thinking about Hosier, and how he would exploit this to his own advantage. He would claim that the loss of the *Atlantic Conveyor* now vindicated his earlier suggestions of an Entebbe-style raid. And there was little doubt into whose ear he would whisper such an opinion, if he got half a chance.

'Nor can we take a warship within Rigid Raider-range of the mainland. That, given that they must be flying defence patrols, would be suicidal, even without the possibility of a flaming Exocet missile. So it has to be entry by submarine.'

'That will take time,' said Vere Symington. 'We've got to get the sub here, get the men loaded and get them back to Tierra del Fuego. It could be over a week before they are operational.'

'No choice Vere. We can't activate A Squadron, since that will denude our Ulster ops, and leave us without a CT team. David, what's the state of Boat Troop?'

'We were, as usual, less than full strength when the balloon went up, and since then we've lost three people. The two who went on the Rio Grande recce, and Sam Clark.'

There was nothing unusual in that – troops and squadrons were very rarely up to their true establishment number at any time. The normal drill was to draw in men from the other troops to make up the numbers.

Their designations – Air, Mountain, Mobility and Boat – referred to particular skills in an environment, in Boat Troop's case to the specialist ability to use the sea as a means of entry into hostile territory. Once ashore, any SAS trooper had the same ability to move and fight. But JRM had paused for a bit, thinking hard.

'Who's the new troop sergeant?'

'That would fall to Blue Harding.'

'How do you think he would feel about having Sam Clark along and above him?'

'That leaves me without an SSM,' said Vere Symington. It wasn't said very forcibly: the OC was just making the point.

'He's a trained Boat Troop instructor,' JRM replied, 'and the chaps are not going to have many attempts at honing their skills on the way in. The Mount Kent operation is a less specialist job.'

'I don't think Harding would object, sir,' said Lowry.

He imparted that without adding that it would do him no good anyway. If JRM wanted Sam Clark on the sub, then that was what he would have. Besides, the two sergeants were good friends. Blue would probably welcome it. And David Lowry, as the officer leading the patrol, would be glad to have a man like Sam along. The only problem JRM had was with Sam himself. He could refuse.

'Right, David, get your troop strength up to sixteen, and plan for a landing on Tierra del Fuego. Target, the Rio Grande air base, with the same objectives as before. Destroy the Exocets or the means of delivery.'

Not much of the planning that they'd done before was much good for this new operation. For a start, they were going in on foot, from a position well away from the airfield. That had a serious impact on the number of targets they could engage. Fifty men might have a great time going after the pilots and the garrison. Sixteen men had to get inside that perimeter without the enemy knowing they were there until the first charge went off.

And there was new information to add, from Captain Heering, that made the whole appreciation of the risk that much greater. Having got to Santiago, Heering had used the Embassy line to pass back the information about the quality of the border guards. In fact, he had given Headquarters chapter and verse about them, information on numbers, quality and location. There were three whole battalions of marines in Tierra del Fuego, facing the same number on the other side of the border. It showed just how much Galtieri and his mates cared about that potential conflict. Those troops should have been based in the Falklands.

HMS *Onyx* was patrolling the Falklands exclusion zone, and could be brought back to San Carlos Water within four days. Lowry, Sam Clark, Blue Harding and the other troop senior, Robbie Knox, began to formulate a plan. They wanted to land well away from the base, though not too far, at a point where the coastal road turned away from the shore, giving them the room to get in without being observed. That put them to the south of the airfield, leaving a river to cross.

'How big do you think that bugger is?' asked Sam, pointing to the thin blue strip of the river on the map.

'How's your Spanish?'

'Useless.'

'Well with the number of John Wayne movies you've seen, even you must know what "Rio Grande" means.'

'That could be a bummer.'

'The first of many,' said Blue. 'Like three battalions of marines who might not have calmed down yet. We might have to fight our way to Rio Grande.'

'We don't fight, Blue,' said Lowry. 'Killing Argies is secondary. Our job is to take out the Exocet threat, either by destroying the missiles or the means of delivery. And that, with sixteen guys, is going to be hard enough without risking casualties.'

'Too right!' Sam Clark added. 'Time has to be allowed for reconnaissance. With the limitations on numbers, we have to be sure we hit what we want to. If we go in at the charge and don't hit the primary target, I don't think we'll get a second go.'

It was Blue Harding's turn to speak. 'So we really have to plan for our entry and approach. Outside the equipment we need all the other info is going to come on the spot.'

'Do we have a time frame?' asked Robbie Knox.

Lowry looked at the square-jawed ex-Royal Marine. 'How does yesterday sound!'

The seniors went back to the troop, where the whole day was spent arguing. Not in any state of rancour, but about who would take what.

Sam Clark laid out the bones of the operation, the timings and distances, plus the level of opposition, reminding them that evasion would be a real bastard, and that they had to take along the kit necessary to make that as successful as the main attack.

'Heering didn't think they had helis, but if we see any sheds that look like they might have them they need to be mullah'd. We don't want choppers on our tail when we are tabbing out.'

A night attack was essential, given their numbers. There were hangars, storerooms, headquarters block, control tower, radio room, recreation, sleeping and cookhouse blocks. But this time the aim was to neutralize or stay away from them. Any sentries would have to be killed without noise, which pleased Dinger Bell, who was a great lover of Welrod silenced pistols.

'Do we trash the vehicle park or leave it so we can use the trucks to evade?' asked Marty Roper.

'Not my preference,' said Blue. 'They're too easy to spot from the air. And all we have to do is leave one jet intact to have it shooting rockets up our arse.'

'We had this on the other op,' said Robbie Knox. 'We reckoned the ammo and fuel dumps would have to be well away from the rest of the buildings. We're on foot, so we might need to nick some transport just to get to them.'

Workshops and firefighting gear stood as high-priority secondary targets, since they were designed to minimize the damage the troopers intended to inflict. AA defences would have to be dealt with. The Rolands were useless against a land attack. But the anti-aircraft guns, depressed, would take out their machine gun teams in seconds. But most vital of all, there were the planes.

'They will be a bugger to see in the dark,' said Sam as he passed round the recognition sheets. 'I asked for PNG kits, which would help if we got close, but the best they can offer is one set, so I told them to stuff it.'

'We've got those new Yank night sights you air dropped us,' said Blue. 'They're not much on wide vision, but they're brill at close quarters. We might have to hunt around for batteries, though.'

'We'll distribute those out,' Sam said, 'one to each patrol senior. Meantime we study these. Look for a feature that stands out, like the long snout on the Etendards. They are bogey *numero uno*, and we stand more chance of getting close to them before the balloon goes up than anything else. Without those, the Exocets are fucked.'

'Have they got them anywhere else?' asked Graunch.

'They might have.'

'So the missiles should come first.'

'Right, but will we know where they are?'

'So, unless we can identify the buggers when we get close, we'll just have to blow every silo and ammo dump, and pray we've got the bastards. They're bound to be guarded, and I don't think we'll get time for a quiet shufty.'

'They'll have heavy steel doors and probably be sited well underground.'

'Then we need armour-piercing rockets.'

'We were going to use Milans mounted on Pinkies,' said Robbie Knox.

'Something like a Law 80 would come in right handy against the buildings, like,' added Dinger Bell. 'They'll go awf if'n they hit a proper bloody wall.'

'Law 80s are too heavy for this job,' said Blue. 'We've got too far to tab.'

'66s if we can get hold of them, then?' Sam proposed. 'Three per man for two of the patrols.'

'Three's too fucking many,' said Serious Sid, who suspected he was going to be in one of the unlucky four-man groups. 'Fifteen and a half pounds is murder with all the other kit we'll be carrying.'

That received nods and shakes. The American M72 throwaway anti-tank missile was a favourite weapon. It didn't go through as much armour as some of the others, but it was the most easily portable.

'Can't be helped. We have to have something to go through a steel door, but it won't be just the bunkers we need them for. There's going to be a rate of targets we might not get close to. And push comes to shove, a sixty-six-millimetre rocket can totally fuck a plane. No point in going there at all if we can't deliver the goods.'

They went on and on, going over the same things again and again. Finally Sam turned to the approach. 'We'll be tabbing at least twenty Ks. The Bergens will be murderous, especially with the anti-tank missiles and the ammo for the Gimpies. But we can carry a lot of kit in to the target that we'll leave behind, used ammo and weaponry. So when we do E&E, we will be a lot lighter.'

'Ground?' said Robbie. 'Is it soft, hard, or boggy?'

'I asked JRM.'

'And?'

'I was fucking told to get on with it.'

'No maps?'

'None better than the one you're looking at.'

'What about that river crossing?' asked Don Campbell, a short, tough Glaswegian corporal from Mobility, who'd been assigned to the Troop.

'It'll have to be nick something or a Bergen raft,' said Sam. 'So we need an Allison bag to keep the ammo and explosives dry.'

The number of radios was agreed at the normal four, one per patrol, so that when they E&E'd they would be able to do so, if necessary, in standard patrol groups. Likewise machine guns. One team would carry GPMGs, and during the assault, when the enemy realized what was going on, lay down the kind of covering fire that would keep the Argies occupied while the infiltration groups carried out the sabotage.

Everybody spoke and everybody was equal. Sam controlled the meeting, but with a very light touch. He wanted these guys to have their say. To feel it was their operation not the Headshed's; that their arguments had been listened to, and if not agreed with, that at least they'd participated in the process. The floor was littered with paper: lists drawn up and discarded, sketch drawings of airports they'd seen or worked on, details of weapons and equipment, plus the distribution that would make the team effective. Then the plan went to Lowry.

'Naturally,' Sam said, 'this might alter. There's a load of ifs and buts. As you can see, we are carrying enough PE to take out the town. If we get the chance we'll lay delayed fuse charges to catch out the guys trying to sort out the chaos.'

'We should take some of it with us, Sam. We might have to blast our way into Chile.'

'Have we got a call sign yet?' asked Blue.

'Bravo one one.'

While they were planning, 2 Para hit Goose Green and took it after a bloody encounter, while 3 Para and the Marines headed out for Teal

Inlet. The SAS had gone off to capture Mount Kent. Boat Troop were the only men left on *Lancelot*, eager each morning to catch the sound of 'Lillabullero' on the World Service, so that they could be told by voices eight thousand miles away what was happening ten miles from their table. And they searched San Carlos Water for the first sighting of the hull of their sub.

It was a clear crisp morning when she finally arrived, the kind of day that the Argie air force should have been able to make good use of. They had just after the landings, clobbering and sinking the Type 21 frigates *Antelope* and *Ardent* as well as dropping a bomb into the *Lancelot* which failed to explode. That had cost them dear. But the pilots, real heroes and terrific flyers, probably thought it was worth it. Now San Carlos Water was as tranquil as a marina, only the ships were bigger. The water was like glass, reflecting the mixed greens and blues of the surrounding hills.

Up on those hills the air defence guys had set up their Rapiers, mobile missile batteries that had initially caused trouble, prone, as all new systems were, to teething trouble. But now they were working a treat. They provided a shield that made any air attack almost suicidal. The odd supersonic Mirage still raced through the Sound, spinning and weaving to avoid the ack-ack from the ships. But they never hung around or slowed enough to offer a serious threat. Those Rapiers were too hot.

They cross-decked to *Onyx* as soon as she arrived, the launch weaving through the Navy ships and fleet auxiliary transports. Between the ships and the shore, it was different, endless assault craft ferrying back and forth, carrying the supplies needed to keep the advance going. Once aboard *Onyx* it was a case of sixteen men and the mass of their equipment going into a space already seriously overcrowded. The submariners had been on duty for nearly two months now, the best part of it underwater, and the effect on their nerves showed. They were always a bit tetchy when their space was invaded. But they were tired now, weary from constant patrolling and the watch-keeping routine that kind of duty entailed. So it wasn't like Boat Troop got the red carpet.

As soon as the sub was refuelled and had taken on stores they were away, diving the minute they reached the edge of the shallow shelf that surrounded the Falklands. The trip was three hundred miles, and the maximum speed of *Onyx*, submerged, was twenty knots. Once off the coast of Tierra del Fuego they would have to get ashore, a job that would have to be done with care, otherwise they'd get compromised before they'd achieved a thing.

The last letters had been sent again. They tended to be similar. Don't mourn for a guy who loved danger so much. That wives adored or tolerated shouldn't hang about, but find another man. Remember me to the kids, tell them about their dad, and put on the mantelpiece or the piano the kind of photograph that shows me at my best. Don't let them think I'm a hero, just one of the good guys. Have a decent wake after the funeral service, and put enough dough across the bar to buy the whole squadron a good drink!

Life on board the sub was not good. No matter how hard a man tried he was forever in the way, while in the forward compartments the three Geminis and the Bergens made it near impossible for the crew to move. The monotony got to the guys very quickly, making them wonder how the submariners could stand it. Hot bunking was standard, one man lying down as soon as the other moved out. The galley was tiny and served endless fried food, so much that the air conditioning was severely challenged by the quantity of farting. And all the time they were going over their options on the operation. Again and again, discussing scenarios and alternatives so that everyone carried in their heads the sum total of all the Boat Troop knowledge on the sub.

Being good is about being careful, and being trained. Every night, *Onyx* surfaced for an hour so that they could practise a float-off. They'd go through the drills verbally and by mime, then do an actual exercise so that each man reached the peak of his possible efficiency. Float-on was a much more hazardous job than leaving a sub. It was during one of those that David Lowry, as much a member of the team as anyone else, dropped a Johnston outboard he was stripping off the inflatable. He slipped trying to hold it, and the whole weight of it came down on his wrist. The break was audible and, according to the boat's medical officer, clean. But it rendered him useless as far as the operation was concerned.

'Never mind, boss,' said Sam, trying to cheer him up. 'If we pull it off you'll still get a medal.'

'Sure, Sam,' Lowry replied. He was low and depressed, but was not about to be beaten in the sarcasm stakes. 'The more of you get slotted, the bigger my gong will be.'

'Then I should get a Bullworker,' Sam snapped, for once rising to the bait, 'and add some inches to that excuse for a chest.'

Behind them, the battle intensified. 42 Commando arrived on Mount Kent, a highly strategic point, only to find that, instead of a battle to secure the position, it was to be handed over to them by 22 SAS. 2 Para were leapfrogging to Bluff Cove and 5 Brigade were transshipping in South Georgia. And still the Argies stayed in their defences around Port Stanley, inviting the Brits to attack them. To the enemy, it made sense. The normal ratio of attacker to defenders held that a minimum of three to one was necessary. The British forces would need massive reinforcements to achieve that superiority. And the Junta knew how fragile things were for a government already in economic trouble. The trick was to hold them, not defeat them!

And at sea the fleet showed great caution. With the land battle joined and all the troops ashore, their role was diminished. But they had to stay close enough to offer air and gunfire support, all the time wondering if, over the horizon, would appear another Super Etendard, and another six-hundred-mile-an-hour Exocet. And the question of how many they had was still unanswered.

Everybody exercised as much as they could; press-ups in the gangway, followed by deep knee bends. Running on the spot if they could find somewhere quiet; lifting weights and stretching muscles that would be under severe strain as soon as they went ashore. And they talked, of old times and old mates as well as operations they'd been on. They had their thoughts too, of home and loved ones, some wondering how their garden was doing, others troubled by the effect their absence was already having on strained relationships. They should have been showing signs of the pressure, but that was absent. These were a group supremely confident of their skills, men who knew they could act collectively and individually.

So by the time the skipper of *Onyx* had reached the Argentine coast, they were hyper but ready, annoyed that he spent a whole day lying on the seabed. He surfaced in darkness. David Lowry and Sam Clark were called forward to the control room, to look through the periscope and check the coastline against the Admiralty outline the captain provided.

There wasn't much to see: a flat, slight plateau, the coast itself the kind of jagged worn cliff that looks as though half of it has recently dropped off. Looking for the kind of features that would distinguish it from the next bay or inlet was hard.

Tierra del Fuego, in English, means 'Land of Fire'. Looking through the sub's periscope, it seemed that if there had ever been a blaze, it had long since gone out. Sam Clark looked at the outside air temperature, which was just a few points above freezing, and that in the middle of the day.

'Maybe it means you need a fire to stay alive.'

'I'm not about to throw you out,' said the bearded skipper. 'But the sooner you're off the better, I imagine. The sea state is good, our position is close to the one you gave us for a landfall, and I rather suspect one bay round here will be much like another.'

Roughly translated, that meant he was in no mood for speculations. The sooner he could get these pongos off his boat the better.

'Do you want to recce it Sam?' asked Lowry.

'No point, boss. The skipper's right.'

The hiss of the hatches opening was followed by a blast of icy fresh air that had the tang of ozone in it. That was accompanied by cold water, first rushing, then dripping into the forward engine compartment. The Chief Petty Officer overseeing the exit was, short of the screams, like a woman in labour. He had his fists clenched and he ground his teeth as he tried by some form of osmosis or levitation to push both Boat Troop and the equipment they needed out of the hatch and off his property. Nightly practice had obviously done very little for his nerves.

A folded Gemini is still a big, bulky object, one that was very close to the size of the hatch through which it had to exit on an 'O' class submarine. So getting the boats out onto the deck was no easy matter. They wanted to be quick as well. That wasn't because of the sailors, who knew that a submarine's place was under water not sitting on top of it; that the more time spent floating on the surface, even in the dark, the greater the danger of discovery. The greatest fear was the arrival of an anti-submarine aircraft, which could close on them before they'd dived. Surface vessels were almost as bad. In moonlight any hard object, like the big conning tower, shows black and clear on the sea, providing a definite point from which to depth charge. But the men toiling on the deck had an added fear to that which bothered the sailors, like not being in the boats when the sub blew its tanks.

Every man, even though he was major busy, had a second to relish that first moment. When you exit from a sub, after days of packaged air, in a tin can programmed for claustrophobia, a cold wind on the face is bliss. Stiff from too little exercise, the feeling of space, the realization that there is nothing around you for miles, is fantastic. It's only an impression, because there's no time for anyone to fuck about and indulge themselves in deep and lasting appreciation.

Onyx began to blow her tanks as soon as the signal was given that the boats were inflated. It was a timed action, not a visually observed one. The Geminis had to be loaded with the troop's Bergens in six minutes; outboards connected but raised, the men aboard and ready to go in fewer than ten. There were no shouted commands or people tripping over each other. Everybody knew individually what they had to do, as well as the sequence in which each function should be performed. Silence, though not total, was important. The best way to avoid compromise is to eliminate risk. The shore of Tierra del Fuego might be three miles away, but you never knew how sound travelled off the sea to the land.

The sub's hull sank beneath the waves, leaving the three Geminis floating in the water. Blue Harding was in the lead boat, the old Spitfire compass once more strapped to the port side. Glowing a dull green in the dark, it was easy to read, allowing him to remain alert for other dangers that might lurk on the surface. Behind him, in the other two Geminis, the outboards fired up, the muted roar shattering in such a noise-free environment. That sound was an acceptable risk. There was always the chance of running into an Argie patrol boat. But that was something you could take a visual on, with the knowledge that if they were moving at any kind of speed their engines would be noisier than a Johnston.

The sky was clear, the air crisp, with intermittent cloud cover, the sea a long even swell running into the black silent shore. The point of entry had been fixed, and they were heading in to it. But there's always an element of drift when a sub is on the surface. This can throw out compass calculations a fraction, so a visual fix was essential. Precise distances are difficult when a boat is so low in the water, so the shortening of the waves, caused by the seabed shelving, is a good indication of the proximity of land. The next clue is aural: the sound of surf breaking on a sand or shingle shore.

No lights at all confirmed that they'd picked a point well clear of human habitation. SOP was to kill the revs of the outboards as soon as the sound of breakers registered. A 40bhp engine makes practically no noise when ticking over. But it will still allow the inflatable to maintain a degree of forward motion. Then the only patrol members occupied are on the tillers. The rest of the troop aim some firepower at the shore, and use every sense they possess to pick up any hint of a threat.

The breakers were light, hissing up the narrow strand of the shell-encrusted beach. But the phosphorescence was a sharp white line as the spume picked up and magnified the ambient light. With eyes perfectly adjusted, the whole troop was at peak performance, keyed up to do the thing they'd trained for, to get on to a hostile beach without so much as scaring a nervous cat. There was no haste. Everything was done with deliberation.

The method by which they worked was not from some manual cooked up in an office. It was the distilled experience of every man who'd ever carried out a beach landing. Communication was by taps and signals. No one spoke, nor would they until they had established a safe LUP on shore. Sam Clark, who was i/c of the lead boat, had one of the new-generation night sights to his eye, and could see more than anyone. He indicated a course that would take them to a point where rocks pushed out to form the arm of a narrow bay.

It might be easy to ground in the middle of a beach. But they had a tidal rise and fall related to depth of strand that represented an unknown quantity. It made no sense to land there. Why leave an M1 of footprints, which could be seen from a long way off in daylight, in the middle of a bay? Much safer to land near the rocks, to see if it was possible to exfil the landing site without leaving the imprint of a single boot. Seaweed was another positive. A trooper could move through that and leave no discernible trace for a shore patrol to see.

Galtieri's goons were not lined up to greet them. So they increased the revs on the engine and began to work crabwise along the shore, still hyped up for any danger. Two boats lay off while Blue took his slowly towards the silent shore. The strand was visible now, a pale strip of grey between the white of the surf and the black of the rocks. Blue was edging in on a rising tide that still had two hours to peak. Once the decision has been made to go in, there are several ways to operate. You can send in swimmers, as they had done on the Murrell Peninsula. Another is with oars, taking it really easy, while maintaining total silence. The best is a strong preference. Most troopers like to have the engine running, ready to rev up and evade, while laying down some firepower at whatever has posed the threat.

And when you do close the shore to your selected landing point, you go with as much speed as is consistent with maintaining safety. That way you hit the shore with a bit of pace. It's the old 'Who Dares Wins' philosophy, which says that if you're going to get in a firefight, you want to bring down maximum force on your opponent as quickly as possible. To impose your will on the waiting enemy, rather than the reverse! There are few things worse than sitting in an inflatable being shot at.

They got close to the promontory where the bay closed off, Blue was seeking a landing point where the water wasn't excessively disturbed, a route that would avoid any broken underwater rocks that could damage the Gemini. Blue and Luke Tuikabe were out and on the shore as soon as the base of the boat touched the seabed, on their knees, weapons trained forward, heads moving slowly as their eyes traversed the edge of the bluffs. Behind them Digger and Graunch, having grounded the boat, were likewise on alert.

Five minutes passed, in which the patrol stayed rock still. Then, at a signal from Blue Harding, they began to edge up the beach, close to the rocks and the bed of dried seaweed, which would cover their passage until they reached the high water mark. That allowed two men to check the beach, while the others sought out a way to get off it. The heights had to be declared secure before the rest of Boat Troop could be called in. Nothing was rushed, as they climbed the ten feet of slope that took them onto the top. Once there, they edged along in both directions to a distance of a hundred metres, then returned to confirm the landing zone was safe.

Blue raised his torch and flashed twice, an infra-red signal that would only be picked up by Sam Clark on his night sight. Within minutes the rest of the troop was ashore. Two sentries were still out, on the high ground. The rest were busy deflating the Geminis and seeking out a hide. The pair on stag were replaced as soon as the troopers had their dry suits off, and they too removed them and stuffed them into the Allison bags. Then, with Bergens on and weapons ready, the patrol made their way off the beach in single file.

Sam Clark put the night sight away, not wishing to waste batteries on a piece of equipment that might prove vital during the actual assault. He called a meet as soon as everybody was ready, establishing their position, going over the route and the pacing, designating the stops. The group moved out, twin files of eight men, heading for their first obstacle, the road that ran south from Rio Grande to the end of the earth at a place called Ushuaia.

The men were five metres apart, each with a clear idea of the compass heading, all using their private method to count off their pacing so that they knew how far they'd marched. Contact was kept at all times, halts made every thirty minutes to listen for any threat. The land they were tabbing across was soft and spongy, but not wet like the Falklands. The few trees they passed, ghostly leafless shapes, were bent over by the prevailing wind, the same hurricanes that blew round Cape Horn to the south.

It was essential to leave enough time to create a LUP. The plan was not to cross the road on the first day, but to use the time to lay up and observe the level of traffic. Boat Troop were under pressure, they knew that. But they were also operating in the unknown, with precious little hard information. The ground might be flat here, but was it the same on the other side? The piss-poor maps they had showed no habitations around here, but that was not guaranteed, and it needed to be.

The level of traffic on the road would tell them a great deal. Did the Argentine Army patrol it? And if so, how often, and in what strength? Was there any evidence of troops being moved to reinforce the air base, or of weapons being brought in to beef up the defences? It wasn't just military information they needed, but civilian as well. This might be the end of the earth, but it was dotted with sheep ranches, huge *estancias*. They, the property of rich owners, must either have telephones or radio. And where there were sheep they usually had shepherds, sharp-eyed individuals who could easily spot and report a strange entity on their patch. There was no way they were going to go stumbling around and walk into an unknown piece of terrain without checking it out first.

Sam Clark called a halt for the bulk of the troop, told them to ease their Bergens, then went forward with Paul Hill to locate the road. It was a thin, two-lane strip of tarmac, with the kind of high camber that can deal with torrential rain. He quickly established that it was in decent repair. There had been potholes, and erosion at the edges, but they'd been properly filled in. That said traffic. That this was a major comms route for the defence of the border. It could mean the troops at the air base were of sufficient strength to require that they be moved in tactical support.

'We'll find out soon enough.'

He whispered this conclusion to Paul. The new boy was, according to the Sergeant, receiving on-the-job training. Sam intended to keep Paul close to him. As a recently badged trooper, he was bound to be on edge, wondering if he could hack it with the more experienced men. Sam could have told him to relax, but he didn't bother. Paul would find out, soon enough, how good he was. He wouldn't be here if he weren't!

The pair made their way back, counting the paces on the flat ground to ensure that they would have the road in view when dawn broke. In the meantime, Blue Harding had established a RV position, and a possible LUP, in a small series of undulations in the ground. It was shallow, but provided there were no hills to command the position, they should be able to stay there out of sight. As half the troop covered the approaches, the rest found some dust and rubbed their cam netting in it, so that as it got light, they could hide under something which would blend with the landscape.

As soon as he got back, Sam joined Graunch, who had set up the comms for the evening Sked. Time to tell Headshed they were in, their location, and that they could expect to close to within striking distance of the Rio Grande air base on the next night's tab. Meanwhile Blue organized the stags, and a rota that allowed everyone to sort out their feet, eat their emergency rations, and to get some sleep.

CHAPTER FOURTEEN

'Clear the net, clear the net. All airborne helicopter units close Port Fitzroy immediately. Assault ship Galahad listing and on fire with casualties still aboard and in the water.'

The increase in the wind, as the night passed, was a mixed blessing. In such an arid landscape it created dust, which obscured vision. That worked in the troopers' favour, colouring their cam nets. A clear, crisp winter dawn was the last thing they wanted – one of those sunrises that throws everything into sharp relief. But the dust did get everywhere, and the noise of the wind made the idea of hearing anyone approaching impossible, which brought the odd expletive from Sam Clark.

'What the fuck,' Digger whispered to Blue, and he snuggled down in his Gonk bag to try and get some sleep. 'If it was everything perfect Clarkie would still moan.'

'He's just tryin' to keep us alive.'

They stood to an hour before dawn. Sunrise, which seemed to last for ever, left them under a grey, cloudy sky, in a dry landscape that showed no signs of human habitation. It was flat to the north and south, but there was the shape of some low hills, about a mile away on the opposite side of the road. They were humps really, worn away by aeons of wind, with no vegetation at all, providing poor cover. In their favour was the fact that they could see not a single house or even a shepherd's hut, though there were animals dotted around where some green showed through.

At their low elevation the road didn't show, and it was a whole hour before the men left on lookout spotted the first piece of traffic, an old truck that Sam Clark reckoned must have had a part in *The Grapes of Wrath*. It even had the right kind of horn, which the driver blasted occasionally, though there wasn't another vehicle in sight. The field of vision, even lying down, was several miles. Sam used his binos to check out the whole area, marking rocks, bent trees and clumps of bushes on the map he was drawing. They would cross the road tonight, and make their way through those hills to the Rio Grande River, well to the west of both the town and the air base.

'Bus,' said a quiet voice after about an hour.

That seemed to streak across their arc of view, a high-wheeled American job made for hard driving in rough terrain. They saw three more throughout the rest of the day, another southbound and two going north. The odd car appeared as well, one of which looked military. But no sign of soldiers being moved around. More to the point, no sign of patrols out searching the countryside for sixteen blokes from Boat Troop. They took turns to stand stag, sleep and eat, took care with their waste so that no one passing this spot later would know they'd stopped and waited for darkness to fall. The last job, before the light faded, was to get ready to move out, and to check that the site they were leaving behind was free of any telltale sign of their presence. Then they sent the evening Sked, to say they were moving, and stood to while darkness fell.

The rain began just after they'd crossed the road: light drizzle at first which steadily increased until it was a steady downpour. You can wrap up as much as you like against that, but it still gets inside your clothes, and runs down the arms of your waterproof jacket to soak the gloves on your hand. But it's the wind that does the damage. The chill from that is a serious factor when dry. But that's multiplied tenfold in wet conditions.

The ground beneath their boots had very low absorption, and was thus slippery. This made tabbing difficult and used up a lot of the troopers' energy. The distance they had to march wasn't immense: some fifteen kilometres in a straight line. But they were operating in undulating hill country, moving with extreme caution, staying off the crests, which increased the distance by a third. They were also carrying packs that had an average weight of 100 pounds. That was still well within the range the men were trained to operate in, but you can never be sure what effect a march is having on even the fittest guy, so Sam made a point of checking everybody out at each halt.

When the patrol leader asks you how you are feeling, there is no way a trooper can avoid the truth. Every man is responsible for himself. He chooses the kit he carries and the clothes he wears, and the law of

200

averages says that sometimes the wrong decisions are made. Weights are too high, boots the wrong fit, or clothing inappropriate. Blue, Digger and Graunch, who still had problems with their feet, were suffering but coping. There were others with minor moans about their Bergen straps cutting into their shoulders. But discomfort aside, the patrol was in decent shape.

But the weather could change that. So far it wasn't serious, but with the temperature dropping, the rain getting heavier and the wind increasing in force, it could get that way. There was lightning too, in the far distance, an ongoing electrical storm, though no sound of thunder. The gale was the real problem, the same howler that blew round Cape Horn and provided a whole raft of seafaring writers with tales of ships, windbound in the Magellan Straits for weeks at a time. Sam Clark was aware of that variable. It could blow out in an hour, and it could blast across the landscape for a month. There was no way of knowing. What was not in question was the need to consolidate. Pushing on was important, but not at the risk of destroying the Boat Troop's effectiveness as a fighting force.

Most of the guys were in reasonable shape, cursing the elements to themselves, but moving properly and staying alert. The real problem would be if one man or more went down badly. They were in barren, open country, a place with poor and shallow topsoil over hard rock. To construct a hide with enough depth to protect against the elements would be difficult, and then there were all the risks of separation and degradation. Once a man starts to go down, getting him back to his peak is really tough. It is nearly impossible without shelter and warmth. Yet every soldier was needed to carry out the job they'd been tasked with. Sure, they would go ahead depleted, but that shortened the odds for everyone, and was not good news.

'There should be a ranch house off to the left,' said Sam, his voice muffled by the hood of his camouflage parka. He'd pulled out the PNG goggles again, even though the teeming rain rendered them less effective, and had a good look round.

Blue Harding, crouched beside him, was carrying the same map, and had calculated the compass bearings at the same time as Sam. He had his finger, and his pencil torch, on the spot where the Estancia Silvana should be. In the whole of the Argentine part of Tierra del Fuego there

201

were no more than a dozen of these *estancias*, testimony to the size of the individual holding each sheep ranch covered. They were enormous – as big as Texas cattle ranches. The house should be substantial, even in these conditions a well-lit beacon that would help the troop fix their positions. You don't put corrugated iron huts on the map, even in a pisshole like Tierra del Fuego. If it's shown, it should be huge.

'Maybe they go to bed early,' said Sam.

'They're like the Spanish, mate,' Blue replied. 'They have dinner at midnight.'

'This place is only just over a kilometre from the river. I want a confirmed fix on it so that we know exactly where we are. We find an inland slope that gives us a bit of protection against the wind, and a team goes out and finds the fucker.'

'Me?'

Sam's nod was minimal. As patrol commander he couldn't go. But he needed a decision-maker he could trust.

'Then I'll use my night sight, and hope we've got enough batteries to keep it going.'

The other two patrol seniors, huddled a few feet away, were called in. Compass bearings and march times were compared, so that there could be no doubt that they were in the place they thought. The variations, inevitable, were so slight as to be unimportant.

'Luke,' Blue called, as the Fijian scurried over. 'We're goin' walkabout, old son.'

Both men slipped off their Bergens. They would go with the weapons and belt kit, using the American night sights they'd been gifted, now fixed to their rifles. These would have to be used sparingly, to preserve battery power. Callbacks were fixed, RVs discussed, and re-entry signals confirmed. Then, as the rest of the troop hunkered down out of the wind, Blue and Luke headed out on an easterly compass bearing, looking for the first sign of human habitation, which should, even out here, be some kind of fence.

They found that quick enough. It was, surprisingly, in very poor repair. That made getting through it a doddle. Both men moved forward a foot at a time, aware that, if there were humans about, then there were likely to be dogs as well. In this case the wind and rain were a positive bonus.

Not even sheepdogs stand out in the pissing rain. They find somewhere dry and sheltered and, if left alone, go to sleep.

Blue tapped Luke and halted him as soon as he saw the outline of the house through his night sight, a high, crenellated Spanish gable. The silence was unnerving, the feeling that this place, which should be inhabited, appeared empty. The suspicion that some kind of trap was just waiting to be sprung. They waited for a whole five minutes, not moving, ears attuned for the slightest noise. Apart from the sound of falling rain, and the swish of the strong gusts of wind around the building, there was nothing. Both men swept the area around them with their night scopes, trying to get a clear picture of what the teeming rain allowed them to see.

Blue tapped Luke again and pointed towards the side of the house. At a nod he was up and moving towards it, his back pressed against the stone as Luke Tuikabe covered him. Edging along the wall, out of the wind and rain, he soon found why there was no light spillage. His fingers found the edge of the heavy wooden shutter. Paint was peeling off the wood, and Blue could finger at the base the points where the timber had rotted slightly. Feeling safer, he called Luke on, and they crept round the exterior of the *estancia*. It was drill they both knew well, Blue searching, Luke providing cover, that reversed as they leap-frogged. Roughly, Blue Harding estimated the size of the building, which was square and of two storeys, at around thirty metres per wall. He also counted the windows: evenly spaced, three on each side, and from what he could make out, the same on each floor.

There was a verandah along the front, with a slatted wooden floor and a carved handrail. They stayed off that, moving along the face till they encountered a stone balustrade. This enclosed a set of stone steps that led up to what had to be the main entrance. That consisted of a set of double doors, high and carved, with a huge padlock and hasp across the join on the outside. They performed another night sight search, then moved away from the front of the building to check that the area was secure.

Luke heard the voices first, faint but audible, carried towards them on the strong wind, interrupted by the occasional tinkle of music, then laughter. He tapped Blue then cupped a hand over his ear to tell him to listen. A repeat had to wait till the wind blew, and carried the noise to them. With the silent, dark house at their backs, they went down on their bellies and crawled down a slight grassy, water-soaked incline towards the source, the noise increasing as they progressed. Blue sussed it was a radio or television long before they got close enough to confirm it. The mix of noises sounded like a gameshow or some form of variety. It didn't matter. What did was the line of light that edged an ill-fitting door, one that faced away from the main building behind them.

Blue touched Luke to advise caution, and both troopers lay still, the rain bouncing off their backs, listening for another few minutes. No sounds of live voices disturbed the endless stream of electronic noise. No conversation or human reaction to what was going on punctuated the flow. Indicating that the Fijian should stay still, Blue edged closer. The walls of the building were not cold stone this time, but a kind of tarred substance over what was probably board, the walls angled inwards slightly to deflect some of the force of the elements. There were shutters too, leaking light through those points at which they didn't fit. Blue could smell food, a sharp tangy aroma of something cooked, that mixed with the odour of burning oil.

Peering through one of the shutter cracks, nose crinkling at the strong smell of unwashed humanity, he could see very little. Some poor furniture, a high, single bed with lots of embroidered coverings, and an oil lamp emitting poor quality light. Electricity for a radio or a television, but none for lighting? Unlikely! The radio must work on battery power. But there had to be a generator somewhere, one that would be used to supply the main house. The absence of noise, of the popping sound of a machine, added to his original impressions. The bulk that filled his slim line of vision was bulky and black, and it was only as it moved on that Blue had a quick glimpse of a grey-haired woman, old, fat and slow.

It's a commonplace that you don't know why you arrived at certain conclusions. It just happens. Blue was crouching down, waiting for his eyes to readjust, when the thoughts formed. He felt certain that the main house was empty and likely to remain so. Was this old dear in the tarred hut some kind of caretaker? There was no indication of anything else about, human or otherwise. Wet himself, he knew the rest of the patrol would be in the same state. He also knew what they had to do. To launch, from an exterior LUP, the kind of operation they intended to perform, was perfectly possible. It would happen even if the guys were wet, tired and cold. Which they would be in this part of the world, regardless of whether the rain stopped and the wind dropped. They were committed to lying up all through the daylight hours, and they'd never get dry in any kind of underground hide.

Possible, but not desirable? When they went into that air base, it would be so much better to be dry, rested and in good physical shape. Creeping away, he tapped Luke to follow, and made his way back up the slope to the main building, hand touching the wooden rail that led along the front. He followed the walls, on the opposite side of the house, neither seeing nor hearing any other evidence of human or animal life, right back to the first shutter he'd touched. The feeling round it for the signs of rot was, this time, more thorough. He also tugged at the bottom, creating a gap between it and the wall that seemed to be further evidence of poor repair. Ear pressed to the wood, he heard the slight grinding sound as metal tapped against timber. The locking bar would probably be on the inside; a simple metal strip dropped on to two holding plates. Was there a window behind it?

'I want to break in,' he whispered to Luke. All he heard was his Fijian companion suck in his breath.

If Luke had reservations, then they were perfectly practical. There was no hard and fast SAS rule. But basically, if you wanted to stay uncompromised, you avoided human habitations. They wouldn't have come close to this one if there had been any sign of life, just registered its location as an aid to positioning themselves on the map. But here it was, empty, and only a few kilometres from their target. A possible LUP that was dry, warm by the standards of the outside temperature, and seemingly deserted.

Blue had his knife out, still pulling the shutter out slightly so that a gap was created at the point where they overlapped. If Luke was worried about what his patrol commander was up to, he didn't say so. He just accepted that Blue Harding had a good idea what he was about and let him get on with it. Blue reckoned he could break in without leaving much in the way of evidence. It didn't matter if there were marks on the shutters, caused by him using his knife as a lever. This wasn't the kind of place where Sherlock Holmes lived round the corner, ready to come and deduce from the minute signs and scratches that there were British Special Forces in the area. Entirely by touch, Blue slid up the bar, opened the free side of the shutter, and lifted the metal strip clear. Now both shutters were ajar, and he could feel, on his fingertips, the dirt-encrusted panes of glass, small and square, on the casements.

The SAS teaches you many things, and since covert surveillance was a heavy part of the Northern Ireland experience, the troopers were taught breaking and entering techniques as well. These windows had never been designed to withstand any serious attempt at forcing them. The catches were simple affairs of a pattern made to keep the casements closed. There had probably never been a burglary round here. Where would anyone go when they stole something? But once they were inside, shutters closed behind them and, their torches lit and shaded, they soon discovered there was plenty to pinch, especially if you had a truck.

They were in a large rectangular room, musty from lack of occupation, what furniture there was draped with white cloths. A quick scan revealed the shut door on the opposite wall. Blue took a chance and unshaded his torch, keeping it pointing towards the floor so that there was no bounce that could be picked up by an exterior eyeline. Luke followed suit, the spill of light from both showing panelled walls dotted with portraits. In the middle was a huge table, and on one wall a rack of cues.

'It's a fuckin' billiard room,' Blue whispered, circling round to try the door. Having established that it opened inwards, he leant against it, jamming it into its frame, and slowly turned the handle. He didn't pull, but eased his body weight off the door, feeling the lock stop it immediately. The handle was let go with the same care he'd used to turn it, his finger doing a quick check to ensure that there was no interior key.

His nose, itching slightly from the dust he'd disturbed, told him they were in a room rarely used. The door was locked on the outside, which implied it was also rarely visited. The way all the window shutters were closed around the house suggested the whole place was deserted. In such a barren landscape, there would be few if any other buildings apart from that tarred hut. Perhaps a barn somewhere, or a housing for the generator. Could it be a perfect, ready-made patrol base?

The odds had to be assessed. There might be more people around, but if he could get Sam and the rest of the guys into this room, with the shutters replaced behind them, they would be out of sight. Footprints from sixteen pairs of boots presented a problem, but the rain might wash that away. Inhabitants? None. Caretakers, at least one. But she was no threat to Special Forces troopers, and neither would anyone else be as long as they could avoid contact, or neutralize them if it happened. Worst case, they would find, in daylight, that they were in the middle of a working sheep farm, be discovered and have to kill someone. Best case, they would be safe from the elements, free to send out recces and plan in some comfort.

Sam Clark, when they rejoined, didn't ask for a full explanation. He merely requested his appreciation from John Harding, and, having been given it by a man he trusted, he was willing to comply.

'There's only one question that needs to be asked,' said Sam to the assembled troop seniors. 'Should we leave a couple of guys on stag outside during daylight?'

Robbie Knox replied. 'Once we're inside we won't be able to see jack shit. They can find an OP and check out the integrity of the place then give us some kind of signal to E&E if we look like being bounced. Or they can come in and give us the good news when it's dark again.'

'I don't think it's necessary,' Blue replied. 'If there's any activity we'll hear it. I don't like splitting us up, and maybe those guys outside will be more at risk of compromise than we are. And they're bound to suffer from the wet and cold.'

Sam had a quick look into the cammed faces. In the end it was his decision. 'Stay together!' he said, before going over patrol orders again.

The rest of the troop were briefed, and with Blue and Luke Tuikabe leading the way they headed back, approaching the Estancia Silvana with as much stealth as he and Luke Tuikabe had shown the first time. The shutter had been left deliberately open. If the place was patrolled, it would have been spotted, and some indication of that should have been obvious before their arrival.

Getting out of the wind and rain was a real bonus. They had to stay silent, sixteen troopers who quietly stacked their Bergens, then, using shaded torches, found a place to lay down. Those not on stag sorted themselves out, then went to sleep. The men assigned to the shutters and the door had their ears pressed against the wood, listening for the first sign of a threat.

Cornelius Hosier was at Special Forces' HQ when the figures were confirmed for the disaster at Fitzroy. Fifty-one Guardsmen had died in what was clearly a total cock-up. The apportioning of blame hadn't really got going yet, though he'd seen, on a visit to Northwood, that the Kennel Club and their staff were already manoeuvring to wriggle out of what was clearly a naval responsibility. The troops should never have been dispatched in anything other than dedicated assault ships. But they were putting about the notion that the Army was at fault because of the slow rate of their disembarkation, crowing about how quickly the Marines would have got ashore.

What it did prove, most comprehensively, was what a continuing threat the Argentine air force posed. Never mind specialist weapons like sea-skimmers. Those pilots had the ability to strike at vulnerable points in the British battle plan, even if, in doing so, they had lost four of their number. Matters were approaching a climax, the troops already in place for the final battle. Nerves were stretched to breaking point, as all three services waited to see how the Argies would respond.

There was not a single senior officer who believed that the war could be won with ease. They all worried that the advance would falter, that the soldiers and marines would become bogged down in the mountains, a fighting force of inferior strength to the enemy, at the end of a supply snake that was dangerously over-extended. The Argentines, they suspected, must have some shock response up their sleeve. Hardly surprising, then, that Bob Brotherton had asked him daily, on behalf of the Old Man, about the progress of the Rio Grande operation.

Impatient as he himself was, Cornelius Hosier presented, at headquarters, an imperturbable front, repeating his formula that the troops were in on the ground, and would attack as soon as they could possibly do so. That was not the tone of his communications with both Hereford and Jamie Robertson-Macleod. He made it clear he was under pressure to get results, and demanded that the patrol commander be told in no uncertain terms that, even if it increased his risk factor, an attack should go in immediately. These orders were duly passed on to Sam Clark, who did his very best to ignore them.

It was still dark in the room, but there was a marginal spill round the shutter edges. They knew, by the brightness of that, and the sound of bird song, that the rain had eased. The sun, rising in the east, was shining right on their side of the house. The wind was harder to call, they being on the sheltered elevation of the *estancia*. There was a terrible temptation to look outside, to try and find out what they could see. Sam Clark was more interested in the interior and the roof. If they could get up there, and set up an observation point, they might actually be able to see the Rio Grande base.

The lock was heavy and old, harder for Blue to pick than the newer, smaller types. But he got it eventually, easing open the door without so much as a creak from the well-oiled hinges. Using torches, when it was light outside, was fairly safe. They wouldn't show. What they revealed, as they swung them around, was a large central area, a sort of lounge, full of what seemed to be tables and couches, they too being covered. There was no avoiding the trail they left in the dust. But that, in itself, was reassuring, showing as it did how rarely the place was visited. Various doors opened off the lounge, all locked, and all picked, one showing a set of stone steps that led to a cellar kitchen that contained utensils but no food. There was a wide staircase off to the right that led up to the spacious landing, various bedrooms, bathrooms, a library and what appeared to be a changing room. It was there that they found the wardrobe full of well-cut clothes.

'These are no fuckin' good,' said Sam, as he rifled through the rack of hangers.

The flat, featureless landscape presented a real difficulty. Sam had been hoping to find some garments that would allow at least one of his reconnaissance team to stand upright, perhaps even to walk past the entrance to the base. Silk shirts and ties, suits stripped and plain, dark and light, were not what was required. There were shoes too, the kind worn by a rich man, each with its own wooden tree, a device that bore the trademark of Lobbs, the London shoemaker. Blue, a smart and expensive dresser, was impressed.

'This guy's got bundles. These are about a grand a pair.'

'Well heeled,' joked Sam, holding up a fine brogue. 'Why hasn't he got a pair of jeans and a checked shirt? That would really come in handy.'

Blue was fingering the stitching on a navy pin-striped lapel. 'This guy wouldn't be seen dead in jeans.'

'They might work if they're scuffed up, the clothes and the shoes.'

'Sacrilege,' Blue replied, but he was nodding.

Sam looked up at the flat ceiling. 'Let's have a look-see and find out if we can get any higher.'

'It might be a flat roof.'

'If it had a wall round it that would be the business.'

It wasn't flat: it was quite steeply pitched, so that snow, which must come to these parts every year, would slide off. They found the access in a packed box room, using the trunks it contained to get through the trapdoor into the void. After a quick directional check, Sam pushed his knife under a tile, easing it up. The noise, as the stone cracked on the restraining nails, was loud right by their ear. They just had to hope it wasn't outside.

'Bingo!' Sam said softly, as he pushed his binos into the tiny gap he'd created. Blue had a look, his eyes picking up the perimeter fence of the air base as soon as he readjusted the focus.

There was the tip of what looked like a guard tower – not very high, but placed at a point that gave some indication of the distance to the main buildings. Guarding an air base is hell. The amount of space the runways occupy means they can only really be covered by mobile patrols. At least from here they could pick up some of the timings on those from observing the headlights. The real guards, the static ones, needed to be near the points that required protection, well away from the fence that they could see.

It ran along the slope by the river, then turned at right angles some two hundred metres away from the road, and the bridge which crossed the river. The route then headed for the coast and the settlements that lay to the south of the Rio Grande estuary. Beyond that Blue could see the last section of the runway, a black tarmac strip rising on a slight incline. There were marker lights there to guide aircraft in, and off to his very left a windsock pointing east, and standing nearly parallel to the earth, evidence that the wind was still blowing strong. A couple of trucks were parked up, painted in red and white chequer. But not much else! He couldn't see any of the buildings. They were hidden by the incline, a slight slope that ran all the way down to the shallow valley that held the Rio Grande.

'Why can't they build airstrips on flat ground?' Blue said. 'There must be tons of it round here.'

But there is, of course, very rarely absolutely flat land. And high as they were, the elevation added to the distance showed them very little. Sam, when Blue looked, was examining the tiles at the very highest point of the roof. An additional few feet would increase their visual range enormously. And Sam, if he was going to set up an observation point, wanted to do so from as high a point as possible. The bummer was that the best place would be on the roof standing up, this adding another couple of miles to their line of view. But that wasn't on. Also, you had to be careful dislodging tiles at the very apex of a steep roof. If anyone looked at a building, even casually, that was one of the features they picked up on.

'I thought for a minute,' Sam said, 'we were going to be able to do the biz without patrolling.'

Blue reckoned that was pushing it a bit. He would have wanted a patrol out just for a terrain appreciation of the ground on the other side of the river. Getting clear was just as important as getting in, and it showed that Sam was more concerned with one than the other.

They heard the engines begin their sharp whine, and both took turns looking through the gap. The jet had extra fuel tanks slung under each wing. It used most of the runway to lift off, screamed down the tarmac, nose and front wheel rising. Then it parted with the ground, shooting up into the sky at an acute angle, turning to the east at the same time.

'Skyhawk,' said Blue.

They watched as the first plane was followed by three others, each one banking in the wake of the leader. It was clearly a combat air sortie, and it didn't take much brain to figure out where they were off to. Neither man said it, but they guessed that on the evening Sked they'd get another heavy hint from Headshed about getting in and doing the job.

They got more than that. With the battle for Port Stanley actually under way, the Headshed could brief them without breaching security. That didn't include any tactics, troop numbers, or progress, but merely acted as a precursor to the increasing worry regarding a last-ditch attempt by the Argentinian Junta to reverse matters in their favour. The nature of that didn't have to be spelt out. If the enemy had any more Exocet missiles, this would be the time to throw them into the battle.

But there was no way Sam Clark, without some knowledge of location of targets, was going to launch an attack. As he briefed Robbie Knox and his team, he made it plain what they needed. A point of entry on the northern side of the river, one that could get the bulk of the men, unseen, onto the base, inside the perimeter. Some appreciation of the layout so that cover could be provided for the assault teams, and an indication of what they would face in the way of defences and guards, plus the strength of the non-specialist personnel on the base.

The difficulty for the recce patrol was the sheer flat nature of the landscape. There seemed to be no elevated ground close by that would give them the kind of view they needed. And that in turn meant that they might have to stay out for more than one night, moving their position to try and get a reasonably comprehensive layout of what the attacking group would face. That would leave the rest of them sitting in this billiard room, at risk of discovery, for forty-eight hours, at the mercy of the increasingly strident commands of the Headshed.

The allocation of the night sights to Robbie Knox made sense, especially given the ground he was operating in. Even if he used all the battery power, including the spares, it would be worth it, allowing him to move in to parts of the base unseen during darkness and make some close-up observations. They were going in at night. It was as important to know what kind of activity happened during the hours of darkness as it was to spot locations and targets in daylight.

Blue had sussed that the man who owned the clothes was no giant. So he sorted out Digger as the man who would go out on foot, wearing the high-quality clothes that Blue had turned into something approaching rags. The shirt had lost its collar, and a few of its buttons. Several pairs of SAS boots had given the jacket, purchased from a Savile Row tailor, the treatment. Trousers from a different outfit had got the same. Digger was tasked to stay between the road and the river, and if he could, to use some of the trees to get up and have a look at the south elevation of the base. Apart from water, he took with him one of the Welrod silenced pistols, just in case he got jumped.

His secondary task was to get near enough to the bridge to tell the others what they would face if, pursued, they tried to cross it. But he couldn't get too close, just in case a suspicious guard called him to ask some questions. As he got ready, they could hear Digger practising his Spanish. Judging by the way he emphasized certain expressions, the language seemed to contain as many swearwords as English.

Sam had set up four OPs in the roof, one facing in each direction, which confirmed that the house was fairly secure. What should have been a working ranch house wasn't. Why didn't matter. There was that little tarred hut at the bottom of the slope, occupied by a black-clad old lady. But throughout the day, as she'd gone about her various tasks, she hadn't even looked at the Estancia Silvana. To the west and the south the land stretched away, mainly flat, the odd slight rise with an occasional tree. It was Paul Hill's opinion, because he'd once had a house near Heathrow airport, that the owner had moved out to get away from the noise of jet aircraft.

They took off and landed throughout the day, all Skyhawks or Mirages, and no Super Etendards, counted out and in by the man set to observe what could be seen of the base. He calculated two less returned than employed. If they'd been downed that was, on balance, to the good – not just for the loss of the pilots or the reduction in targets. An active air base taking losses was not going to be an upbeat place. There would be a certain amount of doom and gloom, the kind of scenes at the dinner table you saw in the movies, the empty places where the lost flyers had once sat.

The downside was with maintenance crews, who might be active well into the night. So too the armourers. As Sam Clark flicked through his *aide-mémoire* book, he made notes detailing these thoughts, so that when it came to making the final briefing, he would have every piece of information to hand. It was battered now, that book – one which he'd had since joining the Regiment, a hundred or more pages containing the distilled wisdom of the SAS. Every trooper carried one, and they all consulted it regularly. Really, a lot of it was just repetitious common sense. But no one person could carry everything in their head and the ones who tried usually ended up making a right Horlicks of some operation.

'Sid,' he called. 'How many pages are there in the standard *aide-mémoire* book?'

'One hundred and forty-seven,' Serious Sid replied, without hesitation. Then he broke it down into sections in such comprehensive detail that Sam Clark was sorry he'd asked.

Digger went out with the recce patrol, to lie up until daylight before going for a walk. They saw him from the roof, ambling about like an unemployed peasant, then suddenly disappearing into the trees. He looked very obvious to the men watching him. What was against him wasn't his appearance. Digger looked the part. It was the lack of other traffic, pedestrian or wheeled, that made him look a bit obvious. But he did the business, returning as ordered during the hours of darkness.

On that evening's Sked, they heard about the Exocet attack on HMS *Gloucester*. The Headshed had been jittery before. They were doubly so now, seeing in the dispatch of the land-based missile evidence that the enemy had more of the weapons than they were letting on. But Sam just responded with the fact that he couldn't move without some kind of appreciation, and that with everything sorted the attack would go in within the next forty-eight hours. He would have smiled if, when his Morse signal was decoded, he'd heard Cornelius Hosier cursing the operation for the lack of a compliant Rupert who would do his bidding.

Robbie Knox was out two nights. His patrol spent one day to the north of the base, and one lying up to the west, silently watching. The first had included an appreciation of the level of traffic on the road from Rio Grande town to the base. He'd gone in both nights alone, right up to the perimeter wire. To locate and evaluate a point of entry, as well as to time and number sentries. What they'd got wasn't all-encompassing. But it was a big advance on the information they'd set out with. Everybody gathered round for the debrief. Working with the patrol, they began to draw a map of the base on the green baize of the billiard table. As Robbie and his men talked, Sam worked out his own ideas on the attack. Then, when the guys had finished their reports, and answered all the questions they could, he called everybody to order and set in motion a Chinese parliament, an animated discussion that had, for once, to be carried out in hushed tones.

Every possibility was discussed, every avenue explored. This, like every other SAS job, was a one-shot operation. If somebody suggested a course of action that seemed a bit weird, there was no laughter or piss-taking. It was examined fully, and either accepted or discarded on its own merits. The aim was simple: to carry out the task given to them by the Headshed, then to get out and E&E in one piece. So time spent now was time well used. Sam was patient, allowing more discussion than was strictly necessary, because time wasn't a problem. He wanted them all to feel sure everything had been covered. But he summed up finally, then began to outline his plan.

CHAPTER FIFTEEN

Land Force Commander to OCs of all units: 13/5/82 16.00 hrs: Gains are being made in all sectors. It is my belief that one final heave will bring a solution to the battle. Good Luck.

Sam started by going over the mission again, only this time, using a cue, he was able to point to some definite features on the map they'd drawn. Robbie Knox had brought back one definite measurement to give some indication of the scale. That gave some accuracy to the distance between the tower position, which with a tall radio mast obviously included the communications centre, the main accommodation blocks, the hard standing for aircraft and their hangars. The sentry posts were marked, as well as the times for changes. Two hours on, four off, normal Green Army routine. The runway, a single long tarmac strip running from east to west, was between those and the river, with the western landing beacons on the edge of the town of Rio Grande.

Anti-aircraft guns, identified by Serious Sid from Robbie's sketch as four Bofors 40mm L/60 batteries, were concentrated at that end of the runway. Of World War Two vintage, they would definitely have added fire-control systems. But according to Robbie, they were without wheels, to aid firing stability, and thus were static. More important, they were unmanned, the assumption surely being that any warning system would allow the gunners to get to them in time to take on any incoming threat. The estimated distance from the main gate to the nearest houses was marked in kilometres.

Ideally it should have been to scale, the kind of model that the Green Slime would occasionally produce in Hereford. But few were gifted in that direction and, stuck out here in the middle of nowhere, they lacked the tools to compensate. Nor was there enough battery power in the patrol torches for the time it would have taken to formulate such a thing. There was a big N on the far side of the green baize so that everybody knew the whereabouts of north.

Surrounded by faces made ethereal by the torchlight, Sam went through the necessary appreciation of the ground they would cover, the kind of going they should encounter, what enemy dispositions Robbie and his team had sussed and the nature of the sentries they had posted. To this was added the information that Digger had brought back. He'd done better than expected, spotting first a guard tower that overlooked the southern approaches to the main accommodation area, then what looked like a pair of earth-covered bunkers on the opposite corner of the field to the room they were now in. They had a guard of their own, housed in a flimsy-looking breezeblock hut. Sam provided a schedule of what they'd observed from the house, the perimeter patrol timings made by jeep.

Sam stated twenty minutes as the time within which the mission would have to be completed once it went noisy, before detailing the team tasks. That was standard SOP. The only way you could hold to a timed plan, and make sure it was feasible, was to work back from completion. There was a slot allocated to each section of the plan, from the moment of departure from the *estancia*, through the river crossing, to the FRV from which the bulk of the patrol would execute the assault. These included speed of movement, rates of advance and approximate distances to be covered. The group would then split up, the GPMG parties taking up stations to provide covering and suppression fire. That was followed by an outline of possible enemy reactions.

There's no such thing as a perfect plan, and no one listening to Sam Clark expected one. But the biggest grey area was how the Argies would respond, especially since they were still unclear as to how many they would face. Robbie had reported the maintenance hangars to be lit up and seemingly working through most of the night. That meant people awake and alert close to some of their targets, aircraft undergoing servicing or repair. The single Roland battery he'd seen was operational twenty-four-hours and mounted on armoured carriers. This, according to Serious Sid, was probably a French AMX 30 tank chassis. Would they stay where they lay, or use their mobility to interfere? The missiles would be useless, but an armoured vehicle was always tricky to handle for ground troops in what would be a messy, uncertain environment. Unless you knew their orders, you couldn't tell.

The level of traffic between the base and the town was another variable. It consisted of two fully laden trucks, which probably carried ordinary jundies, and cars and jeeps which must contain officers, some of them the pilots they should be trying to kill. Return times varied, but the trucks came back first, and the others drifted in throughout the next few hours. All it indicated was that a lot of the Rupertinos were out enjoying themselves, when they should have been either sleeping or supervising their troops.

Sam talked for about three-quarters of an hour, rarely pausing, doing so only to answer the odd question put by one of the troopers. Robbie's patrol was designated as the gun team on the GPMGs and would work in pairs. Sam would lead the main assault group, ten of the twelve men who would go in and divide inside the wire, which sounded like a strong party until you outlined the tasks. The means of entry and exfil had to be held, and the main gate too must be secure. Blue was taking one patrol after the bunkers, which left only four men to take on the rest of the mission, the planes and the people who might be working on them. Movement was to be silent up to the point when action would be initiated. The signal to go noisy was simple. The first bang, either from a gun or an explosive charge.

'At its very lowest, it falls into three objectives and one aim. To gain access to the base, to go for the targets while part of the patrol holds open the window in which we have to operate. The targets are dispersed, so we need to either hold off going noisy to allow time to cover ground, or just go for it as soon as possible. That depends on being able to take possession of a vehicle. If we can achieve that, all teams are to operate simultaneously. If not, the assault goes in on the aircraft and everyone will then try and divert attention away from the men assigned to the bunkers. Our final task is to get out and slow any pursuit. I will tell the Headshed that we are moving out as soon as it gets dark, at around 17.30 hours. Time to get your kit sorted out.'

Most of the troopers stayed at the table, taking a final look at the rough map, before moving away to redistribute the weaponry, so that those tasked to the specific jobs had what was needed. Guns were checked as well as the magazines, the pre-prepared explosive charges with adhesive tape loaded into the dry sack. The 66mm anti-tank rockets, their main firepower, were redistributed. One-shot, throwaway weapons, they had a big fire signature that told everybody and their mother where you were coming from. That didn't matter as long as the man firing it was gone as soon as the rocket left the tube.

In every headquarters from Northwood to Hereford, in Ascension Island, aboard *Hermes* and in Downing Street, the last forty-eight hours had been agony, as the battle for Port Stanley reached a climax. The only people who managed to maintain an air of calm were in the field headquarters of the Land Force Commander. They saw the same picture unfold on their maps, the steady progress of British troops as they dislodged the Argentine defenders from their prepared positions.

They were taking casualties but inflicting more. The British Army was fighting in appalling conditions – wet, hungry and cold – yet still taking ground. But there was another reason for their air of confidence, and that was the one that Cornelius Hosier, in the War Room at Hereford, was watching, having specifically requested to be kept informed. The prisoner count! Nothing tells a general more about the state of his opponents than that. And a collapse is usually proceeded by a rash of surrenders. With Special Forces troops in on the ground in Argentina, he had a right to be told that vital figure.

A hint had been dropped by the Intelligence Officer in the War Room that B Squadron's attack might prove unnecessary. The glare he earned for that not only silenced the Green Slime but anyone else who doubted the Director's wisdom. They had all seen how ruthless he could be with dissent, and were well aware of his dissatisfaction with the way the Rio Grande operation was being handled. Sergeant Sam Clark was watering down his increasingly tart instructions, which Hosier believed any officer would have obeyed. So his name and abilities were added to the mental file of those who said that discretion was the better part of valour.

But no one could doubt, seeing position after position fall, that the Argies were on the rack. If Hosier and some of the other brass hats were right, and there was some last throw prepared, then surely this was the time to launch it. In fact, to most of the people present, unless the enemy air force had a suicide plan, it was already too late.

'Read your history books, gentlemen,' Hosier said suddenly. He'd not turned round, but he must have picked up the vibrations of the room. 'Even with the surrenders we have achieved, our troops have a bare parity with the enemy. If they decide to hold a shrinking perimeter, we could be in for a bloody few days.'

Sam Clark led the way out of the billiard room, with Blue Harding even closing the shutters so that no one would suspect they'd been forced until they saw the bar missing from the inside. The table had been re-covered, though the attempts to erase the plan had proved difficult. The chalk left a faint stain that only a stiff brush would remove. The only evidence that the room had been occupied was the lack of dust on the floor. Everything else had been removed, just in case. A long shot, but for the sake of the time it took to clear up, not one worth taking.

The sky was five-eighths cloudy, perfect conditions for what they had to do, with a light breeze just cold enough to keep anybody standing stag inside the nearest shelter. Hoods would be up on their parkas as well, cutting off a high percentage of their ability to hear. They followed a single path, close together, till they were a hundred metres from the *estancia*, so that no one looking at the ground could count their number by boot impressions. Then, at a signal from Sam, they got themselves into normal patrol order and headed for the river.

The next stage had been one of the most hotly disputed in the Chinese parliament. It was necessary to make a Bergen cache, which would also act as an emergency rendezvous point, in any area clear of obstacles. No one could persuade Sam Clark of the sense of carting the heavy rucksacks across the river, only to dump them on the other side. Yet many hated the idea of being separated from their kit by a natural obstacle. Sam argued his corner, then took a decision that was, anyway, his to make as patrol commander. Bergens would be cached this side, and a secondary ERV would be set up on the opposite bank, using one patrol radio as the meeting point. The rope line they'd use to cross would be left in the water, so that they could evade quickly on their return.

They were all going to get wet, but the poor bastard who took the rope over would be soaked, and so would the last man, who'd have to cross using a submerged line. Luke Tuikabe put himself up for the first job, joking that since he didn't need to be cammed up, there was no way the river water could wash his off. Dinger Bell, an Olympic standard swimmer, would bring up the rear.

The trees both ends were tied to hardly rated the name. They were stunted bent affairs, pointing to the west, growths that achieved so little height that most troopers were in up to their waist. The water, in a river wide and slow, was ice cold, the kind that comes off a mountain glacier. That made the move even quicker than standard, no one wanting their body temperature to be dropped by lengthy immersion in the kind of chill from which they could not recover.

Even without their Bergens, each trooper bore a heavy load. The 66mm carriers had their own personal weapons and ammo to transport as well. The gun teams had belts strapped round their waist so heavy that it had been a moot point whether to take them off and ship them over on their own, using a loop of rope to hold them, and another to pull. But that was discarded. Best to take everything with you: then you knew where it was at all times. While this was going on, those men who would cross last set up a stag to protect the position. The first over the other side afforded the same.

As soon as Dinger joined, Sam restated the tasks and times, checked watches and compass settings, then led the way off to the arranged ERV. In two groups, the troopers moved forward, slow and careful, some of the lights from the air base indicating the location of their target.

'Signal, sir', said the scaley, as he exited the comms room and approached Hosier's back. The Brigadier read it, not once, but twice. He then stood up, and turned slowly, a smile on his face.

'Gentleman, this is from 2 Para, routed through HQ. The Argentine forces have hoisted a white flag, and are requesting negotiations to cover a formal surrender.'

There was no cheering, but a lot of quiet smiling, before the Green Slime spoke. 'Permission to send a signal to Bravo One One, sir.'

That clouded Hosier's brow, causing him to hesitate. He was being asked to bin an operation that stood as his sole contribution to the conflict. Without that raid, the kudos for Special Forces success would reside elsewhere. The scaley coughed, which brought Jock the Sock back to the present. Asked later by his superiors, he justified his action with the same words he used now.

'It may well be some kind of trick.'

As a position to defend, the ERV was crap: not dead ground, just a point on a compass with no cover to speak of. Twelve of the sixteen men formed an all-round defence, as Sam went over the orders for Robbie Knox's gun teams. They, with their GPMGs, were tasked to move out thirty minutes before the main party. Two would seek a position to the west of the main operational area of the airfield, while the other pair would move on to the designated position Digger had spotted, which would allow them to pour down suppression fire on most of the main targets. There were no final handshakes or thumbs up. All that had been done back at the *estancia*. Good luck wasn't going to help anyone. Good soldiering would.

The men who remained were totally silent, a visual appreciation of what was about to happen running through each of their minds. If a bomb exploded in this personal vision, it was only as a prelude to a trained reaction. All their SAS life ran in a seamless film before them; all the agony and the practice, the things they'd learned easily and those they'd found hard. Every one of them would be tested on this operation. The breathing was easy and controlled, the puff of steam from each throat even. But the heartbeats were a little racy, and the nerve ends on the skin absorbed the increased blood flow. The minutes counted off, only twenty, seemed like hours, until Sam called them in to issue his final briefing.

'Blue on point as agreed, with Luke at number two. Fire Team Alpha just behind me and Paul, at three and four. 66s in the centre, exfil demolition team next, Digger and Graunch bringing up the rear. You all know your spot. Second man aim right, third aim left. You have your grid reference for the first and second forward assault position. Any man goes down on the way, for whatever reason, to inform the trooper to his front, pull out and head back to the ERV.'

They all stood as Sam looked at his watch, Blue moving just before he gave him the nod. They had two kilometres to cover and no set time to do it in. The signal for suppression support was noise, which meant they would hold their fire until the assault teams either initiated the attack or responded to a compromise. So they could move slowly and carefully, with Blue Harding setting an easy pace. The headlights on the road had them all crouching down. And they were flat as the truck, turning towards the bridge over the Rio Grande River, swept the twin beams weakly across their inert shapes. As they faded, Blue stood up and signalled with his arm that they should proceed.

He had to halt once more, for much the same reason, as the jeep patrolling the perimeter swept round inside the wire fence. The halt that caused was used to check the timings. Observation had shown that they were haphazard, but only within a limited time frame, which indicated a lack of punctuality rather than staggered runs designed to catch out potential intruders.

They stayed to the north of the road, far enough away to be invisible to anyone walking. Traffic was so light to the east of the air base, and the terrain so flat, that they had ample warning of any threat. The vehicles that were around, exiting from the air base, tended to turn towards the town, not away from it. The point of greatest danger was the minute at which they crossed in front of the main gate. This was dimly illuminated, just enough to allow the sentries to identify anyone approaching. So Blue tended north, to stay well out of the arc of light, until he reached the point at which they were designated to turn due south. That brought Sam Clark forward to restate the tasks. It was a full minute before he spoke, the time used to check the security of the environment.

'We go from here. Fire Team Alpha first. The rest of us will move forward as the jeep goes past. We need to be near the fence when Alpha take out the sentries.'

That was a calculated risk, based on what Robbie Knox and his team had observed. That the Argies headed for town before seven and that the gate was generally quiet until well after ten, when the first of the revellers, the ordinary Joes in the trucks, returned. Not once had a car or jeep preceded the trucks, the officers staying out longer than the men. If anyone inadvertently broke that pattern, they would probably die before they got inside the wire.

Dinger Bell and Tony D'Ambrosio made up Fire Team Alpha. They were tasked to crawl to the wire mesh fence, crossing the road to the east of the main gate, signalling when they were in position with an infra-red filtered torch. The wire would be cut immediately the response was communicated, the point at which the rest of the patrol would prepare to move forward. The sign to do that was the passing of the perimeter patrolling jeep. Robbie Knox had observed that they had a habit of stopping at the main gate so that the driver could exchange a bit of gossip, perhaps to have a moan, or pass on jokes at the expense of the static sentries.

The distraction of that exchange would get Alpha through the wire. The supporting teams would use the noise to get to the gap in the fence, ready to infil when advised it was safe to do so. Dinger and Tony strapped their M203s round their backs, checked that their Welrods were secure, and at a tap signal from Sam, set off. They had a time for this, at least to get in position. Blue reckoned they were safe enough. He couldn't see them after five seconds, and he was looking. Five minutes later, Sam Clark saw the tiny flash in his goggles, and tapped Blue to be ready to move out, a signal he passed on. Now all they needed was the jeep.

A Mercedes based on the old World War Two design for the Kubelwagen, it swept past the point where Fire Team Alpha lay, using the wire and the longish grass that accumulated near the base to avoid detection. As soon as the headlight glare faded Blue moved out at a crouch. This was no time for crawling, it would take too long. The ping of the cutters on the wire was audible enough to induce haste, though they had to hope the idling engine of the jeep would drown that out.

A quick look through his night sight confirmed to Blue that Dinger and Tony were through the fence, inching towards the gate, where the sentries could be heard exchanging laughing insults with the mobile patrol. As the jeep drove away, they raised themselves up, walked quietly but confidently towards the two sentries, whose eyes were fixed on the shrinking red taillights.

A Welrod makes little sound, the level of which can be drowned out by a decent wind or the muted roar of a departing engine. Given those conditions you can fire it past someone's ear when their back is turned and they will not react. Developed during the war for quiet assassination, it had never been surpassed for silence, and was a favourite weapon of many SAS troopers. The two sentries, simultaneously, took a bullet right in the back of their heads. One of them was still chortling at some joke he'd made, the sound of laughter dying in his throat as the front of his head was blown off.

They hit the ground without noise, crumpling rather than falling. Another advantage of the Welrod was a low muzzle velocity, enough to tear apart flesh and bone, but insufficient to throw the body violently forward. There were two more sentries in the gatehouse. They didn't hear Dinger and Tony pull back and twist the mechanism of the pistols to put another bullet in the chamber. But at least they saw they were going to die.

The troopers stepped through the open door, Welrods out, arms extended in the classic firing position. To men trained in counterterrorism, fighting in dark, confined spaces, the sentries were sitting ducks, taking the four remaining rounds at a decreasing range, the only sound that of the single-shot Welrods being re-cocked, immediately followed by the noise of the bullets hitting the bodies.

Taking his cue from the same set of disappearing taillights, Blue Harding was through the wire before the sentries died, followed by the rest of the patrol. The exfil team dropped back to lay the charges that would act to protect them when they bugged out, Claymore mines set as booby traps, which could either be detonated by remotes, or by interference. Sam stopped everyone inside, on the edge of the perimeter road, his hand tapping a shoulder and giving a direction to each team.

Blue, Digger and two of the 66mm carriers headed for the guardhouse to join Tony and Dinger, taking the Argentine forage caps that had been removed from the dead sentries and sticking them on their heads. The 66mms went inside, laid away their tubes and, re-emerging, used their rifles to cover the approaches from the town to the gate, at a point practically invisible from the inside of the camp.

Sam Clark moved over the road with the rest, moving through a narrow alley behind a set of what Robbie Knox reckoned were storerooms. There all four men removed their anti-tank missiles, too bulky for the surreptitious approach they wanted to make, laying them with some care in the deep grass right against the wall. Then they fell in behind Sam Clark, who'd recced the way out into the open and pronounced it clear. As silently and as swiftly as they could, all four men dashed across the open space towards the hangars. Two of these were dark, while the other showed a rim of light around the huge sliding door.

There should have been sentries on the darkened hangars, which had to contain the aircraft they'd seen flying that day. If there were guards, it was certain they were not doing their job. If too many of their superiors were off the base, enjoying themselves in town, then their inferiors would skive off. And who could blame them? To Sam the real worry was that the sentries were on the inside of the doors, keeping out of the wind, and would be alerted as soon as he tried to prise them open.

The noise of the sliding door opening was a blessing. It moved and creaked long before enough of a gap opened up for anyone to see through. By the time the light spilled out onto the concourse in front, Sam and his men were well concealed. Two men in greasy overalls emerged, one stopping to pull the door shut, the other talking loudly. Then, lighting cigarettes, they set off towards the main building block, a square, brick-built construction dominated by the glass-fronted tower, still chatting as they walked.

Blue Harding, standing by the main gate, had a brief sight of them until the lack of light cut them off. But the direction they were heading was a worry. A quick check on his watch put them very close to the road when the jeep was due to return. He had to decide whether they represented a threat, and what to do about it.

'Digger,' he whispered, 'clock the two that have just left the workshops. Get close to them. If they react when we go to work, take them out.'

Digger nodded and was off, while Blue looked into the darkness, towards the two positions that should, by now, be occupied by the fire support teams.

Robbie Knox and his mate had the toughest task. They'd penetrated the wire with ease, right at the western end of the base, bending it back into position and taping it so that even a suspicious sentry would have trouble spotting that a gap had been cut. They'd seen the jeep pass, as arranged, then moved forward along the edge of the tarmac. But Robbie's location for the coming assault was manned. He had to take out the two men guarding the tower before he could perform his function, and how to do that was a decision that could only be taken on the spot.

There was a ladder, but it had been raised so that it was beyond reach. The structure of the tower was flimsy enough to register any movement, so if they tried to climb the frame to release the ladder it would alert the men above them. Dopey they might be, since they didn't seem to be moving around much, but that wouldn't stop them raising the alarm, quite possibly by field telephone. They had to take that position, because it had such a commanding view of the main buildings. It faced directly on to the front door, some five hundred metres distant, of what Digger and Robbie had identified as the accommodation block. As a kill point, when the action started, it was priceless.

Robbie and his number two, Glynn Davies, crouched below it, hidden in the shadows. By a series of taps and moves, they discussed the next move. Glynn had a grenade, while Robbie lifted the GPMG, indicating that he could fire it upwards if he could wedge the muzzle in the guard tower frame to steady it. The only bummer would be if Glynn missed his throw and slung the grenade down their own throats. But he was an ex-fly half for Welsh schoolboys, so Robbie was prepared to trust him.

Over the other side, Tommy Laidlaw and Frank Mills were as happy as pigs in shit. They had a clear field of fire, decent cover to the rear of an undesignated outbuilding. The GPMG was on its bipod, ready and waiting for the fun to start. Tommy had already whispered that they were so well off that he felt they could stir up a brew.

The lock on the hangar doors reassured Sam Clark. If they were secured on the outside, that guaranteed there was no lazy bastard slumbering inside. But each one was a big, complex bugger, too difficult to pick in the dark. They would have to be blown, with no idea if there was anything worthwhile to trash on the other side. He put Luke and Graunch on the workshops. Initially, he'd wanted to leave them till he set his charges in the others. But when he blew the padlocks, that was going to be the closest point of interference. You had to figure that if those two flung the door open, one huge black bastard, and one really ugly white man, it would scare the shit out of those on the inside.

The jeep was late. Not by much, but definitely not on time. Digger had seen the two overalled individuals into the accommodation block, getting close enough to the swinging door to hear the babble of voices from inside. There were a lot of guys in there, all of whom were going to be coming out that door when they heard a boom. They'd be well fucked if Robbie was in place, and doubly so if Dinger and Tony D'Ambrosio got in amongst them.

The distant headlights made him move, and he was back with Blue before they got close enough to pick him out.

'Shit!' Blue exclaimed, as he saw the jeep pull up outside the door Digger had just moved away from. The driver went inside, leaving the engine running. He made a sign to the two hidden troopers, telling them to wait. They'd been doing that already, but neither moved so much as an inch, staying in the shadows into which they'd retreated once Blue had arrived.

The engine revved as the driver climbed back in, and he swung round heading for the gate. Blue and Digger stayed out of the light, guns loose but loaded, waiting as the Kubelwagen approached. The guy was gunning the engine, showing off a bit, and even slewed the tyres round in a mild screech as he drew alongside what he thought were two fellow countrymen. That thought died in his eyes as they slowly turned, rifles pushed forward, their cammed up faces startling in the orange glow of the sodium lighting. Tony and Dinger were behind them, firing their reloaded Welrods before either man could open his mouth. Within a second that option was removed, permanently.

Silently, they were lifted out, Blue catching the Coke bottle the driver had stopped to buy. Dry in his own mouth, he took a slug, before passing it to the others. Funnily enough, it was Dinger, the roughest of the bunch, who declined to drink a dead man's beverage. The 66mms were loaded into the jeep within seconds and Blue and Digger climbed into a vehicle that still had its engine running. Then they were off, leaving the two assassins to set up their M203 grenade launchers, and to take a sight on the nearby buildings.

Did one of them contain pilots, men who'd decided on a night in? None of the patrol knew. If they did kill any flyers it would be by luck. Sam had decided, regardless of what the Headshed thought, that he had no time to look for their billet. If they came across them well and good – if not, so be it. The aircraft would suffice for him. That and getting all of his patrol out alive.

Blue killed the lights on the jeep before he spun it out onto a hard standing that ran onto the runway. The target he had was at the other end of the base. Typical of the kind of berks who built these things, to put their bunkers on the town side of the base, when all that lay to the west was wilderness. As he crawled along, he was mentally preparing himself for the next stage of the assault. When the balloon went up, he would drive like buggery, headlights blazing, for that small satellite guard post Digger had spotted. The hope was that there was only one. If Digger was wrong, then being along for the ride he would pay for it.

Sam Clark looked at his watch. Timed it wasn't, but there was a limit to how long he could wait. Quite apart from the danger of discovery, there

227

was the need for a decent period of darkness to get clear of the area. He signalled to the guy with him to set his charges on the padlocks, then to take cover. That done, he offered up a silent prayer, looked at his watch to check the time, waited till the second hand reached twelve, then flicked the timer on his own.

CHAPTER SIXTEEN

The explosions shattered the silence, sending great orange flashes and clouds of smoke into the air. Robbie Knox dropped the muzzle of his machine gun into the frame and cocked it, kicking clear the ammo belt that hung down. Glynn Davies stepped out from under the guard platform, pulled back his arm and threw, repeating the action as he tossed two grenades into the roofed platform. He was back under, taking hold of and extending the belt, when they detonated, the sound accompanied by a long burst from the GPMG.

Tony D'Ambrosio and Dinger Bell looked up from their watches and fired off the first of their grenades, aiming for the front door of the accommodation block, the intention to deter anyone inside from venturing out. The tracer opening up from the roadside sentry post, aimed at the hangars, fixed their main target. That had them reaching for the 66mms that had been left behind in the guardhouse, these aimed at the guard tower. It didn't matter if they were spot on. They only had to take away the legs of the thing, aiming for the point at which they joined with the upper structure, something Dinger Bell managed on his second attempt.

That was just as well, since the explosive flash of rocket discharge had fixed their position, which brought the fire from the tower machine gun down on them. The tracer from that ceased abruptly as the structure leant sideways, creaking and groaning, before it toppled over, bringing down with it the large radio mast on the roof. That done, they engaged with rapid rifle fire on the other buildings, the offices and storerooms, first shooting out the window glass. Next, using the 40mm underslung grenade launchers, they fired through the gaps to start fires.

The exfil team, Marty Roper and Don Kavanagh, had their weapons trained down the road, having just come back from laying charges and tripwires. The explosions would be heard in the town, and every officer or jundie there would be rushing back to the base, either out of curiosity or to try and help out. Whichever, they were going to get a very nasty surprise.

Sam Clark heaved on the hangar door, the sound of Graunch and Luke Tuikabe firing loud in his ears as they sprayed the inside of the workshops. He had a day bag on his shoulders, full of pre-prepared charges, plastic explosives with enough of a kick to wreck an air-frame, plus destroy the engine and avionics it contained beyond repair. There would be no firing bullets at the buggers. They were designed to withstand that and more. The aviation fuel wouldn't go up even with an incendiary bullet, since it was of deliberately low combustibility.

Instead, he and his team ran around, barely registering the kind of plane they were working on, an almost impossible task in the dark anyway. The masking tape was used in long strips to fix the charges, each timer set, the whole operation taking half a minute. The hangar was crowded with craft, clearly a command decision that got them out of the elements during the hours of darkness. Sam, as he worked, felt a flash of anger as he contemplated what should have been. An all-out air attack by bombers would have caught these planes cold. All the RAF had to do was bomb the hangars to destroy their contents. Instead, lives were being risked on the ground to achieve the same purpose.

When Graunch pulled the door and Luke Tuikabe stepped through, everyone inside dived for safety. There were plenty of places to hide, and if they had weapons standing in the doorway was pretty stupid. Graunch hit Luke's body as he came through the gap, careering into the Fijian and driving him bodily towards some kind of cover. The doorway behind them was suddenly filled with pinging bullets. Swearing and shouting, both men returned fire. But unable to clearly see their targets, they could not impose themselves in the way that they wanted.

'I think we found the fuckin' sentries, Luke,' Graunch shouted, as the firing eased.

Blue marked the time as he gunned the engine hard. Beside him Digger switched on the lights. The jeep wasn't built for speed, and on the open surface of the runway they didn't seem to be making much. But they closed with the flimsy guard post eventually, to find the two goons in charge standing out in the open staring and pointing. Seeing their own jeep arrive they obviously felt no immediate threat. But something must have alerted one of them – perhaps four men instead of two, or the lack of the right caps – because he raised his rifle and started firing.

Digger was already standing, his Armalite pumping away, getting his retaliation in early. Blue, steering with one hand, was firing off his MI6 with the other, hoping that his fire would distract rather than hit anyone. The two guys they were carrying, Serious Sid and Tommy Seaman, had their weapons up too, trying to aim round the men in front of them. It could only have been a lucky shot that took Digger in the shoulder, because the two sentries looked nothing like marksman.

It knocked him right back into the jeep, his weight taking down the man behind him, Serious Sid. Blue was still firing, and the two Argies were busy trying to get away from him, pushing each other as they tried to find some shelter in their flimsy box. A grenade in the hand of Tommy Seaman suddenly appeared over his shoulder, accompanied by a hard tap. Words were superfluous. All the guy was asking him to do was to steer past the hut, and let him do the needful.

Blue swung the wheel hard, which didn't help Serious Sid, as he tried to pull the wounded man's morphine syrette off his neck. Digger was sprawled back, eyes closed, a great wound in his shoulder, moaning and cursing as the shock wore off and the pain took hold. Sid got the drug into him just as Tommy tossed the grenade. Blue was well past it when the L2 went off. When he spun round to look the hut wasn't there. It was gone, only the two twitching bodies on the ground evidence that it had ever existed.

Robbie and Glynn had got into position and set up their weapon. They had no defined targets, just a job to do. They began to spray bullets around like there was no tomorrow, firing at height to avoid hitting their own men with friendly fire. They were second storey men, tasked to hit the upper floors of everything that had them. Windows were going out everywhere, but they couldn't hear it. Only the sound of their gun was audible, as they shot the place up with gleeful abandon.

They came out on the ground floor eventually, the deterrence of the grenades that Tony and Dinger had launched wearing off. Frank Mills let them out, but only so far, and then he pulled the trigger. The arc of his fire went across the face of the building, so that even the bullets which missed ricocheted off the walls to cause wounds. The bright orange tracer split the darkness, bisecting that of the other GPMG as they laid down enough flying metal to suppress any desire in the Argentine breast to come out and fight.

Sam Clark had clocked seven minutes on his watch as he went in to rescue Luke Tuikabe and Graunch, which he did with grenades lobbed towards the aircraft under repair. He could chuck them from the door; they were pinned down and found it hard to get enough swing. But once they went off Luke was up and charging, diving into the smoke without the least regard for what might be on the other side. Graunch had no choice but to follow, Sam Clark's voice ringing in his ears reminding him that nearly half their time was gone and they still had the anti-tank rockets to fire.

It really didn't matter who fell back to engage with the 66mms, as long as the patrol were sticking to the timings. Out by the bunkers, Blue had jumped out of the now-stationary jeep, taking one of the tubes. He fired a flare to illuminate his target, a double steel door several feet below ground level. It was a chancy business, the elevation forcing him to stand closer than he would have liked while his finger located the rubber detent which formed the firing mechanism. As soon as he pressed the trigger, and felt the rocket depart the tube, he threw himself down and tried to crawl away. The blast, even though it went over his body, moved him several feet, as a great orange plume lit the night sky. He had no idea if it was an Exocet: he just knew that whatever that bunker had contained was no more.

Tommy Seaman wasn't so lucky. He hit his target as well, but if he tried to avoid the blast he failed. Blue saw the 66mm go off, and heard the great bang that accompanied its firing. But the blast that followed dwarfed that. It also lifted a man just beginning to crouch off his feet and carried him thirty feet before slamming him down hard on the tarmac. Both Blue and Serious Sid got to him in seconds, but one look was enough to show that nothing could be done. There was almost nothing left above the shoulders on one side.

'Fuck!' Blue yelled, as first a flare exploded, quickly followed by a series of bangs that went off around his ears. He knew, by the sound signature, that they weren't bullets but shells, and they were being aimed at the jeep. A lot can go through your mind in a second. The fire could only be coming from the Bofors firing over open sights. Who was firing the bastards if they were supposed to be unmanned? And were they trying to get them with HE designed to down aircraft, or did the guns have a supply of anti-personnel shells for a surface-to-surface role? Thinking was one thing, conclusions another. With Digger wounded they had to use the jeep to get him out, knowing that if a shell from a Bofors caught them, regardless of what type it was, they'd be eviscerated.

Their job was done and the clock was running. By now they should have been well on their way back. Both men ran for the jeep. Blue thanked God that the engine was still running, and that he was able to slip the clutch and get moving. That meant they'd need a deflection shot to get them. He was just congratulating himself when he realized that anti-aircraft gunners were specifically trained in that department. That made him brake, then accelerate again. Behind him, the top layer of the tarmac was ripped off like paper.

Blue slewed the jeep to a halt and jammed it into reverse, well aware that he was never going to outrun that gun. Serious Sid had the good sense to chuck out the remaining 66mms before they came to a halt. It was only luck that saved them, either some malfunction on the Bofors or the gunner taking his finger off the trigger for ten seconds to adjust his aim on a target moving at variable speed and in the wrong direction. Digger, full of his own morphine, probably felt nothing as Blue and Serious Sid dragged him clear of the vehicle. The shells began to rip into it before they'd gone five feet, Sid dropping to one knee as a piece of the wing took him on the back of his knee.

The firing stopped as the jeep blew up, sending a huge flash of orange light that was visible for miles. Sam Clark had been in the process of falling back, obeying his own orders. Ten minutes from first bang time to the point at which he'd begin to withdraw. It made absolute sense, because no matter how good they were, sixteen men could never fight the number they had on the base. He and Paul Hill had just retrieved the stashed 66s, and rounded the building, planning to take aim in the direction of the smashed control tower.

One look showed that to be unnecessary. Though not utterly destroyed it was at an angle, clearly out of commission, with bullets from one of the gun teams slamming into it just below the already shattered windows. The earlier booms from down the runway were what he'd expected. The flash from the second flare hadn't distracted him, since he assumed it was from the team attacking the now-burning bunkers, making sure the job was complete. But the thud of the exploding jeep made him concentrate; the orange ball, like a huge expanding flower, ballooned into the night sky. He knew it was Blue, but the sinking feeling he had in his gut was removed by the sight of the three struggling figures in the glow from the flare and the burning vehicle. The Bofors opened up again. Even if it had a conical flash eliminator, firing low it still sent out pinpricks of light. With the 66mm already at his shoulder, Sam took a quick aim and fired.

Frank Mills felt the tap on his shoulder, and looked into the watch Tommy Laidlaw had pushed towards his face. It was hard to stop firing, but that was the deal. And they might have the furthest to travel, with the option of making for the ERV or the Bergen cache if they could get across the river. They were just about to be up and off when the Bofors opened up on Blue Harding. There was light from the bunkers as well as the flare and the gun position was visible. Frank was back on his belly right away, firing off the last belt of ammunition. It wouldn't do much against the protective shield, but it might distract them.

Robbie Knox had another two minutes to go, but was running short of ammo. He was firing bursts rather than long arcs, trying hard to keep up the suppressing fire until he was out of time. The scene in front of him was changed now, and not just by the succession of massive blasts from the other end of the field. Most of the buildings, including the control tower, were alight. The upper storeys of the offices and admin blocks were ablaze. Just then the taped PE charges went off, sending huge fingers of flame out of the narrow space left by the open hangar doors.

That blast nearly did for Graunch and Luke. The Scouser had to haul off his woolly hat, because it had caught fire. Luke lost half his hair because he didn't wear one, and both of them were thrown to their knees by the blast. Graunch had been pushing Luke, who was so fired up for battle that he wanted to personally kill every spanner in the workshops. Now that was changed. The huge Fijian hauled him to his feet and half dragged, half carried him towards the exfil point in the fence, until a signal from Sam Clark told them to get down behind him.

Sam's anti-tank rocket had missed the target by yards, though the sight of it passing must have given them pause. Frank Mills' GPMG fire was different; pinging off the protective shield it must have concentrated their minds, since the barrel swung to aim at them. With no ammo left they were on their feet running for the perimeter fence when the shell cut Tommy Laidlaw in half. Frank Mills stopped in shock, tasting the blood in his mouth as he hit the ground, feeling at his own body for a wound until he realized it was Tommy's blood he was licking.

Sam Clark had seen his rocket miss, and was waiting for the Bofors to turn on him, given that the gunners could not have missed the fire signature on the 66. By aiming away, it allowed him time to move and to think. He could still see Blue in the dying light from the flare, crouched over one inert body and another half on his knees. Only three meant that one had already been lost. The decision Sam had to make was what to do about the survivors.

'Where the fuck did those gunners come from?' Graunch demanded, raising another 66mm. He had to duck back quick as shells started to rip into the front of the building shielding them. Even worse, the explosions to their rear had started several fires, all of which were rapidly forming into one huge blaze. The aviation fuel was alight now, set off by the sheer heat from the burning planes.

'God only knows,' Sam replied. Maybe Robbie had been wrong, or perhaps they'd been returning from the town when the balloon went up and just crashed through the fence to man the weapon. It really made no difference. They had to be taken down. He had no way of knowing how acute was their angle of fire. But if the Bofors could traverse to the exfil point, with the amount of light being created by the fires, they'd never get away from here. He knew he had five 66mm tubes left, and four guys to fire them. Part of his plan had been to save some to discourage pursuit. That would now have to be just one.

'Don't aim for the gun, aim for the ground just in front. We shoot at the next traverse.'

The Bofors gunners sent another set of shells towards the building. This time they had to be HE, with fuses set at the lowest point, since when they hit they exploded, sending brick and roof sections flying. Sam didn't yell they'd only get one shot. He didn't have to. The four rockets went off within the space of a second, their flash bringing the Bofors swinging back on its traverse so quickly that they had to dive for cover. They didn't see the effect of their shot, and if they had it would have been impossible to tell which of the rockets had struck the ground and ricocheted into the gun position. By the time they looked it was no more, just a twisted heap of burning metal, with some of the remaining shells exploding harmlessly.

'Paul, back to the exfil. Tell them we are going after Blue and we want some covering fire to keep the jundies' heads down.'

If there were rules in the Regiment, then this was strictly against them. You didn't risk three men's lives to rescue three others. But that was Blue out there, a good mate. Graunch and Luke didn't even hesitate to follow Sam. They ran, firing to their left from the hip – not aiming just hoping to suppress. Blue saw them coming, and he helped Serious Sid to his feet. One leg was gone, cut at the back of the knee, but he stood on the good leg, his weapon up, ready to keep fighting. Digger was mumbling to himself words that were jumbled but clear enough to let Blue know that he was alive.

There was no talking when the guys arrived. Luke just lifted Digger while Blue and Graunch got an arm each under Serious Sid. Sam Clark had a simple job now, and that was to get all of them inside the guns of Marty Roper and Don Kavanagh, who had control of the exfil point in the wire. The battle, as far as Boat Troop was concerned, was over. Now it was pure survival.

The bulk of the accommodation block was in the way, a place full of what defenders were returning fire. In fact it seemed like half the Argie garrison was in the front of that building, aiming at anything that moved, and since they were moving more than most they began to draw a lot of fire. It was the concentration of the rest of the troopers that made the difference. Five men in all, they still managed to lay down the kind of suppression fire that kept the Argies' heads down, even putting the last of the 66mms into the ground floor. That created just enough of a window to get them past and, careful to stay out of the arc of friendly fire, they closed on the exfil point at a staggering run.

'Right,' shouted Sam Clark, looking around at the burning buildings, 'let's get the fuck out of here.'

Marty Roper hauled back the fencing to make it easy for the guys to get through. Just then a huge blast came from outside the wire, as a vehicle coming along the road from the town ran into his booby trap. As the Troop staggered across the road they saw the blazing lorry, on its side, blocking the route. It was only then that John Harding realized that any notion of taking out the vehicle park had been a myth. It was the one thing they'd missed in their briefing. All the transport was used at night to take the jundies to town. They were on foot, and likely to stay that way.

'Holy shit!' screamed Marty Roper. 'A fuckin tank!'

The roar of the huge diesel was clearly audible as it ploughed its way through the burning remains of the truck. The guy in charge had been shrewd, sending the poor bastard in the truck forward to take out any traps these attackers had set. Marty's exclamation was understandable. But Serious Sid, even hobbling, knew what it was, and he shouted as the rest opened fire, their bullets bouncing harmlessly off the armour plate.

'It's the chassis for the Rolands. There are no fucking guns.'

'How the fuck do we stop it?' yelled Sam.

Blue hadn't waited. Having blasted the bunker doors with 66s neither he nor Sid had used their pre-prepared charges. He grabbed at Sid's day sack to extract a taped cube of PE, hauling a grenade off his belt as he ran forward. It was crude way to do what was necessary, but even without guns that armoured chassis represented a threat to a patrol without anti-tank weapons. The Argies could use it for cover to pursue them, leaving the men in the open very vulnerable.

The tape on the charge seemed to stick to his fingers, and Blue had to slow his actions to avoid fumbling. He knew what he wanted to do, best to give himself the time to get it right. The AMX 30 had slowed slightly, as it ground its way over the bulk of the truck body. Blue taped his grenade to the charge, then stepped forward until he was nearly under the body of the Roland chassis, ready to slide it under the tracks as the vehicle dropped down. He pulled the pin just as he placed it, then slipped on spilled fuel as he tried to spin away.

Blue was on his hands and feet, scrabbling for what seemed like an age before his boots got enough purchase to put some distance between him and the charge. The blast was timed at seven seconds, too close for comfort even if most of it was contained by the weight of the vehicle. He knew he was hurt as it slammed him back down on the road. He passed out, so didn't see the AMX 30 chassis slew round, the track clattering off the wheels to render it useless.

There was now no doubt about it: the Argentine forces around Port

Stanley were determined to surrender. The talk of terms was a smoke-screen for the fact that there was only available whatever option suited the British government. There was still sporadic fighting on the 5 Brigade front around Tumbledown and Sapper Hill. But a report had come through that the Paras had discarded their steel helmets in favour of their red berets, and were even now in the island capital. There was, in fact, no shortage of cheerful signal traffic, except from one place – Tierra del Fuego.

Hosier had finally conceded the need to abort the mission when it was, if Sam Clark's plan was in motion, clearly too late. There wasn't a man in the War Room at Hereford who didn't feel that he'd exceeded his responsibilities. That he had sent men to die for no purpose other than personal gratification. Everyone avoided his eye, not willing even to exchange a disappointed glance with him. And the insensitivity of his parting shot was breathtaking.

'My being here serves little purpose, Archie. This little operation was really down to Jamie and the command on *Fearless*. I must be getting back to London, you know. There are bound to be inquests, and it will do no harm to have someone on the spot who can defend the interests of Special Forces.'

'As you wish, sir,' Archie Grosvenor replied, so tight-lipped he almost didn't get it out.

Thick skinned as he was, even Jock the Sock knew he was an embarrassment. That produced his slightly goofy smile, a slap of his trews with his swagger stick, and a single word with which to say goodbye.

'Quite.'

Blue came to before they'd covered half a kilometre, aching in every part of his upper body. Sam Clark grunted a question, and when Blue replied he could walk he enquired no further. Sam was a man with a lot on his mind. He had no time to stop and send out signals indicating success. He had three wounded men and half of Argentina on his tail, with only a few hours of darkness to get some air between him and the pursuit. It was only when he joined up with the gun teams that he found out there were two dead troopers instead of one.

Digger was the worst, but it had been a joint decision not to leave him behind. As Marty Roper said, there were just enough fit bastards left to carry him provided they could get across the river. Sam's solution to that was typical. Fuck crossing by rope! He decided to attack the bridge, only to find when he got there that whoever was supposed to be guarding it had scarpered, no doubt scared shitless by the noise of explosions coming from the air base.

They retrieved their Bergens and headed out west, almost running, Sid hopping and Blue staggering a bit, the fit taking turns to carry Digger, all of them in that quiet after-action mood in which they felt totally drained. They hadn't really thought through this part, which was a sort of fear, the knowledge that a positive outcome was so unlikely that to mention it was to invite a jinx. Yet there was no sign of pursuit, and this was while they were in sight of any headlights on the road, heading for the only hilly area they knew, the one they'd occupied before using the Estancia Silvana.

These hills weren't much to write home about and setting up a decent hide here was chancy. But that was all they could do. To try and keep moving in daylight went against every tenet of their survival training. And they had to report in, to tell the Headshed that the raid had been a success, an absolute must before they were captured. Sam Clark left the rest to dig and cam up a fold in the hills while he and Graunch opened the console to compose a Sked. Graunch switched on the PRC320 to power it up. As soon as he offered his signal, he was informed there was a 'message for you.'

They cheered on *Fearless* when Sam's original signal came in, and even louder in the War Room at Hereford. But both sets of celebrations were more from relief than exultation. Jamie Robertson-Macleod ordered them to keep the line open to send a reply himself, and stood over the signaller who sent it. Had he known the response to the earlier signal he might not have bothered.

'The dirty rotten no-good bastards,' Sam Clark had shouted, as he decoded the first message. 'It's a signal to abort.'

'There's another one coming through.'

Sam had the console to decode it, and Graunch looked at him for enlightenment. But the SSM just shook his head and waved a hand to indicate that he should follow. The guys working to improve the hide must have sensed there was something up, since their Patrol Commander a stickler for good routine in a cammed up basha, barged in noisily.

'I've got a message here from the Headshed that is going to either make you laugh or cry.'

Digger, still for some time, had come round. He was weak and pallid, but the tongue was still working. 'You've been made a Rupert.'

'Fuck that and fuck them,' said Sam, holding up the paper he'd written on. It read as follows:

Sitrep 14/6/82 A: Well done Rio Grande: B: Am pleased to inform you that white flags are flying over Stanley: C: Proceed to infil landing site and await surface arrival of HMS Oberon:' D: RV visual and open.